THE RIGHT SWIPE

J.D. ELLIS

Copyright © 2021 J.D. Ellis

All rights reserved

ISBN: 9798467244556

The characters and events portrayed in this book are fictitious. Any similarity to real persons, living or dead, is coincidental and not intended by the author.

No part of this book may be reproduced, or stored in a retrieval system, or transmitted in any form or by any means, electronic, mechanical, photocopying, recording, or otherwise, without express written permission of the author.

Cover design by: Agnese Priekule

TABLE OF CONTENTS

MAPS AND A NOTE ON LANGUAGE 7

CHAPTER 1 GEORGETOWN, DC, DECEMBER 25 13

CHAPTER 2 GALLERY PLACE, DC, DECEMBER 25 19

CHAPTER 3 K STREET, DC, DECEMBER 26 28

CHAPTER 4 GEORGETOWN, DC, DECEMBER 26 37

CHAPTER 5 I-66, NORTHERN VIRGINIA, DECEMBER 27 43

CHAPTER 6 K STREET, DC, DECEMBER 27 53

CHAPTER 7 K STREET, DC, DECEMBER 28 59

CHAPTER 8 CAPITOL HILL, DC, DECEMBER 28 67

CHAPTER 9 I-95, NORTHERN VIRGINIA, DECEMBER 29 75

CHAPTER 10 OCRACOKE, NORTH CAROLINA, DECEMBER 29 85

CHAPTER 11 OCRACOKE, NORTH CAROLINA, DECEMBER 29 91

CHAPTER 12 OCRACOKE FERRY, NORTH CAROLINA, DEC. 30 94

CHAPTER 13 FBI HEADQUARTERS, DC, DECEMBER 31 102

CHAPTER 14 NORTHWEST, DC, DECEMBER 31 108

CHAPTER 15 DULLES AIRPORT, VIRGINIA, JANUARY 6 114

CHAPTER 16 OUTSIDE RĪGA, LATVIA, JANUARY 8 120

CHAPTER 17 DAUGAVPILS, LATVIA, JANUARY 8 127

CHAPTER 18 DAUGAVPILS, LATVIA, JANUARY 9 135

CHAPTER 19 DAUGAVPILS, LATVIA, JANUARY 9 145

CHAPTER 20 DAUGAVPILS, LATVIA, JANUARY 10 151

CHAPTER 21 DAUGAVPILS, LATVIA, JANUARY 10 159

CHAPTER 22 DAUGAVPILS, LATVIA, JANUARY 10 168

CHAPTER 23 DAUGAVPILS, LATVIA, JANUARY 10 176

CHAPTER 24 DAUGAVPILS, LATVIA, JANUARY 11 182

CHAPTER 25 DAUGAVPILS, LATVIA, JANUARY 11 190

CHAPTER 26 DAUGAVPILS, LATVIA, JANUARY 11 197

CHAPTER 27 OUTSKIRTS OF DAUGAVPILS, LATVIA, JAN. 11 204

CHAPTER 28 OUTSKIRTS OF DAUGAVPILS, LATVIA, JAN. 11 215

CHAPTER 29 DAUGAVPILS, LATVIA, JANUARY 11 227

CHAPTER 30 DAUGAVPILS, LATVIA, JANUARY 11 237

CHAPTER 31 JFK INTERNATIONAL, NEW YORK CITY, JAN. 12 246

CHAPTER 32 BROOKLYN, NEW YORK CITY, JANUARY 12 252

CHAPTER 33 GREENWICH VILLAGE, NEW YORK CITY, JAN. 13 ... 257

CHAPTER 34 ACELA, NEW JERSEY, JANUARY 16 262

CHAPTER 35 NORTHWEST, DC, JANUARY 16 267

CHAPTER 36 FBI HEADQUARTERS, DC, MARCH 6 272

AFTERWORD 277

ACKNOWLEDGEMENTS 278

ABOUT THE AUTHOR 280

MAPS AND A NOTE ON LANGUAGE

It would be the height of insensitivity for a story drawing on the subtle interplay of language and identity to bowdlerize the very tongues it describes. Yet to a reader unfamiliar with the unique script of the Latvian language, the use of original spellings may present some confusion. I have made every effort to present non-English terms in a generic, phonetic form, but for several words the original spelling was most appropriate. The name Bērziņš, notably, is pronounced "BEAR-zinsh." One of the most common Latvian surnames, it means "little birch tree."

Daugavpils & The Baltics

* Maps are stylized and for illustration purposes only

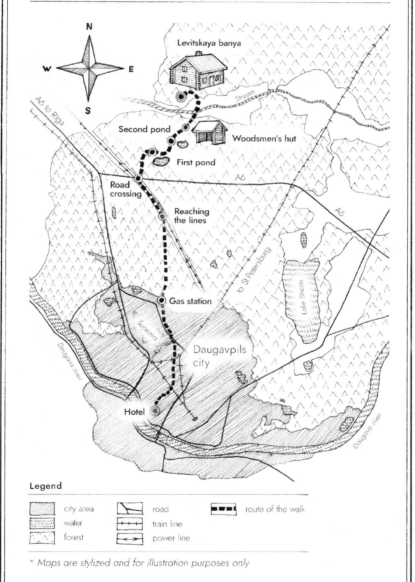

CHAPTER 1
Georgetown, DC, December 25

Breathe, just breathe.

Charlotte leaned back against the bathroom door, exhaling in relief as she locked the world outside. She closed the lid on the toilet, gratefully sinking down to the seat with a sigh. *Two minutes*, she promised herself. *Just two minutes, and then I'll go back out there. Inhale.* From the dining room, she could hear her father's loud laugh, followed by her mother's higher, more excited tones. They were happy. That was good. Two out of three kids now engaged or married; that reflected well on them, she supposed. She caught herself. She wasn't trying to judge. They lived according to their principles; she was trying to live according to hers. *So breathe.*

Charlotte closed her eyes and tried to clear her mind. How long before she could leave? Maybe thirty more minutes? Congratulate her sister; hug her soon-to-be brother-in-law, say work was calling, get out of here. Her family would give her a hard time—it was Christmas dinner, after all—but she could plead innocent. Her boss's inflexibility was no secret.

As if to make the lie real, Charlotte reached for her phone. No new messages. She mindlessly opened her news app and scrolled through the headlines ... gruesome images of the massive Australian bush fires ... the latest impeachment gossip ... protests on the snowy streets of an eastern European country. Charlotte shook her head, shook herself out of it. *But what about ...* Almost inadvertently, Charlotte opened Bumble. *Two minutes*, she reminded herself. *Just to get my mind off of all of this ...*

Jared, 31. *Ugh, what a bro.* Left.

Charles, 28. Handsome ... but posed with a tiger. Left.

Robert, 35. *Just ...* Left.

It wasn't a pity party here in the bathroom, Charlotte tried to convince herself. She was doing great. OK, not as great as her baby sister, on the other side of that door. A year Charlotte's junior at twenty-nine, Caitlin was already a senior associate at the firm where she'd worked since finishing law school. She'd bought this historic townhouse in Georgetown with her boyfriend — now fiancée! — Ted, whom she'd met on her first day of work. Of course they had to announce their engagement at the family Christmas party, Charlotte thought, again reminding herself to breathe.

Kevin, 25. Look at those abs! Let's see the other pics. But ... 25. Left.

Tim, 34. "It's not the six feet that matters, it's the four inches." Charlotte guffawed. Left.

Evan, 30. *Could it be?!?* Charlotte felt the uncomfortable rush of recognition as she swiped nervously through the photos, each one a reminder of a person she knew so well. *It's him all right.*

Charlotte sighed and leaned back against the toilet. How many years? Ten since they met in college and fell in love. Eight since they moved from Providence to DC, both to start internships — his on the Hill, hers with an NGO — living on beans and love, it seemed at the time. Six since he made the earth-shattering decision to leave their shared lives and join the Army. Five since that awful breakup at Fort Bragg, five since she left for grad school abroad, five since they had seen or heard from each other at all. Five years of not-thinking about Evan, five years of making her own way and finding her own path. *But damn, look at those eyes,* Charlotte thought, allowing herself to dwell on one of his particularly flattering pictures. *It's over. It's been over. I know I'm in a vulnerable moment and probably shouldn't do this, but ...* she swiped right. It was done.

Once she committed, it wasn't a second before the match popped up. *What the hell. Let's just take this train-wreck of day as far as it can go.* She started a message: "hi Evan! what a pleasure to remake your acquaintance." He instantly replied: "Charlotte! Are you in DC? Let's meet up." His enthusiasm seemed harmless and infectious, a welcome change from the forced camaraderie outside. Charlotte tried to conjure up her best self. *What am I doing??* she asked herself. But she had the easy answer on hand. "Yes I'm in town! Been back stateside about 4 months. What about you?" Just then, a knock on the door. Charlotte jumped up guiltily, as though caught, her phone clattering to the ground.

"Just a moment!" she called out, grabbing her phone and running the water to wash her hands. Stepping out of the bathroom, she nearly collided with her uncle Walter, her dad's brother and co-partner at their hedge fund. "Uncle Walter!" she said, realizing as it came out that her voice was a little too high and a little too loud. She slipped past his massive bulk and slid down the hallway, ducking into the guestroom. Her phone lit up with three messages: all Bumble, all from Evan. Giddy in spite of herself, cheeks burning, she read them quickly:

"I'm here in DC! In grad school. It's good

Wanna hang out? Denson's is open tonight

Where did you go???"

Smiling to herself, she wrote back: "Denson's sounds great. Soon? I can be there in 30." His reply was quick, confirming the time. Charlotte stood up and straightened her dress, judging herself in the mirror. Her lithe, six-foot frame was hardly flattered by the blue silk number — low-cut, but not sexy — she'd chosen to signal to her parents that she was a reasonable adult they could stop worrying about. She flipped her dark blonde hair onto her shoulders, checked her face for makeup blemishes, so obvious against her pale skin, and forced herself to smile until the glint came into her grey eyes. It wasn't the look she would have chosen if she'd known she'd be seeing her ex for the first time in five years, but it would have to do. She nodded to herself and grabbed her coat. Her family might find her abrupt farewell odd, but now she had somewhere else to be.

Charlotte's Uber was still two minutes away when her phone rang. She frowned; the only people who actually called her were her mom and her boss, Margaret. She had just said goodbye to her mom, so …

"Hello, Margaret." Charlotte tried to keep the tension out of her voice. It's not that Margaret was calling on Christmas, but that she, Charlotte, was actually answering. Charlotte had only been back in the US for four months, and she needed her job at Margaret's corporate investigation firm in order to apply for what she'd decided would come next: becoming an FBI agent. The work was interesting but not, Charlotte felt, important; sometimes it even felt like swimming with the bottom-feeders. That said, she was learning a lot, not the least of which was how to survive as a professional woman in DC. Margaret modeled that for her with aplomb and sometimes took the lessons too far. Tonight, Margaret's tone was professional, clipped. She dispensed with formalities, not even bothering to acknowledge the holiday, and got straight to the point. "I assume you've seen the news?"

"Um, yes, of course. What are you referring to?"

"It's this business in Latvia. A week or so ago a Latvian policeman murdered a Russian father and daughter in their home. Russians across Latvia — there are quite a few of them, I suppose — are going off the wire. It's all quite … Ferguson-esque, really. Thugs all over the place, broken windows, vague complaints, you know the drill." Charlotte sighed inside — Margaret may have been a pioneer in her field, a steely-eyed breaker of glass ceilings, but her politics often seemed to be based on the latest clickbait from the Drudge Report.

Margaret continued. "I imagine Russia has its fingers all over this business, but the only reason we care is that we've been retained to advise a representative of the Latvian police." Charlotte's interest was piqued. Charlotte couldn't quite grasp what the Latvian police would want with a small American investigative firm, especially one that specialized in Beltway due diligence. "Our client contacted us through our Munich affiliates. She is the retained counsel for the Latvian police in Daugavpils, the city at the epicenter of the protests. It seems that this whole murder and protest affair has some connection here in the United States."

Charlotte was scrunching her eyebrows together, getting ready to ask the obvious question when Margaret continued. "I know what you want to ask. I don't know what the connection is, and I'm well aware that we're right on the edge when it comes to doing work that's best left to the FBI. But let's hear what she has to say. Be in tomorrow morning at nine. We'll sign Non-Disclosure Agreements and decide from there." Despite all her wishes for a restful long weekend, Charlotte was intrigued and couldn't help but accede. A barely polite "Merry Christmas" and a click ended the conversation. It would be easy to make overtime this week, even with the holiday.

It wasn't until she was in her Uber that Charlotte reflected on what she was about to do. Seeing Evan, especially after only being back in DC for a few months, felt like insanity. She couldn't admit it at the time, but he was the reason she left five years ago. They had been so in love—so in love—and their future had felt so big and bright. He, with his legislative internship, activism on campus and then in the community, his skill and compassion with nearly every person he met, not to mention his amazing brain. She, with her—with her what? What had she brought to the relationship? Who had she been in those days? Lost, in many ways—rich, yes, privileged as hell, check. But uninformed, even unformed. When she met Evan she had been ready to change her life, and he had helped her find the direction and means to do that. They had been shiny, the two of them. They had glowed with possibility, with desire, with potential. The future had been bright, and then it hadn't. She still blamed him, in spite of herself.

The car slowed down as it approached the bar. One of their old haunts. She checked her makeup in her compact, afraid to see her own eyes, doing her best to banish the insecurities and ambitions and doubts and regrets rushing through her mind. *Breathe, just breathe.*

CHAPTER 2
Gallery Place, DC, December 25

They were lucky: the Denson liquor bar would have been a pleasurable spot for a sorta-date in the best of circumstances, but on Christmas afternoon—when even the grossest undergrad Irish bars were closed—it was a godsend. Charlotte descended into its underground cave and saw Evan almost immediately. *Damnit, damnit, damnit,* she thought, smile plastered across her face, *he looks really good.*

Evan's face opened into a warm smile as she approached, a lock of his unkempt brown hair falling across his forehead. He stood from the bar and opened his arms for a hug, and then dropped them again as she approached, instead gesturing to ask if she wanted to hug.

"No, no, it's OK," she said, laughing in a way she hoped sounded natural, and their bodies pressed against one another for a moment. A moment when Charlotte felt the familiar warmth of his torso, the place where her face fit against his chest, the perfect embrace of his arms. She pulled away quickly, still laughing, and drew up a stool next to his. "Wow," she said, taking him in, "it's been a long time."

"Too long," he said, and again Charlotte got the impression that he was being genuine. She felt herself relax a bit and allowed herself a chance to really look at him. He had the same tall, broad build and looked every bit the part of scruffy grad student—lumpy sweater, worn jeans, old boots—but he held himself with a new poise and confidence. Must have been that Army training, she supposed.

"So …" Evan said, and they both laughed again. Charlotte turned to the barman and ordered an Old Fashioned.

"Tell me about you," Charlotte said. "What is this school thing you're up to?"

"Georgetown," he answered. "I'm doing my master's in foreign affairs. I'm just getting started. The Army was good to me — or, I should say, I was lucky in the Army." Evan had said that line before, she could tell, but it seemed honest. "There wasn't a day I didn't hate it and love it all at once. Oh my god, Charlotte — the stupidity. Do you remember when I was in training, the stories I'd tell? The pointless hours, the haphazard exercises, the heart-breaking waste … that was only the beginning of it. I thought it would be better once I made it to the more … specialized side of things, but — god it was just mind numbingly stupid. They trained me to speak Russian, then sent me to Afghanistan two times. But you know, I wouldn't trade it for anything. The values, the challenge, the people I served with — the adventure. Long story short, I loved my time … but at a certain point it was either stay in forever or get out. I just didn't see myself living the twenty-year, three-divorce plan. So I got out."

Charlotte swallowed hard. This was both easier and harder than she expected. Easier because she was genuinely interested in seeing Evan and hearing about his life. Harder because, in her mind, he had chosen the Army over her. And now he'd been out of the Army for months.

"So — why grad school?" she asked.

"Since I was stupid enough to pay for my own education and then join the Army, I had my full GI Bill," he continued with a chagrined look. "So a master's program was a way to … give myself some space to figure out what's next, I guess. And I just kept on from there. It's been wonderful. Char," —she noted he had slipped back to using her nickname—"they give you a piece of paper at the beginning of the year and it tells you everything you have to do to succeed. Read this, write this, done!"

Charlotte smiled at his discovery. Evan had always been on the energetic side.

"So what about you?" Evan asked. "You left for school and—."

"Yes ..." Charlotte hesitated, unsure how to narrate the last five years. Evan wasn't on Facebook, or any other social media it seemed, so as far as she could tell, he knew nothing about her life. "Well, after ... I did the master's in economics at the University of Singapore. After graduation I got a job with a small nonprofit doing rural microfinance in northern India, which led to a gig lecturing at the University of Delhi. It was fine, interesting work, but ... after three years, time to come home." *Don't ask any more questions*, she pled silently. She had no desire to revisit the loneliness, the intensity of those years. She had been good—better than good, great—at her work, but nothing about it had been easy. She had witnessed too many of her talented female colleagues crushed under the weight of their own expectations, expectations exceeded only by the obstacles to their advancement. Too many well-intentioned aid programs foundered on unmovable bureaucracies and entrenched interests. Too many people like her, people who started life on third base, strolling across home plate and thinking they'd hit a home run while the stadium burned.

Evan's eyes lingered on hers, and she felt him plumb the layers of loneliness and jadedness she was trying to repress.

Her anxiety rising to the surface, she nervously glanced around the room, noticing for the first time the contrast between the classy, speakeasy-style décor and the scattered sad few folks who'd trudged there to avoid whatever holiday misery haunted them at home. Or maybe that was just her projection.

Evan glazed over Charlotte's discomfort and continued. "But DC isn't home. Why'd you end up here and not NYC?"

The question threw Charlotte right back into her twisting self-doubt. Despite all their ideological disagreements, her father, Bill, had always made it clear to Charlotte that there would be a place for her at his hedge fund when she got all this wandering out of her system. But after her gilded childhood of exclusive Upper East Side private schools and high expectations, she'd never recovered from the shock of the financial crisis, when she saw exactly how it was her father made his millions. As a college sophomore, she'd been ill-equipped to handle the shame of meeting people like Evan, whose parents were working two jobs only to lose their house, when she could pop down to New York to have their housekeeper do her laundry on the weekend. From then on she'd been on a quest to prove, or perhaps redeem, herself: first through campus activism and radical politics, then through an embrace of sustainable development and the expatriate NGO life—always through trying to escape her privilege. Her older brother Chuck had no such qualms and was well along the path to partner. But Charlotte just wasn't ready to enjoy a decent quality of life if it meant giving up on a decade of living her principles.

"I guess …" she began, tentatively. "It started to seem like no matter the project, no matter the numbers or the investment or the protections or whatnot, the same type of person would always find a way to benefit. Sometimes it was bigwig investors like my dad, whose mistakes cost the world trillions of dollars during the recession but who still walked away with a TARP bailout instead of in handcuffs. Or maybe it was just the ubiquitous village strongmen who managed to take a cut of every loan we issued. But I started to realize that it wasn't enough to just make the system a little less unjust. I wanted to go after people who were trying to keep it that way."

Charlotte felt her confidence returning as she found a familiar strength in the righteousness that had drawn her to DC. "So I've decided to be one of the good guys. I'm going to join the FBI. I can't even apply until I've been back in the States for six months, so in the meantime I'm working at a corporate private investigation practice. It's definitely a few rungs down on the traditional ladder, but I'm learning the ropes and making contacts. And I'm going to make a difference." She left the statement hanging, hoping Evan wouldn't pick up on just how much Charlotte felt like she'd thrown away years of experience and privilege to pursue this path.

Evan gazed at her, appraising. "Special fucking Agent Charlotte fucking Sorenson. Badass, Char." He was smiling. Charlotte suppressed a twinge of joy at his approval as she felt the corners of her eyes crinkle. No one — not her parents, her siblings, not even her closest friends — had expressed support for the path she'd chosen. "So what kind of stuff does a detective agency have someone with almost a decade's experience in microfinance doing? Anything juicy?"

Charlotte paused for a moment, thinking of how the boss whose example she'd once looked up to seemed to live a soulless, ungrounded life of manipulation, eighty-five-hour workweeks, and shady dealings. She resolved to order another round, gesturing a "two" sign at the barman as she weighed her professional loyalty against the joy she'd get from telling Evan about her new project.

In the Uber, she'd had a moment to do a bit of reading on the Latvia protests. The reputable news outlets agreed on a few salient points. On December 18, the police in Daugavpils, a majority ethnic-Russian town in eastern Latvia, had received a call about a burglary at one of the dilapidated Soviet-era apartment blocks on the outskirts of town. The ethnically Latvian Sergeant Aleksandrs Bērziņš was dispatched to investigate. A short time later, others in the building called the police, reporting hearing three gunshots; when the response team arrived, they found two people dead in the apartment Bērziņš had visited. The two were later identified as forty-four-year-old Dimitri Evgeniev and his fifteen-year-old daughter Svetlana, who lived alone in the small one-bedroom unit. There was no trace of Bērziņš.

In the following hours, cell phone footage emerged showing a Latvian policeman resembling Bērziņš fighting with Dimitri Evgeniev — evidently filmed by Svetlana, it was clear from the dialogue that Dimitri had walked in on Bērziņš trying to force himself on her. The clip graphically culminated with Bērziņš shooting Evgeniev twice point-blank, then turning to Svetlana and raising his pistol. The image played in Charlotte's mind as she felt her closeness to Evan overcome her common sense.

"Have you seen these Latvian protests on the news?" she inquired.

"The Russia ones?" he answered. "Feels a lot like Ferguson, if you ask me."

Charlotte was stunned — it was the second time she'd heard the comparison. "Why do you say that?"

"Well, I was reading a bit about it on the BBC. I had no clue there was this entire underclass of Russians in Latvia."

"Underclass? How so?"

"I'm sure it's no news to you, but this whole 'non-citizens' thing—that there are hundreds of thousands of ethnically Russian residents of Latvia who lack citizenship on the basis of their heritage. A decision made when Latvia became independent in '91. The idea that there is a member of NATO, of the EU—a democracy—that can uphold a policy like that? It boggles the mind. And then something like this murder happens, some super-nationalist wacko acting out his insecurities. The father does what any father would do, and boom, they're dead. Mr. Wackjob disappears, the Latvian government has no answers, no desire to provide any answers, only seems to care about who leaked the video—of course these Russian 'non-citizens' are rioting on the street. It's what I'd be doing. So I saw some meme on Facebook, it had a picture of the Paris Arab riots, Ferguson burning, and the Latvian protests. To me the parallel is obvious."

Charlotte needed a minute to process what Evan had said, a moment she was granted by the arrival of their drinks and a cup of goldfish. For one, she'd only just started her research, and much of what he'd referred to—'non-citizens,' Bērziņš's nationalist ties, the lack of Latvian government response—was new to her. She didn't want to let him know she didn't yet have a formed opinion. Especially when Evan was so ... plugged in. His upbringing had always lent his outrage a degree of authenticity that eluded her limousine liberal values, but she'd imagined the Army had squeezed some of that out of him. Evidently the opposite. But most striking was that Margaret and Evan, two people with totally divergent values, had made the same comparison to make opposing points.

"It's interesting. My conservative boss also compared it to Ferguson. But I got the impression it was a negative comparison to her."

Evan sipped his Old Fashioned and tilted his head in thought. "Honestly, maybe she even saw the exact same meme. I'm realizing now that it made no point, only the comparison. What a genius piece of propaganda—if you want to sympathize with the protestors, it fills you with righteous outrage. If you want to see the protestors as lawless hooligans, it fills you with righteous outrage."

Charlotte felt the bourbon hitting her veins, the warmth of the basement bar and the heavy liquor and comfortable company surging through her despite the depressing topic. She could see that Evan had made up his mind about where he wanted the evening to go, and try as she might to pretend, she knew she felt the same. It was going to take every bit of discipline she had not to walk down that path, her deep yearning for the type of connection and comfort and support she'd once felt with Evan piggybacking on the alcohol to make her feel like everything was OK. But it wasn't, and she felt her eyes empty as she drew within herself to a familiar place, an inside where she could feel in control and squash the kinds of emotions that were dragging her towards him.

"Well Evan, I've got an early morning and a hell of a day tomorrow. I don't think I've got much in me beyond this round …" She could see the disappointment in Evan's eyes. He clearly thought their history and chemistry and her quick response had meant she was on the same page. Which they were, it was just …

Thirty minutes later she was in an Uber home, wondering if she should have jumped in harder than just making a vague plan to hang out soon. And thirty minutes after that, she was in bed, cursing her loneliness.

CHAPTER 3
K Street, DC, December 26

The conference room was silent save for the incessant whistle of the air vent and Charlotte's intermittent sighs. Aside from an old coffee stain on the carpet and a smattering of corporate logos, there was nothing to distinguish it from conference rooms in the exact same spot on the lower seven floors of the enormous office building, or for that matter any conference room in any twenty-first century cookie cutter office building. Charlotte's utter disgust at losing a day of vacation made the expensive chairs, the state-of-the-art smart board, and even the expansive views of K Street and DC beyond seem like a miserable imposition, simple capitalist artifacts meant to sooth the raw truth that she was bound by reputation, contract, and rent to be sitting in this soulless cell.

She'd arrived at work a smidge before nine, leaving just enough time to make a cup of coffee and settle into her office before Margaret barged in, precisely on the hour, her diminutive form projecting a dominant energy that filled the room.

"Here's your NDA," she said, plopping the pages on Charlotte's desk. "Sign it, and be in the conference room at nine thirty. I trust you've done some preparation." There wasn't a hint of empathy in Margaret's husky voice, well trained by decades in one of the three-letter agencies to conceal anything but exactly that which she meant to convey. This one sounded like "I'm tired too, but you'd better be ready to work your ass off." Not content with the federal pension that accompanied the end of her twenty-five-year career as a field intelligence officer, Margaret had directed her ruthless energy toward starting a private due-diligence firm. Known for her vast network and indefatigable discretion, Margaret offered her clients an insider's perspective on potential business partners and an informal channel between parties who couldn't be seen communicating. As Margaret's senior analyst, Charlotte participated in almost every part of the spy-of-fortune operation. She wasn't sure how comfortable she was working on behalf of the highest bidder rather than the national interest, but it was a necessary step to build a reputation in her field. Margaret turned on her heel and breezed out of the conference room.

Getting home late, Charlotte had lay in bed and read more about the situation in Daugavpils. Evan's description had been correct, if limited. At the time of its independence in 1991, Latvia was faced with a dilemma similar to one faced by all the post-Soviet states: What to do with all the non-Latvians who had moved there since the USSR had first invaded at the beginning of World War II? Should they be granted citizenship, regardless of ethnicity or affiliation with what many saw as the occupying regime? Or should they be expelled, Stalin-like, to their ethnic homeland? In other words, would Latvia be a non-Latvian democracy, or a Latvian non-democracy?

The solution kicked the problem down the road: No one whose ancestors moved to Latvia after 1940 would be granted citizenship. They would be "non-citizens," denied most of the rights of a democratic regime but allowed to stay and, if they so desired, work toward Latvian citizenship. In 1991, there were more than 715,000 non-citizens—mainly Russians, but also Belarussians, Ukrainians, Poles, anyone resettled during the Soviet era—almost 35 percent of the population. With generational change, that number in 2017 was down to 14 percent, or just under 300,000.

But with restrictions on the official use of the Russian language and escalating ethnic tensions across eastern Europe, the issue had become more divisive with time, not less. Ethnic Russians came to see themselves as victims of an oppressive, nationalist regime that inherited a fascist legacy and wrote off their legitimate grievances in a rush to join a hypocritical NATO and EU. And Latvians, worried about a resurgent Russia that had invaded Latvia three times in the past century and attacked four of its neighbors in the past decade, saw ethnic Russians as a fifth column working against them from the inside.

Into this powder keg dropped the spark of Aleksandrs Bērziņš. A rabid Facebook user with decidedly anti-Russian, pro-Latvian, and far-right political views, Bērziņš's track record included disciplinary action for inflammatory remarks at work. Something must have snapped, and between his well-documented online rants and the shocking video of his crime, the event had triggered massive protests across Daugavpils, a town only fifty miles from the Russian border where a mere 15 percent of the 95,000 citizens identify as ethnically Latvian.

In the week of unrest, there had been minor clashes between protestors and police, but as a whole, the situation had settled into a kind of stalemate. The protestors, well-organized and disciplined from the look of it, had simple if vague demands: bring Bērziņš to justice, grant equality to non-citizens, and recognize Russian as an official language. The Latvian government, on the other hand, had been haphazard and sluggish in its response. Some police units had made aggressive one-off stands against crowds, but the national government didn't even acknowledge anything was happening. The whole thing felt murky, one of those complex issues that slipped away from you any way you grabbed at it, but on one thing Charlotte was clear: there was no question these non-citizens had a compelling grievance.

The sharp click of heels on the tiled hallways brought Charlotte back to the present; she sat up in her chair and straightened her blouse. Charlotte could tell Margaret's quiet pad from the many times she'd appeared quite suddenly around a door corner or doorway, leaving Charlotte unsure just how long she'd been there. These footfalls, on the other hand, had an efficient "snap" to the steps that told her the owner was officious, dominant, and clad in stilettos. Sure enough, Margaret silently entered the conference room, trailed by a yet shorter, black haired woman in her mid-forties, her wiry figure apparent through a shapeless grey pantsuit. Her four-inch heels, grossly out of place in the office, were the sign that made the mark: this woman couldn't be anything but Slavic.

Charlotte rose to greet her boss and the visitor, surprised that the client had come all this way just to brief them in person. Even Gulf oil magnates preferred to Skype these days.

"Natalya, this is Charlotte, our top investigator." Margaret introduced them with a gracious voice, sticky with sweet undertones and featuring a compliment she would never have given Charlotte to her face. The distinctive first name confirmed Charlotte's initial appraisal: even if she worked for the Latvian police, this woman was ethnically Russian to the core. "Charlotte, this is Natalya Lubachevsky, our client. She is counsel for the Latvian police. Natalya, can we get you anything?"

The implication was clear that it would be Charlotte who would be doing the getting, but as they shook hands, Natalya declined. "No thank you, Margaret. Charlotte, it is a pleasure to meet you." She had an extremely thick Russian accent, the *r* of Charlotte's name sounding like she had swallowed it and the *ee* sounds of *is* and *meet* reaching a sharp, high pitch.

"Let us get right down to business," Natalya continued. "My supervisor expects me back at work tomorrow afternoon, and my flight leaves in just a few hours." Charlotte was impressed by Natalya's command of English, belying such a thick accent, and appreciated her directness. This was someone she could work with.

"I assume I do not need to review what one of our policemen, Aleksandrs Bērziņš, did last week, or the chaos that has overtaken our beautiful city. I would like to be able to tell you there is a resolution in sight, but unfortunately I only see things getting worse. To be honest, Bērziņš's opinions, misguided though they may have been, were not far from the norm among our policemen. The police commander in Daugavpils has been … less than energetic in his search for Bērziņš."

"It is such a shame," Margaret interjected. "I can't imagine how it must feel to be Russian in Latvia today." It took all of Charlotte's willpower not to let out a guffaw at Margaret's bald-faced pandering. *What was it, twelve hours ago she'd been parroting right-wing mockery of the protests?* "What is to be done about it?"

"I appreciate your sympathy," Natalya replied. "But it is your expertise here in the States I seek." Charlotte grinned on the inside at the implied snub. She was liking Natalya more and more. "Those of us within the Daugavpils police who are more … sympathetic to the non-citizen point of view have not been inactive, even if we must be careful not to exceed our superiors' tolerances. We can't ever be seen to walk faster than their dragging feet, but that's not to say there aren't steps we can take.

"Three days ago, the Latvian cyber intelligence bureau intercepted a phone call from a close friend of Bērziņš's to a number in the United States. They forwarded the transcript to the Daugavpils police, but my colleagues tell me the report was stifled. Once I was informed of its existence, I was able to obtain a copy through contacts in Rīga. Here is a translation for your consideration."

Natalya slid a single sheet of paper across the table. Margaret glanced at it before shifting it to Charlotte, who was able to take it in at a single look:

```
09GAD2-ER453N-DD0944-DF3342
FROM: +37120242446
TO: +1[UNK]
DTG: 23 DEC 2019 // 0943

// CXN //

R: Speak.

S: He is safe and on the move. He should arrive in the
States on schedule.

R: Understood.

// XCXN //
```

"The American number was blocked by your NSA, of course," Natalya continued, "and the original language was Latvian."

Charlotte was taken aback—this was FBI business, plain and simple. A foreign government representative, a fugitive of the law no less, trying to sneak into the United States? She and Margaret had no business here. She turned to Margaret, looking to her to take the lead on calling a turd a turd. But what she saw shouldn't have surprised her; high risk meant high fees. Margaret knew what she could make off a project like this one, and it showed in the enthusiastic smile she wore.

Natalya remained silent, knowing that the promise of an interesting project and a hefty invoice put the ball in Margaret's court. It took a moment for Margaret to make the next, obvious move. "Natalya," she asked, "why haven't you brought this to the FBI?"

Natalya cracked a smile caked in the raw dominance she'd asserted since she first walked in. "Margaret. Did your Negros go to the FBI when they were being lynched by the dozen in the South?" She paused for a moment, too happy to turn American exceptionalism against itself. "No. The Bureau was too busy chasing Chicago gangsters whose only crime was making profits the government couldn't tax. Ten Negros died from racial terrorism for every Mafioso killed in the wars immortalized by Hollywood. But Americans don't care about Negros. So why would the Latvian police spoil their relationship with the premier law enforcement agency of the greatest superpower on earth for the sake of a few people who weren't even citizens to begin with? So I am simply making steps to ensure there is at least someone following this lead."

Charlotte's defensiveness rose up — *who was she to make judgments?!* — but then she saw Natalya staring blankly at the creases on Margaret's forehead and knew she hadn't made the comparison for the sake of argument. It was just a distraction, a red herring to give Natalya a moment's breathing room — and maintain control.

"You make a fair point," Margaret rejoined conciliatorily. "So what am I to understand you expect out of us, seeing as you have no better lead than a snippet of conversation?"

"You are correct," Natalya responded. "There is nothing to be done in the meantime, except learning as much as you can about the situation. I have contacts across Europe who are helping us pick up Bērziņš's trail as he makes his way here. All I ask is that you be ready to look into things once we find a thread to pull." Natalya turned her intense gaze to Charlotte. "I trust that you will be doing the bulk of the heavy lifting, Charlotte. What support do you need?"

Contentious probing aside, Charlotte's positive impression of Natalya increased with her straightforward manner. "I'll require funding for Latvian and Russian translation services, of course, but otherwise I see nothing unusual about the project."

Natalya smiled. "But of course. I've already discussed your expense account for this project with Margaret, and I assure you it will be sufficient."

Her words hung in the air like an invitation. Charlotte couldn't resist: "You've left out one piece, Natalya. How did you go from hearing about a cell phone intercept to flying to the United States with a blank checkbook?" Margaret shot a wrathful glare across the table.

After a short pause Natalya looked into Charlotte's eyes and replied. "I am overjoyed to have such a sharp mind on my side." Natalya's compliment felt genuine. "Well, Charlotte, I reached out to a Russian-speaking representative in the Latvian Assembly, who was able to allocate funds from a cultural-exchange program. I suppose I should give you a nesting doll to live up to the effort." Charlotte couldn't help but smile. Natalya continued, "I took a few days off from work, and here I am. I didn't dare use any form of electronic communication — our national intelligence bureau is, as you have already seen, quite efficient."

With these words Natalya signaled she had nothing more to say, and after they exchanged a set of formal goodbyes, Margaret walked Natalya to the front desk. Charlotte plopped back down in the fancy chair, looking without seeing out the panoramic windows, unsure what to think about the assignment. Charlotte couldn't help admiring Natalya and found it easy to sympathize with the non-citizens. It was undoubtedly an interesting case, one she'd dive into with relish. But it was also one that fell squarely into the grey area between private intelligence work and a jail cell.

Margaret returned a moment later and didn't waste a moment. "Charlotte, you were far too forward with our client. Leave those questions to me. Your job is to investigate what you are told." Margaret sat back down and avoided her gaze. "That said, you are absolutely correct. This is a hair's breadth from nothing we should have anything to do with. But for the time being, it's just doing open-source research on someone else's dime, within the bounds of a normal NDA. So start learning all you can about Latvia, what's happened, and the Latvian community in the US. If it ever gets sketchy, we'll call it quits."

Charlotte was worried they were on a slippery slope but couldn't argue with Margaret's logic. As she made herself a fresh coffee and wandered back to her office, she did wonder just how big that expense account was, though, and laughed at the idea of making Evan her Russian-speaking assistant.

CHAPTER 4
Georgetown, DC, December 26

Ensconced in one of the overstuffed chairs that graced her sister's Georgetown rowhouse, Charlotte scrutinized every millimeter of Caitlin's face, feeling a disbelief equal to the one that was wrenching Caitlin's pupils open. *She is only 29!!! Botox already?!?* Charlotte couldn't find a trace of the nascent crow's feet that had graced Caitlin's eyes just a few months before, nor a hint of any upward eyebrow movement to match the judgement seared on Caitlin's eyes. *And she didn't even tell me. Well at least the little princess will look perfect in her fucking wedding photos.* But she had to file that one away, for now; there was no doubt Caitlin had her on the ropes.

"Jesus fucking Christ, Charlotte. Did you kiss him goodnight? Evan fucking Roberts. I thought I'd never have to hear that god damn moocher's name ever again."

Insight into the extent of Caitlin's vain insecurities aside, Charlotte was beginning to regret inviting herself over to Caitlin's with a "sorry-I-left-your-party-early" bottle of wine. She'd needed a drink after a long day studying the intricacies of the Bērziņš situation, and genuinely felt bad at having rushed out early after Caitlin's big announcement. For all the rivalry, the resentment, the mutual disdain for life paths chosen, Caitlin was still her little sister and, after so much moving around, the closest thing Charlotte had to a best friend.

"No, I didn't kiss him goodnight, Cait," Charlotte countered, exasperated. "But I wanted to."

Caitlin rolled her eyes, folding her lululemon-clad legs beneath her while holding the oversized glass of rosé aloft to avoid spilling on the off-crème boucle couch that anchored the center of the room. The place could have passed for a spread in a West Elm catalogue, the design as millennially faultless as Charlotte's conviction that half the furniture would be on Craigslist in five years, traded out for the trends of Christmas 2024.

"Why, Char. Just why? After the stunt he pulled?"

Caitlin had always been the one member of the family who wasn't head over heels for Evan. From the moment Charlotte had brought him home from Brown for Thanksgiving their junior fall, Evan had become the adopted son of the family. Bill saw in Evan's energy and drive a worthwhile addition to the family empire, and her mother, Heidi, was convinced that Evan would temper some of what she saw as Charlotte's unusual life priorities. Evan had quickly won over her older brother, Chuck, at a bar one night, but Caitlin had always remained skeptical.

"You're so unfair to him, Cait. You were bent against him from the beginning."

"He was crooked from the beginning! Evan is a user, Char. He's charming and gracious and lovely and works on Things That Matter, but the whole thing is a façade. He grew up poor and knows what side his bread is buttered on. That guy always has an angle, and he freeloaded off you until the second he didn't need you. Then—poof—he disappears?!? C'mon."

Charlotte thought back to the first time Caitlin met Evan, on a weekend when Caitlin had taken the train up from NYC to visit her big sister. Teenage Caitlin was every part the NYC socialite, a gap-year intern with a fake ID and dad's credit card, a newfangled iPhone, and the confidence she was born to rule. Charlotte had thought that the dark glint escaping Caitlin's eyes as she appraised Evan's threadbare wool sweater and unkempt hair over the sticky table at a late-night diner had been jealousy, predatory expressions of their childhood rivalries. But as time went on, Charlotte had come to understand that Caitlin truly saw something more sinister in Evan. A social climber herself, Caitlin couldn't help but see the same schemes in Evan's ceaseless rise, and in his pursuit of Charlotte.

"You forget that it was *I* who broke up with *him*." Even just stating it brought a feeling of revulsion to the back of Charlotte's throat, a visceral memory of how much she'd dreaded cutting it off with Evan. He'd been willing to try to figure out something long distance, thinking a weekend every month or two would be enough to keep them together, but Charlotte had needed the physical closeness of someone actually *in her life*. So it had fallen to her, as their conflicting emotional needs grew messier and messier, to be the one who cut it off.

Caitlin blew a big raspberry that ended with a swig of wine.

"Surrrrree, Char. Whatever you say. But let's review the facts, shall we? You meet in college, where you're his sugar momma. Then you live together for two years in DC in an apartment Daddy paid for. Then all of a sudden he goes home for Christmas and comes back a different person, ready to throw away a five-year relationship for some new path? You were never the most important thing to him, Char. You were just a useful steppingstone while he worked his way up at the Senator's office, so he could go check the box on military service and get his name on a ballot somewhere."

"Fucking harsh, Cait. You know as well as I do that he went home for his best friend's funeral. Remember, Kyle?"

Kyle, Evan's closest childhood friend, someone he only ever spoke of in terms of the highest praise, the only person Evan ever admitted truly looking up to. Kyle, who in a just world would have had a full ride to any college in the country, but who was never mentored to try for anything better than community college. Kyle, who lost his night job and enlisted in the Army to help keep up his mother's underwater mortgage payment. Kyle, who'd been killed in a firefight in Afghanistan on a weekend when Evan and Charlotte were out at her uncle's place in the Hamptons.

"I know, Kyle." Caitlin leaned over to make herself another cracker with brie and jam. "But you can't tell me the whole thing isn't just a tad too perfect. And now he's back here, doing whatever. Maybe he's sincere, maybe not. But one thing I'm sure of is that he is up to something. You're useful to him, Char."

Charlotte was certain Evan was sincere. She'd seen the pain in his eyes after Kyle's death, and borne the brunt of the torment it had thrown him into. When he'd gone back to Washington state for the memorial service—the first time he'd been back to his childhood home in over five years, during which time his parents had lost their jobs, their home, everything—it had come as no surprise that he'd returned to his comfortable, East Coast, privileged life carrying a resentment that spilled into every part of their lives. And no less a surprise when he'd then felt the need to himself serve, to pay back somehow. Even if it meant the agony of realizing he was putting his dreams ahead of her.

Charlotte looked back down at the text message that had put such a big smile on her face as she and Caitlin had first sat down, the smile that had made it impossible to be as reticent about the night before as Caitlin was about her cosmetic surgery: "Wanna go to the Shenandoah tomorrow? I don't have a car." It was typical of Evan, no mention of the night before or even a pleasantry, but in the direct invitation an expression of everything she'd hoped to hear. The Shenandoah had been their refuge from the DC bustle, her mother's family outside Charlottesville serving as a starting point, but the entire valley providing hikes, pies, picnics, and history to help them escape. The long summers she'd spent there as a child and the fond memories of their adventures made it her special place, and her heart jumped at his suggestion.

"So should I go?" she asked. Caitlin sized her up as she licked extra brie off her fingers.

"Why the fuck not," Caitlin replied, surprising Charlotte. "He makes you happy. You're fucking lonely and you suck at making friends and you'll have a good time." Charlotte was touched, honestly, at the loving insult—just a few years ago, Caitlin could have only seen her own opinion and not even begun to empathize with Charlotte's conflicting, subtle emotions. "But friend zone, Char. It won't do you or him or any of us any favors if you go and let him rekindle things. You know he's going to try. Don't even give him an opening."

Caitlin was right, she knew, but even the oblique reference kindled the feeling of warmth that had surged, unbidden, when they'd hugged goodbye. He just smelled so damn good, and Charlotte missed that. But Caitlin was right. She texted back: "I'll pick you up at 10, send your address. Hiking boots or adjustable-waistline pants?" It wasn't a moment before his response popped up: "Both. I have a special hike I wanna try, but let's stop for pie afterwards :)"

By the time she looked up, Caitlin was off and away, scrolling through a Pinterest feed of wedding dresses and floral arrangements. Charlotte closed her phone and skootched over to her, grabbing the wine bottle as she went. Her little sister might be a selfish little twerp, a brainwashed diva who couldn't see beyond her billable hours and next social ploy, but she certainly had a way of cutting to the core of things.

CHAPTER 5
I-66, northern Virginia, December 27

Growing up on the Upper West Side of Manhattan, Charlotte was no stranger to transiting miles of suburban sprawl to leave a city, yet even so, every time she left DC it felt like the blight of strip malls and housing tracts stretched out a little further. *Someday*, she thought, *it will reach all the way to the Shenandoah, and then what's the point.* She was behind the wheel of her beat-up old Outback, struggling to hold sixty as I-66 finally freed itself from the confines of the northern Virginia suburbs and began to climb up toward the Blue Ridge mountains.

"Now with eight horsepower, the 1923 Model T." Evan had instantly resumed his ragging on Charlotte's beloved old hoopdie when he'd loped out of his Georgetown apartment building and hopped in the passenger seat, joyfully identifying the stain from where he'd accidentally dropped a pizza nine years before. The car had been ratty and beat up in college; Evan was ecstatic to see it had acquired another six years of scars to ridicule. Charlotte couldn't care less. A car like this was just right for surviving DC streets. "If she needs a little more help," he continued, "we can stop in at one of these farms and see if they'll hitch a team of oxen to the front."

When Charlotte had finished up discussing the pros and cons of a full-length train with Caitlin, it was well past ten. She retreated homeward but slept fitfully, a fact that was now all too apparent in her sluggish driving. Evan wasn't letting her forget it, either, chiding her as he guided them through Front Royal and onto a picturesque road paralleling the South Fork of the Shenandoah. The last of her road coffee had gone cold, but now that they were on a two-lane road, she had no trouble staying alert as they passed fields dusted with snow under a perfect winter blue sky. "So did you find ole Aleksandrs Bērziņš yet?" Evan chimed in after guiding them across a one-lane bridge.

Charlotte shot him an anxious glance, unsure what he was getting at. She was relieved to see his playful expression — he'd only been making a generalized reference to their conversation the night before. Of course he couldn't know about the NDA, the hours she'd spent researching just that question, the doubts she had about her role. Maybe she'd gotten a bit too into this project.

"If only it was something that exciting," she lied, wanting his input but wary of the signature she'd scrawled. "It's just a lot of tweets and posts and angry rants."

Charlotte felt relieved as Evan took the bait. "I'll say," he replied. "I read more about it yesterday. I think the Ferguson comparison is actually pretty solid. It's easy for people who disagree with the protestors to laugh them off. And it's easy for people who sympathize to see it as a no-holds-barred fight against evil. In both cases, the only winner is people who profit from the chaos."

Evan directed them onto a dirt road as he finished, no parking lot or trailhead in sight. "Evan," Charlotte tried tentatively, "where exactly are we going?"

Evan smiled at her as he leaned forward to look at the ridgeline through the windshield. He scanned the trees to their right, then looked back at her with a grin, gesturing to pull over. "This will do," he smirked.

"We're on the edge of the George Washington National Forest. A buddy of mine in the Virginia National Guard came out here to do some training a couple weeks back and found a gorgeous frozen waterfall off in the woods. I wanna go check it out. It should only be a mile or two from here."

"And ... where's the trail?" Charlotte dreaded the answer, recalling the time Evan had taken a "shortcut" cross-country and led them through a poison ivy patch. To be fair, they had shaved two hours off the return trip — and spent the rest of the week itching.

Evan pulled a plastic sleeve out of the brightly colored backpack between his legs. "I've got the GPS coordinates, a topo map, and a compass." He smiled, the slightest bashful glint showing in his eyes. She met his gaze and let his words linger. "And ... a thermos of hot chocolate?" She struggled to hold her glare, wanting to smile. "No poison ivy, I promise." She cracked, smiling as she opened her door and went around to get her stuff out of the trunk, the cold hitting her face and banishing any remaining shred of sleepiness.

They set off into the woods, heading straight up a hill at a brisk clip. Evan had put away the map and compass and seemed to just be flying by the seat of his pants, chugging up a slope on the side of a stream. Charlotte refused to fall behind, but she could feel the impact of a few years of driving a desk, and needed to slow Evan down.

"So foreign affairs is a big topic. Do you know what you're going to specialize in yet?" Charlotte tried, hoping to get him to waste some air on talking.

"Right now I'm just at the beginning. Last semester was a whole bunch of intro courses, next semester I'll start some more specialized ones on military policy. But I'm looking at writing my thesis on Syria."

"Syria? Like the refugee crisis, or what?"

"More on the war. Pretty much everyone—the Russians, Assad, Iran, the US, even Turkey—has been using it as a sandbox to test out new weapons, new units, new techniques. It's like the Spanish Civil War before World War II, when Hitler tried out blitzkrieg and bombed Guernica and generally gave the world a preview of what would happen a few years later. And sad to say, like then, no one's really paying attention to what's really going on."

They'd reached the top of a wooded ridgeline, and without glancing at his compass or map, Evan turned and continued along the crest. "Which is?"

"Well for one, all sorts of new technologies—drones, cheap guided missiles, mobile phone apps. And the indiscriminate use of horrendously destructive munitions. Plus, most of the fighting is being done by spies and advisors and proxy forces—guerillas, rebels, gangs, you name it. It gives everyone deniability and lets them skirt humanitarian laws. But most of all, it's one of the first wars where the ground truth only matters insomuch as it spreads online—memes and viral videos are a surer way to outmaneuver your enemy than bombs. The Russians flatten city blocks to create refugees to make memes they amplify to stoke anti-immigrant panic in Europe. ISIS anticipated its violent downfall at the hands of the West, and made it a part of their apocalyptic worldview, maintaining their influence beyond the battlefield. To those who are paying attention, it's a model of warfare as revolutionary as blitzkrieg ever was. Only this time, all the battles are fought in your opponents' minds."

"That's scary," Charlotte chimed in, catching her breath with the gentler slope. "And here we are, still talking about aircraft carriers like it's 1944."

"Like France before World War II. They were so blinded by World War I, they relied on the Maginot Line to stave off the Germans, never imagining that new technologies would let the Nazi tanks just … go around their defenses. They had no idea what way the world was going."

"Speaking of which, Evan … where are we?" Charlotte was a bit concerned at how long it had been since Evan had checked a map. He had a GPS, after all—why not just head straight there?

"I'm terrain associating. If you just plug in a destination on the GPS or figure out a bearing on the map, you'll end up taking a route without regard to the type of terrain you're crossing—which means wet boots and sore legs. Instead, I chose a route using the terrain, and I'm just following the signs. First we took a stream up to the ridge, which we are following west. When another ridge comes in from the right, we head due south across a small gully, then walk back east along a new ridge for four hundred meters. Then we cut due south into the draw, and there's the waterfall. Longer walk, but much easier on the legs."

Charlotte had lost track of his description around where they were, but knew from experience exactly what he meant. Sometimes she'd lost the trail on a tough hike and used GPS to link back up with at a checkpoint. But that was terrible—the straight-line route always led through the worst terrain, and she found herself stopping every ten meters to peer into the woods around her, hoping to see the sweet relief of a trail. Evan moved with no such fits and starts—utterly unconcerned with what was around him, he seemed to be navigating by the soles of his feet, moving as quickly as if there had been a paved road.

They crested the top of a small rise and Charlotte saw the ridge coming in from the right, just as Evan had predicted. Evan stopped in his tracks, putting a finger up to his mouth. Ahead of them was a small family of deer, a mother and two fawns. Nothing special—deer were a pest even in urban DC— but somehow, in the morning light with the dusting of snow, it was something wonderful. She looked at Evan, feeling the urge to slip her cold hand into his. A moment later, the trio startled, bounding off up the mountain. Charlotte and Evan shared a glance and, without speaking, continued across the gully side by side.

"It's all very interesting, Evan, and you're clearly passionate about it," Charlotte picked right back up. "But so was your internship at the Pentagon, and you got ... restless. Aren't you worried you'll get bored in academia, or do you think you've got the adventure out of your system?" She hated herself the second the question left her lips. Here she was, alone in the woods with someone she was trying to friend-zone, bringing up whether he was ready for commitment. *Great one, Char.*

Unfortunately, lack of vulnerability was never one of Evan's traits. "I'm not done running, Char, but ... I'm lonely. I need to figure out how to keep some skin in the game but not lose my soul. This is us—four hundred meters west along this ridge."

"How do you measure that?" The question hung in the air. "The meters."

He flashed her a smile. "My gait gives me about fifty-eight

paces per hundred meters at a gentle downhill like this," he explained, starting to count under his breath. "It's not too important if we're right on or not, since it was a rough start point. But I'll err on the side of coming in short — that way once we hit the stream, we know we can continue downstream to hit the waterfall. It's frozen, after all — no using sound to cheat!"

Charlotte loved the outdoors, but this was something else — Evan had a sense for the terrain that baffled the mind. From what she'd seen, she wouldn't have been surprised if he could have navigated blindfolded, using just the slope of the ground under his feet to keep him on track. Charlotte was unsure exactly what he'd been doing in the Army, but whatever it was had certainly taught him how to handle himself in the woods. No more poison ivy with this one.

But she wasn't sure she wanted to dive too deeply into a conversation about loneliness. "I hear you Evan. By the time I can get into government and start doing anything cool, I'll be thirty-three. And I want to have kids — I just don't know how it all fits together."

Evan turned to her. "I'm glad we reconnected, Char."

"Me too, Evan, it's just ..." She paused, aware that her inability to say what needed to be said would only come across as coyness, yet unsure of how to voice what needed to be said. She turned and kept walking.

They continued in silence, Evan continuing to count under his breath. He stopped at 200 and pulled out his compass, sighting due south. They headed off straight down the side of the ridge, at first a gentle slope, then steepening as the vegetation thickened. Soon it was thick enough, even with the bare boughs of winter, that they were having to use their hands to push aside branches. Charlotte was on the brink of castigating Evan for letting one flail back in her face when he stopped short — they were dead on. The frozen waterfall raised ten feet up above them, thawing trickles dripping down dramatic, eerie formations of ice clinging on to boulders coated with rime. It glistened in the shallow winter light, tiny rainbows dancing off the drops of water falling on moss-clad rocks below. Charlotte turned to Evan, utterly incredulous at his navigational feat.

"Not bad," Evan said curtly.

"Not bad? It's gorgeous," Charlotte countered. "And that was fucking impressive, Evan. Where's that hot chocolate?"

They sat on a dry boulder as Evan pulled out the thermos and snacks — a hunk of marzipan chocolate, a square of goat brie, and an apple. "No judging," he said, "it's what I had in the fridge."

"If that's what's in your fridge, I'm going to have to spend more time at your place," Charlotte replied. *Fuck, what did I just do?*

"I'd like that, Char," Evan responded. He started to lean in for a kiss, one that Charlotte knew would feel genuine and magical and warm and comfortable. But … she pushed him away.

"Evan, I'm not … I'm just not there anymore," she lied. She could see the rejection and disappointment in his eyes. What she wanted to say was "take your clothes off" or even "I'm not quite ready yet" but knew she had to be firm.

"Char, I thought …" he grasped.

"I know. I know. I just ... there's a lot of pain, Evan. I want you in my life, I do. Just not like that. I'm sorry."

He looked away at the waterfall, thinking, brooding. He reached for his bag and pulled out the thermos of hot chocolate, passing her the cup.

They sat for a few more minutes, passing the snacks back and forth and talking about nothing in particular. Charlotte loathed the awkward distance, sure she'd ruined everything. She panicked.

"Can we get moving? I'm getting a little cold," she asked.

Without any hesitation, Evan silently started packing up, his body tense from unexpressed emotion, then wordlessly guided them back the way they came. They moved more quickly on the return, covering the mile and a half in under twenty-five minutes. With every step Charlotte felt worse and worse, cursing herself for pushing him away even as she knew it would only make things worse to let him in.

She unlocked the trunk—the beeper had long ago stopped working—and Evan started loading everything up while she went around to the driver's side to start the heater up. As she sat down, she saw the innocuous blue light blinking from her phone. She'd taken a risk spending a few hours away from her ball and chain, but even with the conflicting feelings of guilt and desire that had come with turning Evan down, it had been worth it. She was apprehensive as she picked up the phone and woke it up. Sure enough: eight missed calls, all from Margaret. Six texts, starting with "Give me a call" and escalating all the way up to:

"Need you to call me ASAP and get to the office NOW. Can't

explain on phone. Big changes. Unacceptable you are out of touch."

Charlotte looked over at Evan, who was clearly psyching himself up to be as pleasant as possible for the hour and a half drive while trying to make sense of what happened. She started the car, realized it was late enough that she wouldn't be at the office before five thirty, and steeled herself for the drive to come.

CHAPTER 6
K Street, DC, December 27

"It's OK, Charlotte, really. I understand." They'd pulled over in front of Charlotte's office building, the freezing rain flashing in the warning lights. No matter what he said, Charlotte felt the yawning gulf between them, the chasm of missed expectations and unexpressed emotion. She understood — there was nothing she wanted more than to curl up and spend the night with him, too — but she was a little turned off by the twinge of petulance in his reaction. Still, he was being generous enough, dropping her with a tub of Chinese takeout and shuttling her Outback home. She jumped out of the car, leaving with an awkward "text me?" before running inside. She glanced back to see him looking after her.

She flashed her badge to the night security guard, disgusted she was here on a day off, ashamed to be at work in sweaty hiking clothes, afraid of the tirade she was sure to receive from Margaret. Sure enough, the elevator doors had barely opened when Margaret, somehow apprised of her arrival, tore into her.

"Charlotte, it is absolutely unacceptable for you to be out of touch like that. Was I unclear in saying this was a project of the utmost importance?"

Charlotte knew Margaret's bait-and-tackle open-ended question approach well enough by this point. Nothing to be gained by indulging in self-defense. "You're absolutely right. I thought I was safe taking a few hours off, but I was wrong. I'm prepared to stay as long as it takes," she retorted, gesturing to her takeout containers, "and it won't happen again."

Margaret glared at Charlotte with her arms crossed, clearly cherishing the power that moments of silence like these gave her. It was only then that Charlotte noticed Margaret wasn't wearing her normal bland pantsuit; clad in a somewhat elegant cocktail dress and woolen shawl, it was clear Margaret was on her way to a date. Charlotte knew Margaret had lost a marriage to her career, so this had to be something new. A sliver of empathy poked its head into Charlotte's defensiveness, the humanizing touch reminding her that behind her ruthless, patronizing boss was a person trying to enjoy her weekend, too.

"Come to my office. We have a lot to discuss." Margaret finally broke the silence and turned and walked off. Her imperious gait instantly restored Charlotte's resentment. *This had better be good*, she thought. *Whatever it is, we're both missing out on real life for it.*

Charlotte plopped down into an overstuffed chair in the corner of Margaret's office, plunking her bag down and pulling out a pad of paper. She gazed longingly at her tub of Chinese food, hoping that whatever was to follow would last short enough so her Shrimp and Broccoli wouldn't get cold.

"First tell me what you've found so far," Margaret demanded, her chair squeaking despite her miniscule frame as she leaned back. Charlotte's eye was drawn to the wall of photos—Margaret's "I Love Me" wall—behind her head. Smiling with suits around DC, hefting an assault weapon in the woods, hijab-clad with snowy peaks in the background, alongside shady bearded characters—it was the standard visual resume of a post-9/11 spy, one that seemed to mock Charlotte's slow-starting career.

"Bottom line is nothing." Charlotte knew Margaret would rather hear the raw conclusion first before getting into all the facts and details, even if it wasn't good news. Margaret remained expressionless. "It's as Natalya told us—there isn't much to find. I'm caught up on the ins and outs of the past two weeks of protests and the underlying issues. I understand the positions of the various stakeholders and have identified key influencers. I've mapped out Latvian cultural groups here in the US and started to get a grasp on how they support their homeland."

"What are the influencers saying?" Margaret inquired.

"On the Latvian side, there are several nationalist politicians who are capitalizing on the protests to shore up support. I'd compare their statements to American politicians criticizing the NFL national anthem protests. It's obvious they dismiss the grievance itself, even disparage the protestors, but can't say it outright without attracting enormous controversy. So they use the disorder and perceived rule-breaking to make harsh statements about restoring order, being respectful … questioning why the issue can't be resolved within the system. The inverse is true among ethnic Russians—this is turning into a massive unifying event inside Russia, with even anti-Putin sources coming out in strong support of the protestors, and the extreme Slavophile outlets even calling for an invasion of Latvia to 'save' their brethren.

"That kind of rhetoric is gasoline on the fire of the meme machine. Latvian Facebook has gone nuts—the event is even more divisive and all-consuming than the 2016 elections were here. On the one hand, some nationalist politician makes an inflammatory statement, liberal commentators go nuts screaming bloody murder, nationalists go wild with mocking memes. On the other, some liberal activist demands action to address Bērziņš's disappearance or the protests, nationalists jump on how naïve they are, liberals go wild with outraged headlines. What's lost in the middle of all the shouting is any coherent, consensus plan of action—it's all so emotional, it's impossible for anyone to take even the most reasonable of steps, even deploying the national police."

"What about these groups in the US?"

"There is one formal Latvian-American cultural group, with chapters across the country and a main office here in DC. There's no indication it's anything but a normal affiliation caucus, mainly concerned with exchanges, guest speakers, art exhibitions, some above-board support to Latvia— you know the drill—could be innocent, could be anything. That said, there are some pretty hardcore nationalist groups—all closed—on social media, who exhibit extremism typical of expat and immigrant communities. They've been echoing a lot of the grosser stuff from Latvia, and definitely seem more organized."

"Anything stick out?"

"Judging only from online, I'd say that New York City is the only place where there's really enough of a ground presence for this to be anything more than a meme-and-PayPal operation. There are some communities in California, Chicago, and Raleigh, but none exhibiting the level of passion and organization as in New York. That's the only place where I could see there being an actual community capable of hiding Bērziņš."

"That's a bold assessment based solely off the internet, Charlotte. Let's not go too Howard Dean."

"All I mean is that New York is the first place I'd watch."

"I see." Margaret paused. The sleet was plastering the window with a thin level of verglas, which only served to remind Charlotte of the layer of nasty cold grease that forms on cheap egg rolls when they're not eaten soon enough. She glanced longingly at her pail of takeout. Had Margaret only brought her here for a debrief? What were the six missed calls about, anyhow?

"There's been a significant change in the situation," she continued. *Aha.*

"On December 21, three days after Bērziņš's disappearance, the German police raided a suspected drug house in Hamburg. Initial reports, and interrogation of a junkie arrested at the scene, confirmed the Polizei's appraisal that the site was used only to distribute heroin.

"Subsequent analysis of materials found at the site, however, raised the possibility of a connection with Bērziņš." Margaret paused for a moment, letting the import sink in. *Holy crap,* Charlotte thought. *Holy living crap, this is real.*

"Natalya has obtained, through her connections in the Polizei, access to photographs of the materials in question. Apparently they are the charred remains of documents that the one witness says were burned after a meeting between two men he didn't know or recognize, who spoke a language he couldn't understand. Natalya's contact has DHL'ed them here. They will arrive in the first delivery at seven tomorrow morning."

"Margaret ... is it ... strictly legal for a foreign law enforcement agency to be sending us evidence that is part of an ongoing investigation?" The question took all of Charlotte's backbone, and then some, to squeak out. "Doesn't this cross that ... FBI line?"

"Decidedly not, Charlotte." Margaret shut her down with the most curt, dismissive tone Charlotte had yet heard. "A client is providing us information. The provenance of that information is irrelevant, and once it is in our hands, it is protected by attorney-client privileges. We— you— are to use the information furnished to continue to develop our understanding of the situation. My earlier guidance stands, unchanged. I want you in here tomorrow, first thing, ready to sprint on this. Understood?"

Charlotte hesitated. "Understood."

Margaret stood quickly and packed her purse. "Good. Enjoy your Chinese food. See you at six thirty." She waited for Charlotte to gather her things and step out of the office before exiting and locking her door. "Good night, Charlotte." She turned to walk away before Charlotte could respond "good night."

Charlotte looked down at the bag of cold food in one hand and wet coat in the other, and shuffled, sighing, toward her office. She didn't know how to feel about what they were doing, but she knew one thing: if she was going to have to trudge home in the miserable freezing rain, she sure as hell was going to do it on a full stomach—greasy egg roll or not.

CHAPTER 7
K Street, DC, December 28

Charlotte walked through the same office door she'd left nine hours before, vaguely better rested but certainly better dressed. She'd slept fitfully after making her way home, bone tired after the hike but oozing anxiety about Evan. Evan, who hadn't so much as texted since dropping her off. So she'd tossed and turned, and too soon she'd woken to NPR on her alarm clock, poured herself into slippers and a bathrobe, and brewed a cup of coffee just to make it through a shower. There was no amount of makeup that could even out the bags under her eyes, but she at least felt professional in a grey sweater over a blue dress and tights as she stepped aboard her arch enemy, the Metro train that carried her away from home every morning.

She dumped her bag on her desk and careened back into her chair, not even bothering to doff her coat. The clock on the wall read 6:28 when she booted up her computer, and she stared blankly at the screen as Windows started up. The caller ID lit up on her desk phone a moment before it rang, reading Margaret's office, three doors down. *Goodness, woman, I'm right here.* She lifted the receiver.

"Good morning, Charlotte. Just wanted to make sure you were here," Margaret said, somehow cheerily. *Click* went the other side. *She must have gotten laid last night*, Charlotte thought. *And even then she doesn't care enough to actually just come over here to look over my shoulder.*

Charlotte spent the next half hour looking at pictures of cats on the company's dime. The way she saw it, if she was required to be here at 6:30 on a Saturday ready to work, then they could pay her to be here at 6:30 ready to work. Seven o'clock came and went, punctuated only by the chime of a clock in someone's office. Charlotte's eyes got heavier and heavier with every meme she clicked through, the effort of staying awake only accentuating her increasing ennui as she compulsively checked her phone for new messages. With only the whoosh of the fan to distract her, she couldn't help hearing the elevator open at 7:08 and someone walk down the hall toward Margaret's office. There was a knock and a male voice said, "I have a package for, um, office seventy-three?"

Of course Margaret had anonymized her mailing address, Charlotte thought as she painfully pried herself out of her chair and shoved her anxiety down. Turning the corner, she saw the DHL man walking back to the elevator and breached the threshold of Margaret's office just as her boss was picking up the phone to call her.

"Oh good, you're here. Let's see what we've got here."

Margaret slipped a letter opener into the side of the yellow and red package and pulled out a small stack of papers. She described each one as she examined them in turn.

"A cover letter, no letterhead, simply saying 'N, please see the enclosed five documents, G.' Then five photocopies of photographs. Looks like all five are of charred documents ... a ticket, a map, a handwritten note, an email, and ... a list of some kind."

Margaret put the pile on the table and slid them across to Charlotte, removing the cover letter as she went. "Well, these are yours. Get to work."

"Margaret ... do we even have the address where these documents were recovered? Or when exactly the raid occurred?"

"Only what I told you last night," she snapped. "The raid was on the 21st of December. Beyond that, it's yours to figure out."

Charlotte picked up the pile wordlessly and returned to her office. She paused for a moment and decided another cup of coffee was in order before getting started. She wished there was whiskey in it.

Sitting down, she spread the five documents out on the desk before her. She pulled up the first photo, the remnants of a ticket. It was relatively simple to piece together, even if the most important information was missing. A red logo peeked out from a charred edge, and a few Google image searches later, Charlotte had matched it to Deutsche Bahn, the German railway service. *Well, that only makes sense.* She turned her attention to the numbers along the bottom edge. At the end of a line of unreadable text was a single number that had to be a time—2138. *If the raid was on the 21st, and the murder on the 18th, then this time is probably an arrival into Hamburg on the 19th or 20th.* She pulled up the Deutsche Bahn website, clicked over to the English-language version, and pulled up the timetables. She was relieved to see there was only one main train station in Hamburg: the Hauptbahnhof. It was a simple matter of Ctrl-F to find her train, the RE842 departing Warsaw, Poland, at 1025 on December 19 and arriving Hamburg, Germany, at 2138. *Bingo.*

After determining there was nothing further to be learned from the random digits and letters that showed on the charred ticket, Charlotte turned her attention to the second—and most interesting—document. It was clearly the remnants of a map—but that was pretty much all she could figure out. It portrayed a narrow stretch of land flanked on both sides by water, but whether it was an isthmus or peninsula was impossible to tell. As was the scale—it could have been Florida, or a tiny island. The details were all washed out save for two words. The first, running vertically along the coast and clearly part of a longer text, was "strand." Her first instinct—confusion—was remedied by a universal-translation search, which told her that "strand" was German for "beach." *Good to know,* she mused, *but again, not that helpful.* The second word was more cryptic. It was the middle letters of some word, and the best she could tell it read "crac." No matter what she tried, she couldn't make sense of it, unable to find a likely word in a German dictionary. She put the map down in frustration, glancing at the clock. *Nine thirty already?!?*

She decided to launch into the third document before taking a break, then realized her folly and went to get another coffee before continuing: it was a photo of the remnants of a handwritten note—in Latvian. Piecing this one together would be difficult in English, not to mention a language she had barely even known existed five days before. She couldn't help but chew her nails as the coffee brewed, her foot tapping as she nervously scrolled through the phone. Still nothing from Evan. Should she? Not yet.

After refueling she started about deciphering the note methodically. First she copied the document and sent it out for translation from the service the firm employed. But knowing their turnaround would be two or three days for an inconvenient language at an inconvenient time of year, she started in to do her best. She'd done work like this before and knew that translating one word at a time would only get her a sentence worse than playing "Telephone" with a bunch of French chipmunks. But it was all she had—and worth a shot.

The right side of the document had almost entirely burned, leaving only the faintest trace of a header to indicate it was the printout of an email. But as the charred scrap widened, more and more characters were visible in each line. On three lines she could pick out full words. The first was *ierodaties:* "arrive." On the next, *garām baznīcai*: "past the church." Finally, *zvaniet pie trešā numura un jautājiet:* "ring number 3 and ask for."

Well, that's simple enough, she thought. Instructions to the drug house. It was highly unlikely that, in an eight-word snippet of instructions, the mention of a church and a multi-unit building could refer to anywhere but a dense city like Hamburg. She decided to count that document as a "win" despite the pain it had caused behind her eyes and, glancing at the hour hand making its way past twelve, decided to treat herself to delivery. She was making overtime, after all, and despite all her best intentions, she was enjoying herself. It was like working on an enormous crossword.

The fourth document, the remnants of an email, was extremely straightforward:

```
.......r a small white house with a red door, down the street from the din....
.........ight side there is a small garage, with a door around back. The door ..
.............o a basement where you'll find some food and water. As soo........
................he red handkerchief that's on the water bottles and tie it .........
.............reet sign directly in front of the house. Be ready to go the...........
.......... up the sign.
```

Until I figure out what "crac" means, Charlotte realized, *this is pretty useless*. It's not like she could scour the coastlines of Europe and the US for small white houses. If she could pinpoint a neighborhood, though, this would be a pretty decisive clue to what was going on. Putting out handkerchiefs and waiting until darkness seemed like some pretty conclusively sneaky behavior.

Her sandwich arrived and she took a moment to sit back and think it all over, picking oily eggplant out of an otherwise scrumptious veggie baguette. She reflected guiltily on just how much each soggy circle had cost her but banished that thought in favor of thinking about her hourly rate. It made missing vacation hurt a bit less. Her phone blinked, causing Charlotte's heart to jump, but on unlocking it, she found it was just another swath of Bumble matches. *Traitorous phone.*

Her hands de-oiled, she turned to the fifth document. This one was the most difficult, and even after staring at it for ten minutes, Charlotte could hardly make sense of it. It was a list of names, with numbers beside them, and a simple code by each name—either "F," "D," or "L." But that was it. There was no header or footer to make sense of what it could be.

Frustrated, she leaned back to take it in. She decided to start with an assumption: all of the documents pertained to Aleksandrs Bērziņš making his way from Latvia to the United States. If she put them in that context, could anything emerge?

The obvious first step was the train ticket. So he somehow made it from Daugavpils to Warsaw, where he caught an express train to Hamburg on the 19th. Then he followed the instructions in the note to the drug house, where he crashed that evening. At some point on the 20th he met with someone and received instructions on what to do when he arrived somewhere with a coastline and a small red house, leaving before the raid on the 21st.

The conclusion was so obvious it hurt. Bērziņš had gotten on a cargo ship—the list was a crew manifest.

Charlotte excitedly pulled down her reference tabs, knowing just what she was looking for. Jane's, Zillow ... there it was! MarineTraffic, a website that consolidated all the publicly accessible data every single ship broadcast, and put it on one extremely handy map interface. Her account had long expired, but she quickly paid for a one-month membership, knowing Margaret would gladly pass the fee on to Natalya's expense account.

It took a moment for Charlotte to remember how the interface worked, but once she got the feel back, it was a cinch to find what she was looking for. Bērziņš must have left sometime between very early on the 20th and the evening of the 21st, so she looked at all ships departing Hamburg during that time. It was a big assumption that he'd left out of Hamburg, but she had to start somewhere. She waited for the results ... thirty-eight departures.

Making another leap, she filtered the ships by destination, choosing only those that would take the ship near the United States (she left in Iceland and the Azores just to be sure). That brought it down to twelve ships.

She started paging through each one, not sure what she was looking for but hoping it would pop out at her when she saw it. She made it through all twelve with nothing jumping out; she felt deflated and started to question the assumptions that had led to the list. She switched to the "Route" tab and went back through the list; by the fourth one she realized that any ship headed for South or Central America wouldn't come within a thousand miles of the US coast. Filtering them out, she was left with three ships, all headed for ports in the US.

The first one, the *COSCO Voyager* out of China, was a roll-on, roll-off ship bound for New York with a cargo of vehicles. The second was the *Constellation,* a Maersk container ship heading to Norfolk. The last one was the *Kasimir,* an independent tramp steamer bound for Wilmington, North Carolina, with a hull full of "assorted goods." Zeroing in on this holdover from an earlier age of independent carriers with small cargos, Charlotte wondered just how easy it might be to smuggle a Latvian fugitive amongst assorted goods.

Pulling up the *Kasimir's* route, Charlotte saw it was only twenty-eight hours from reaching Wilmington, with its projected path shown on the map display. Travelling at an excruciatingly slow 8 knots, it was only just approaching the Outer Banks of North Carolina. In a second Charlotte saw it: Ocracoke—"crac." The island and town at the very southern tip of the long, narrow sandbar of the Outer Banks.

Her veins coursing with the adrenalin of the hunt, she pulled up Google Maps and went to Ocracoke. The note had mentioned a "din" which could only be a diner. There was only one in town, with only one street leading off it. She hopped into street view, trembling with excitement. There it was! A small white house, with a red door and garage on the right, and a street sign right out front. She couldn't believe it.

Returning to the *Kasimir's* track, Charlotte confronted the obvious: if Bērziņš was trying to come ashore at Ocracoke, it would only be a few hours before the *Kasimir* was its closest to the town. This wasn't just happening. It was happening *now.*

CHAPTER 8
Capitol Hill, DC, December 28

"I don't know which was worse, his white socks or the mansplaining." Alycia was recounting yet another one of her tales of failed love, her somewhat mysterious ability to catch the eye of every man in the room exceeded only by her utter consistency at then choosing the odd ones. "I was like, dude, we literally met working on a case. We do the same job. But his entire apartment was set up as a prop for him to show off his Important Legal Knowledge. It was a fucking expositorium in there."

Charlotte snorted a bit of her gin and lime at the pun, easily picturing her statuesque lawyer friend crinkling her nose in disgust at what she'd gotten herself into.

"So what did you do?" asked Beth, a struggling journalist who rounded out the closest thing Charlotte had to a lady friend circle in DC. She had plenty of acquaintances, sure, and no shortage of invitations to happy hours and mixers and receptions, but she'd found it tremendously difficult in DC's transactional, itinerant social scene to establish meaningful connections. She tried not to dwell on the fact that Alycia had been a coworker of Evan's, and Beth an introduction through an old colleague in India. Instead, she cherished that she'd brought them together, and she was starting to feel the warmth of true friendship and trust emerging.

"I mean, it's December ..." Alycia trailed off.

"Oh, darling, no ..." Charlotte assumed a disapproving smirk while Beth chuckled into her cocktail.

"Whatever. I'm working seventy-hour weeks at a thankless job as a public servant while my friends in corporate law are pulling in $300K to review contracts. So who cares if he kinda sucks? I'll let him buy me dinner, get what I want, and send him along." Alycia rarely referred to her mid-level job at the Department of Justice, which was in the throes of an impeachment trial; the details of her dating life were less sensitive than any workplace gossip.

"What about you, Charlotte? What's the chance this 'big project' at work is really you just having a hot date and wanting to ditch us?" Beth turned her muckraker's nose for a story against Charlotte's happy façade, and Charlotte felt it working. Charlotte felt a rush of pride that these women, these accomplished women who were living their values and trying their best to do good work in this world, were interested in her and her silly corporate job.

"After suffering through my sister's wedding crazy for two hours the other night, I'm not sure I'll ever date again," she offered in the way of a smoke screen, realizing it had been over twenty-four hours since she'd seen Evan, fighting the desperate urge to check her phone. Even more, she wanted these women to respect her. "But work is actually pretty cool. We're trying to track down this guy in North Carolina, so I'm heading down there tomorrow to poke around a bit."

She'd rushed into Margaret's office at two thirty that afternoon, surprised at how late it had gotten, but proud of her work and excited to have figured the whole thing out. As she walked Margaret through it, the momentous conclusion sank in: Bērziņš was about to be on American soil, illegally.

"Margaret, how is this not crossing the line? This evidence may be protected by attorney-client privilege, but the conclusion it points to is a clear violation of US sovereignty. I don't understand how we *can't* call this one in."

Charlotte began to squirm in her seat as she realized just how bold her statement had been. Maybe she'd done fantastic work, maybe her conclusions were spot on, maybe it was crossing a line ... but she was still talking to her boss, and they'd still both signed the NDA.

"Charlotte, it's time I pulled back the curtain a bit. I protect you and the other investigators here the best I can, but situations like this call for a bit of real talk." Charlotte leaned forward in her chair—this was a side of Margaret that she'd never seen, an honest side. Of course, her first thought was that even what seems like honesty was still part of a carefully crafted image for someone like Margaret, but it was a refreshing image nonetheless.

"It's extremely important that we maintain our reputation as loyal brokers. We only survive as long as clients perceive us as utterly trustworthy. We signed NDAs and that's that. If it gets out that we're ratting our clients out to the FBI—even for something this obvious—we're out of business. My reputation will be shot, and we'll be out of work in weeks. Instead, I'll do exactly what we do for our clients. I still have contacts. I'll make sure this gets in the right hands. I know it's a lot to ask, but I need you to write it up formally for me. And then I need you to get down to Ocracoke first thing in the morning and see if this checks out on the ground."

Charlotte was so overwhelmed by the vote of confidence and support—suspicions of manipulation aside—that it wasn't until she was three pages into the report, Margaret long gone and with the clock inching toward five—that she realized how absolutely and absurdly beyond her comfort zone it was to go to Ocracoke. What in the hell was she supposed to do?! She wasn't a field person. She was just good at pulling things together!

Eager to put off packing, and depressed at the continued lack of a text from Evan, she'd agreed to meet the girls at a bar on Capitol Hill where Beth was wrapping up an interview. The easy joking and shared misery were just what she needed after the cascade of stress.

Beth's reaction to Charlotte's offhand mention of the trip to Ocracoke was incredulity: "Wait, what? So you're going to go down to North Carolina like some kind of ... private eye ... to just 'poke around' a bit? Who exactly are you trying to 'track down?'"

Charlotte felt a defensiveness rise up in her. "It's really not that big a deal, Beth. He's just a ... guy who went missing." She hated the lie, unsure how she really felt but also not comfortable sharing that insecurity with these women.

"Sounds sketchy to me, Charlotte," Alycia chimed in. "People don't just go missing. Could even be dangerous."

"Yeah, you should take a buddy," Beth suggested. "I'd offer to come, but I have plans of my own tomorrow." She winked.

Charlotte's mind jumped ahead to a vision of a small white cottage on the North Carolina coast, and whatever uncertainties lay within.

"I mean, there's this guy I could ask ..." She hated herself for saying it aloud. Caitlin was right about Evan, there was no point in leading him on. And it would be nearly impossible to convince him it wasn't a romantic overture. But Beth was right, she'd feel safer with a friend along. And with the way he'd handled himself in the woods …

"Oh? Who's this? Anyone we know?" Alycia's voice dripped with voyeuristic interest. Charlotte had to tread carefully … Alycia knew Evan, but not the intricacies and ups-and-downs of the past five years. If she got a whiff that Evan was back in Charlotte's life … no use going down that rabbit hole.

"Oh just this guy. The thing is … I wouldn't want him to get the wrong idea, you know? But he's just the type of person you'd want along." Charlotte was letting her own desires color her words.

Beth responded instantly. "Oh, easy. Just invite him along, and tell him he has to get his own hotel room, in a different hotel. Set the terms early, stay in charge."

Alycia's guffaw nearly spilled her drink. "Are you kidding? He's a guy. You could hit him over the head with a crowbar wrapped in a restraining order, and he'd still try. No, if you want to invite him, you need to appeal to some other motivation. Be explicit that you want him around for safety, then any time he so much as glances at you, use it against him."

"Devious." Charlotte admired Alycia's cunning.

"Effective," Alycia replied. Charlotte reached for her phone. *Here goes.*

"Can we chat?" she texted, instantly regretting the pleading tone. Luckily, the reply popped up nearly instantly: "sure."

Without the slightest forethought, she excused herself from the table, raising her eyebrows knowingly, and dialed his number, hoping he wasn't stuck in a library or something.

He picked up on the second ring. She could instantly tell he was at a bar. *Was he on a date?!*

"Hey Char."

"Uh, hi. Um ... what's going on?"

"Sorry it's so loud. I'm at a trivia night with some buddies." Charlotte wasn't sure whether to feel relieved or dubious of what could be a simple white lie. She recognized that jealousy was clouding her emotions—and hated it.

"No, uh ... no problem. I'm, uh ..." She wasn't sure where to take it. *Screw it.* "Hey, I've got to head down to the North Carolina coast for work tomorrow. To be honest it's a little bit of a sketchy situation, and I'd feel a lot safer with someone along. Wanna come?" It came out of her mouth before she'd even thought it. "I, uh ... I'll pay for your hotel room and all. Back to DC Monday." The silence that followed made her feel like a teenager; worse, a teenage dunce.

"Uhh ..." Evan began. "Not gonna lie Char, it's a little weird to go from being turned down on a romantic day together to ... being asked on an overnight trip?"

"Evan, I ..." Charlotte grasped for the right words. *Should have thought this through.* "I meant what I said. It's not like that anymore. But I do want you in my life, and I do want your help on this project. I don't know what else to say."

"Char ... you know how I feel. Isn't this a little cruel?" Charlotte knew he was right, knew that no matter what she did, she was stringing him along a little. But then she thought of Caitlin and felt a surge of power. Evan *had* used her. She *had* spent months pining after him when he chose his adventures over her. So why should she feel any regret asking for what she wanted?

"Evan, I've told you where I stand. What you do with it is up to you. I don't want to send any mixed messages, but I'd like you along." Silence.

"Hm. Let me think on it. When are you leaving?" he asked.

Charlotte hadn't planned it. "I'd pick you up at seven," she blurted out.

"OK. I'll text you before nine tonight. Uh ... thanks for the invite, Char."

"You're welcome. Bye."

"Bye."

Charlotte looked down at the phone, unsure if she'd just put a last nail in the coffin, thrown gasoline on Evan's desire, or hit just the right tone. She slipped the phone away and returned to the booth.

"Aaaaaaaaand?" Alycia frowned, expectant.

"We'll just see," Charlotte said coyly, unsure if she could share the story without spilling all the beans.

The conversation flowed on, with Beth bemoaning the ever-dwindling market for good investigative journalism, and Alycia sharing a series of surprisingly tender texts with someone she'd met on the Metro. Charlotte's phone pinged. She pulled it up and could hardly conceal her pleasure.

"Hey Alycia," Beth opened. "What do you think are the chances Charlotte actually ends up getting a second hotel room when she's got that look just from reading his texts?"

CHAPTER 9
I-95, northern Virginia, December 29

At the crest of each rise, Charlotte could see just how far the red lights stretched south on I-95. She'd picked Evan up at seven, but it was never too early for Virginia traffic—and, apparently, yet another person had found it too difficult to stay between two lines and not hit the person in front of them, so here they were along with thousands of others, stuck in pre-dawn bumper-to-bumper misery two miles from Fredericksburg. The irony that the site of a devastating Civil War battle was now shorthand for cataclysmic traffic was never lost on Charlotte, least of all when she was mired in it. At least it was all south of the Mason-Dixon Line, and they'd been able to stop for Bojangles on the way out of town.

The buttery smell of biscuits and astringent bite of first-batch coffee could have kept Charlotte awake in any circumstance, but the thrill of the chase was powering her better than any stimulant ever could. With how much she'd emphasized wanting him there for her safety, she was having a hard time knowing how much to tell Evan.

Up front, he'd asked what merited the trip, and Charlotte had parried the best she could. It wasn't hard to imagine what Evan's reaction would be to chasing down a criminal attempting to enter the US illegally. Charlotte didn't quite know her own reaction. Was she grossly exceeding the bounds of normal attorney-client privilege, potentially abetting a criminal by not turning him in? Or was she just verifying circumstantial evidence, the situation unclear until there was some firm evidence Bērziņš was actually on the ground? Beyond that, what would she even do if she came face to face with him?

Deciding to expand Evan's usefulness, Charlotte turned the conversation to Russia. Aside from occasionally crossing paths with some embassy types in Delhi, she had an *Economist* reader's understanding of the country's politics.

"So Evan, help me understand something. All this fretting about a resurgent Russia … how much is it the real deal? I mean, isn't it just liberals scrambling for a scapegoat for the 2016 debacle? Or conservative Cold Warriors and their defense-industry cheerleaders unable to let go of the old adversary? C'mon. How much of a threat can a country with half our population and ten percent of our GDP really be?"

Evan sized her up with an impressed nod. "You're absolutely right, Char. Discussion of Russia in the US has more to do with the skeletons in our closet than any reality." He turned, looking out at a rest stop touting four gas stations and six separate fast-food joints, then continued.

"Russia is a mess. Its economy is in shambles; what the West heralded as liberalization in the '90s was really just the transfer of state assets to a few well-connected families, the oligarchs. They run the country to their benefit, the enormous mineral and industrial wealth of the nation flowing into their pockets rather than missile silos. And all the social ills that afflicted the Soviet Union—plummeting birthrate, decreasing life expectancy, rampant corruption—have grown only worse. Young democratic institutions like the free press and elections are just window dressings or, worse, the very Orwellian levers by which the ruling class ensures the proletariat still buy into the system. It's only in this extreme post-modern context that Putin's endless wars—Georgia, Chechnya, Syria, Crimea,

Donbass, Nagorno-Karabakh, Ossetia — make any sense, as a nationalist rallying cry."

"So Russia is a failing state whose implosion at the hands of a selfish ruling class will spell disaster for the region. How does that add up to a threat against the US? Nukes?" Charlotte inquired.

"Sure, nukes. But also something yet more powerful. In the '90s the West was convinced that the end of the Cold War meant the spread of liberal values to the Soviet bloc — democratic institutions, capitalist economies. But what if the opposite were true? What if it meant an export of the Russian model of non-freedom to the US?"

Charlotte's mind reeled. The pattern was plain to see: A political system increasingly concerned with divisive issues of identity and nationalism. Ascendant politicians who, like Putin, capitalized on showmanship and fictional triumphs as much as their connections to an oligarchy. Economies defined by rising inequality and unhindered resource exploitation. And adventurism overseas that had more to do with assuaging domestic insecurities than any long-term strategic interest.

Charlotte made a logical jump. "It would mean ... we're already at war, in a sense. A war we're already losing."

"Like the Union lost the Civil War," Evan retorted.

"Huh?"

"Sure, the North won the battles, and Lincoln preserved the Union. But if the Confederacy's truest political objective was to preserve a certain way of life, to protect the socio-economic power of a certain ruling class ... then by the end of

Reconstruction, you can say they'd won, too."

"The antebellum dream preserved through the KKK, Jim Crow, and the Lost Cause."

"So it was then, as it is now. Russian nostalgia for supposed Soviet greatness preserved through troll farms, crony capitalism, and a newfound nationalism."

"And future generations will talk about the 2016 election the same way we talk about Dred Scott. Fuck." Charlotte sank into silence, stunned by the revelation.

It was past one when they crossed the bridge to the Outer Banks, pulling through Kitty Hawk to the accompaniment of grumbles from their stomachs. Charlotte, taking a break from driving, did a quick GPS versus ferry schedule comparison and made a tough call. "If we stop for lunch, there's no way we can make it to Ocracoke before dark. I'd really prefer to see the place with some light — what do you say we push through?"

Charlotte knew the risk she was taking skipping a meal, but she figured low blood sugar was no match for the excitement she was feeling now that they were getting close. Despite summer trips to Long Island, Cape Cod, and the Chesapeake, she'd had no idea the Outer Banks was so dramatic. Cape Hatteras was quite literally just a huge sandbank. The two-lane highway, half-covered in sand drifts in places, ran just inland of the highest peak. In the misty weather they had a gloomy but regular view of the sound, but only occasionally did the road pop out and afford them a view of the ocean on their left. Strong gusts buffeted the Outback at those moments, with a dramatic stormy coastline showing the sea's force. Charlotte was struck by how calm the sound remained even with the pounding waves just a few hundred feet away — and wondered just how Bērziņš planned to get ashore in conditions like that.

The point was driven home on the ferry from Hatteras, the last town on the southern tip of the Cape, to Ocracoke island proper. Making a wide loop into the Sound to avoid an endangered crab breeding ground, Charlotte could see the ocean crashing onto the sandbank — *above* where she was standing on the second deck twenty feet above the waterline. It was high tide out there, but it took so long to force all that water into the Sound that they were still at low tide, putting them well below the waves hitting the sand bar just a mile away. *Somewhere out there, Aleksandrs Bērziņš got in a boat and came ashore. He certainly couldn't have done it alone — who helped him? What did they do it in? Was it dangerous? It certainly must have been cold.* Charlotte shuddered at the thought and wondered why she was lingering on the exposed observation deck when she could be warm in the car.

Reaching the northern Ocracoke ferry terminal as the clock ticked toward five, Charlotte measured her hunger against the ebbing light. It was a ten-mile drive to town, which would give them only fifteen minutes of gloaming to explore before darkness settled over the village. She had to prioritize. She figured the best approach would be to drive the main road all the way to the southern ferry terminal, then double back along the only other through-connecting road in town before poking out to the lighthouse east of town. That would give her the lay of the land before they found somewhere to gorge.

"Uh, Charlotte, wasn't that the turn for our hotel?" Evan asked as their ever-suffering GPS rerouted them. Charlotte realized she hadn't told Evan her plan — too anxious to let him in on what she was really up to, she'd just made up her mind.

"I want to check out the village real quick. Then we can grab a bite to eat."

Evan looked at her quizzically and remained quiet as she creeped through the cluster of buildings that constituted Ocracoke's downtown. She noticed as they passed the diner on her left but didn't trouble herself to try to pick out the white house—it was enough to note that the diner was open. Score. She was itching with anticipation but didn't want to run into anything unsated.

Charlotte made an awkward K-turn once the southern ferry terminal was in sight, at which point Evan broke the silence. "Nice little reconnaissance route you're running here, Char. Wanna tell me again what kind of work you're doing?"

Charlotte navigated onto a back road that guided her along the western part of town, back toward the diner. They could check in after they ate. "Evan, I'm not comfortable telling you. It's confidential, and I'm not going to compromise myself." It was hard to say—all she wanted to do was tell him everything.

"Does it have anything to do with Aleksandrs Bērziņš?" His tone was skeptical.

Charlotte felt resigned and decided to give him something to chew on to keep him from prying anymore. "It is. There's something here I need to look into. That's all." Of course that wasn't all.

"Well, OK then. Let's get some food." It wasn't hard to tell he was frustrated.

Pulling into the diner, they stepped out of the car into a crushing gust of wind. There was the distinct feel of a coming storm—swooshing trees, the smell of sea salt, a cold that bit through clothing. They hurried inside and were greeted by a fifty-something man who looked like he'd just rolled out of bed. Without a shred of introduction, he gestured them toward the back.

"There's a clean table in back. All I've got tonight is grouper, fries, and slaw. Whaddya want to drink?"

"Uh …" Charlotte hesitated.

"Two beers, please." Evan stepped in.

"Two beers and two grouper plates, on the way." He went back to his cell phone as Evan and Charlotte hesitated, finally deciding the unconventional welcome was a blessing to find their spot. They flopped down and cherished the décor, all photos of old fishermen and their catches, as well as the table sticky from years of happy hours. It was clearly the off-season—there were only four other people, all crowded at the bar up front.

It was only moments later that a different fifty-something man who looked like he'd rolled out of bed showed up with a pitcher of beer and a basket overflowing with fried food.

"You folks look like you need a good meal. We won't charge you for the extra beer, and here's some food to get you started. Just flag me down when you need more," he said as he plopped everything down, the beer sloshing over to form a wet layer atop the stickiness. *This couldn't be better*, Charlotte thought as the first hunk of fish was touching her lips.

A few mouthfuls later, the sharp edge of hunger starting to dull, Evan spoke up. "You've got to tell me a bit more than that, Char. No specifics needed, but what do you mean by 'look into'?"

Charlotte took a swig of the watery beer and shoved a hunk of grouper in her mouth, watching Evan's face all the while. She wanted his help, that was for sure, but how to phrase it? She swallowed and dove in.

"There's a house down this street that's of interest to our client. I just need to check it out."

"Whatever that means." The rebuke stunned Charlotte, and she went silent, concerning herself instead with grouper. "What exactly are you going to check?"

A vision of a red kerchief tied to a signpost crossed Charlotte's mind. It suddenly returned to her, through a hefty mouthful of slaw, that every second she spent here was a second Bērziņš could be getting further away — and covering his tracks. They needed to see the house *now*.

"Why don't you tag along and we'll head there right now?" The glint of excitement in Evan's eyes told Charlotte that including him in the adventure was more than enough to keep him from asking more questions. She told him it was a garage next to a white house three spots down, and they chugged the last of their beer.

They quickly paid the bill — cash only — and headed back out into the storm, which was now pelting rain through the salt spray coming over the dunes. They grabbed rain gear out of the Outback, too late to prevent getting soaked, and headed up the street. "Let's cross to the other side," Evan said. "We'll be able to see it better."

As soon as they'd hopped a puddle to the far side, Charlotte could take in the entire house. It was a gorgeous 1920s craftsman, clearly once cared for but suffering from a decade or two of neglect. She could see the garage to the right, perfectly framed under a magnolia that swayed provocatively in the storm. She turned her eye back to her side of the street—a red handkerchief barely held on to the street sign in the fierce wind. *Shit. He's either still there or just left.*

"The garage, you say?" Even boldly started crossing the street. "Let's check it out."

"Evan, no!" Charlotte ran up and grabbed him. "We have ... no clue who's in there."

"There's no one home, Char. And even if there is, it's only weird if we make it weird. We're just tourists who got lost on the beach." He turned and walked right up to the garage, testing the locked front door before walking around the side. "There's a door here!" She heard him grab the handle and came around the corner just in time to see him push the door open.

"It's a basement—odd. Shall we?" His tone was a challenge. At this point they were committed. She turned on the flashlight on her phone and pushed past him. "Let's."

As she haltingly poked her way down the first few steps under the inadequate light of her phone, the wind and rain pushing through the doorway against her back, the thought crossed her mind that this was very, very stupid. She hadn't meant to break and enter! She'd only wanted to scope the place out. With the handkerchief out front, literally anything could happen. *What if Bērziņš was still there?*

She reached the bottom of the stairs, a quick scan of the room revealing nothing other than a musty, empty basement. She could feel Evan come up behind her. "Nothing much to see, I guess," he said, his hand grazing hers in the darkness.

Charlotte felt her body ready to respond, electrified at Evan's touch, when the door slammed open. Startled, Charlotte turned to see a silhouette in the doorway—and was blinded by the glare of a high-power flashlight. "And just what were you hopin' to see, there?" inquired a man with a thick Carolina accent.

CHAPTER 10
Ocracoke, North Carolina, December 29

For a brief moment, fear coursed through Charlotte's blood, banishing any trace of thought as surely as the flashlight blinded her vision. She found herself picking up Evan's line before he could even chime in.

"I'm so sorry, sir, we were just walking out on the beach and got caught in the storm and were just so cold and wet and lost and were just looking for a dry spot for a second ..." She started to make herself tear up, hoping to play on his sympathies.

"What kind of horseshit is that?!? You just break into someone's house cause you're feeling sorry for yourself?" Charlotte could hear the deep twang in his voice—this guy was as local as it got.

"Hey hey, man, it was totally abandoned. If we'd known it was yours, we wouldn't have come in," Evan added. "We're just here on vacation. It got a little cold out there, we just ... wanted to ... to warm up a bit, you know what I mean?" Charlotte hoped his innuendo landed.

"Y'all know there's a diner just down the street?" the man added.

Evan jumped on the opportunity. "Why don't you show us how to get there, and we'll buy you a beer?"

There was a moment of silence before the flashlight clicked

off. "Fair 'nuff," the man grumbled. "Can't be too mad at a couple of kids enjoyin' themselves."

Charlotte and Evan hurriedly made their way up the stairs, introducing themselves as they reached the top. "Thomas," he growled in response. "Follow me." He turned and led them back to the street. As they walked, Charlotte got a better look at him. He was short, maybe five feet six, and stout. His face wore a few days' stubble over the evidence of forty-five or fifty years of hard outdoor labor, and his stained jeans, worn flannel shirt, and old-style oilskin sent the same message.

Drawing abreast of Evan, Charlotte hissed in his ear. "What are we doing?!"

He whispered back. "You wanted to know about the house, right? Here's your guy."

True enough, she thought, hoping the waiters at Joe's wouldn't say anything that would betray them. She pushed to the front of the group as they approached the door, and before the other two had even crossed inside, she'd explained away their return to the host. He'd given her a quizzical look at first, but her proffered "last place to get another beer" allowed them to breeze past, unquestioned, and establish themselves across from the bar, where the diehards remained clustered.

"So Thomas," Evan opened, as Charlotte ordered them a pitcher of the same nameless watery beer. "Is that your house?"

"To tell the truth, no. I just do a few odd jobs around the place and happened to be … passing by right when you two made a racket opening that back door." *That doesn't add up*, Charlotte thought. *There's no way he could have heard us over the storm.*

"You're from the island?" she asked.

"Born and raised. Hardly ever left, except to take care of business on the mainland. What brings you folks out here this time of year?"

Evan took the question in stride as the beer arrived. "We had some time off from work, so figured we'd spend it somewhere we could cuddle up and be all alone." Thomas eyed their ring fingers, obviously inferring they were up to some kind of affair away from prying eyes. *Nothing I haven't seen before*, his expression said.

They toasted to the misunderstanding and the conversation turned into Evan trying to learn everything he could about Ocracoke, how people fished, the town drama. Maybe it was just the Dutch confidence speaking, but Charlotte started to feel more secure in their position. Thomas was no longer shouting down at them from the top of the stairs — he was the guy who'd been snooping around the pickup site at the same, unlikely time they were. *It's now or never.*

"So Thomas, what kind of odd job had you out on a rainy evening?" she probed.

"Oh, nothing much. Was just passing by on my way back home and saw you two."

Charlotte straightened up in the booth. "I'll give you five hundred dollars to tell me the truth." She felt the words slide off her tongue and felt even more strongly Evan's shocked sideways gaze.

"Say, what the hell is this?!" Thomas protested.

"There's no way you could have heard us open that door in

this rain from around the front of the garage. Which means you were either hiding in the bushes or you watched us go around. Which is it?"

"Well, I'll be." Thomas arched his back, drawing as far away from Charlotte and Evan as he could within the confines of the dingy booth, and crossed his arms. Charlotte could swear she heard the fizzing of the beer, flat as it was, in an awkward silence that seemed to last minutes as Thomas met her eyes in an unbroken, defiant glare. She felt a dampness start in her armpits.

She broke the freeze. "Look, we're not cops. We're just trying to find someone, and I think you can help us."

"Only cops say they're not cops" was Thomas's bitter reply, followed by a return to the détente. Time for a different approach.

She pulled out her wallet and slid her driver's license across the table. "That's me," she started again. "Copy it down. That's my home address. Go ahead, copy it down." Thomas's eyes slid down to the ID, as he picked it up and inspected it closely. "Now you've got me on a leash, and all I know is you say your name is Thomas and you prefer Coors Light. I couldn't care less who you are or how you pay your bills. I'm just trying to find the guy who was hiding out in that basement earlier today."

Evan, who up to this point had held a rigid, ready-for-anything posture with his elbows on the table, broke his composure and shot her a sidelong glance—one that didn't go unnoticed on the other side of the table. *Shit. That's a hell of a way for Evan to find out we're on Bērziņš's trail.*

"Five hundred, you say?" Thomas paused, watching the new tension between Evan and Charlotte. "Make it a grand."

Charlotte measured his gaze, his garb, his gambit against her expense account and made up her mind.

"Done. Keep my ID card 'til I pay you."

"Oh no. There's an ATM right there."

Minutes later Charlotte returned to Evan and Thomas deep in their discussion of fishing, albeit now with a much greater degree of self-conscious awkwardness. She sat down and pushed 50 twenty-dollar bills across the table. *This had better be good or Margaret will have my balls*. Thomas counted the bills, secreted them in his dirty flannel, and looked up.

"No need to beat around the bush, and I ain't gonna give no one away. I get paid every month to check the street sign out front of that garage every morning. If there's a red hanky tied to it, I come back with my pickup after dark, back up to the door, and wait ten minutes. Usually I hear some scuffling 'round, but it ain't my business to ask. Then, I go catch the last ferry to the mainland. By the time I get there, I get a text from a blocked number with an address. I drive where they tell me, park for ten minutes, and drive home. There's always a good bonus and nothing else in the bed." He paused and took a swig of beer. "It ain't none of my business to ask. I always just figured it was some island boys gettin' rid of stuff they stole from tourists like y'all.

"Now, last night was a little different. Usually I can tell its boxes and stuff gettin' stashed back there. But yesterday they had some trouble with the cover, and I could tell from the sound of 'er that it was a person riding back there. Same deal, took him to … er—"

Charlotte slid ten more bills across the table but left her hand covering the pile.

"Well, I only found you young folks 'cause I had some business on the mainland and was late coming back to take down the hanky."

"The address, Thomas?"

"Was a real nice place. 119 Stanfield Street, out in Fayetteville."

Charlotte lifted her hand off the cash and thanked Thomas even as her mind started racing through the daunting possibilities. She only knew Fayetteville as the last place she'd seen Evan, the weekend before she'd finally cut it off. He'd described Fort Bragg as a miserable posting, but it was also home to Joint Special Operations Command and the US Army Special Forces. Where the military trained foreign operators to do its dirty work.

CHAPTER 11
Ocracoke, North Carolina, December 29

Charlotte didn't know what was worse: the already-devastating distance between her and Evan as they finally made their way to the hotel, or her anticipation of the fight to come. She knew she'd done him wrong by keeping him in the dark, but what was she supposed to have done? If she'd told him all, there's no way he would have come with her — not to mention the breach of her Non-Disclosure Agreement. On the other hand, he'd already proven critical to her success, as both a catalyst for inquiry and an emotional buttress.

They walked over a small wooden bridge barely cresting a tiny creek swollen with rainwater, weaving through the magnolias before making it, soaked, to the porch of their bed and breakfast. It was well past ten, and the last thing Charlotte wanted to deal with were any strangers. But the opening of the screen door brought the proprietor to her feet, and it took all of Charlotte's composure to smile through a few pleasantries and "bless your hearts" delivered with a full measure of Southern skepticism.

They escaped upstairs, grudgingly accepting mugs of hot cider and leaving their sodden clothes in the foyer. Reaching the landing, she fumbled with the key, hearing Evan's breaths weigh his next words. She beat him to it.

"I need to call Margaret. I'll come to your room afterwards." Evan grunted his agreement.

"Good" was the closest Margaret gave to an

acknowledgement of Charlotte's success, along with terse instructions to immediately write up a formal report along with her expense report. "And Charlotte," Margaret continued, "I assume you're planning to head to Fayetteville tomorrow?"

Charlotte was dumbfounded. *What?!*

"Margaret ... uh ..." she fumbled. "I'm not sure moving on from here is something I'm, um, comfortable with. Someone broke the law here. There's a foreign agent on US soil, headed to a military base. I think the FBI needs to take it from here." Silence.

"I'll forward your report directly to the Bureau," replied Margaret in a cold, scolding tone. "But needless to say, there's an element of urgency here. You have an opportunity to tie this thing off." *How?!* "All you're doing is gathering information. I don't need to elaborate on the consequences if you're unwilling to comply."

All the frustrations of the past day rose up in Charlotte's chest, her face flushing as she raged at her loss of control. *Who did Margaret think she was? It's my ass on the line. I've already fucked it up with Evan, and for what?* Even then, Charlotte knew the answer: for her future. One call from Margaret would torpedo her chances at ever moving into government service.

"You'll have the report before midnight," she answered, as devoid of emotion as she could.

"Good. I'll be waiting."

Charlotte threw the phone down in rage, balling her fists against her thighs in a silent scream. How could everything, every single thing, be so fucking hard? Knowing she should breathe, relax, consider, she burst out of her room and turned to knock on Evan's door. Her hand paused, held in the air, as a whole new thought crossed her mind. She was wet, angry, alone ... why not just ... no. *Get your shit together, woman.* She knocked.

Evan answered, clad in a hotel robe post-shower. He looked her in the eye. "I'm heading straight to bed, Char," he said. "I don't know the first thing about law enforcement, but what you're up to is wrong. This is the real deal. And I want nothing to do with it."

He's right he's right he's right. She weighed her reply.

"I'm catching the first ferry to the mainland and heading to Fayetteville from there. I'll drop you off at the bus stop and you can head back to DC." She struggled through his silence to find the next words. "Evan, I was wrong not to tell you, but you'd have never come if I told you and ... and I needed you. I still need you. This is something I have to do."

Silence.

"Would you stay up with me to help write my report?"

Silence.

"Good night."

She turned and shuffled back to her room, empty. A scalding shower didn't change a thing except bring her exhaustion to the surface. Mechanically, she pulled out her laptop and sat down at the desk to start working, unable to hold back the tears.

CHAPTER 12
Ocracoke Ferry, North Carolina, December 30

A stiff wind blew across the bow of the ferry, sending up a plume of spray that clouded Charlotte's view of the mainland finally emerging out of the mist that had cocooned them for the entire three-hour journey. Every couple of minutes the ship let out a forlorn bellow from its foghorn, keeping Charlotte awake despite her heavy eyelids.

She and Evan had spoken hardly a word since she'd been jarred awake by the blaring alarm at 4:50 that morning. They'd quickly packed and set off in the Outback, inching their way through a thick fog that seemed to dampen all evidence of last night's storm. It was only the brake lights of a minivan that told them they'd reached the ferry terminal. Paying the fee, they'd loaded aboard the first trip of the day, only to find the ferry was delayed two hours thanks to the fog. Thankful she'd skipped her normal coffee, Charlotte slipped into a catnap while Evan read, each avoiding the other's gaze. With the fog masking all evidence of the outside world, Charlotte had never felt so alone. It was eleven before they reached the mainland, and Charlotte's rumbling stomach told her as well as any alarm that maybe it was time to break the silence, if only to choose somewhere to eat.

"Bojangles?" she probed as they poked their way off the ferry. The sun was burning through the fog, and she could pick out dramatic dunes stretching along the coast.

"We can do better than that, I'd say. I'll Google us a seafood spot." Back to the silence.

It took them almost an hour for Evan to guide them into downtown Beaufort, a tiny resort town perched on a sandbar along the southern edge of the Croatan National Forest. Forest was an interesting choice of words, at least for someone raised spending summers in the Appalachians; even from the elevated highway, Charlotte could see the space between the trees was wet sand at best, impenetrable bog at worst.

Beaufort itself was the opposite, indeed the height of new development. If Ocracoke's isolation allowed it to retain a hint of its historical character, Beaufort's prime location and pristine beaches had led it down the path of summer resort destination. Even in the fading winter mist it was easy to see the town's draw, with piers and berthing spots lined right along the picturesque waterfront. All but abandoned in the offseason, it must have been overflowing on summer weekends with crowds rushing to avoid the humidity of the North Carolina Piedmont.

Evan had found an old-timey seafood spot, and in no time at all they'd been seated and ordered a couple of sandwiches. Charlotte couldn't help but blush when Evan clearly reacted to her disastrously loud stomach rumble. She smiled and looked away.

"That's what I don't get, Char," he began. "You've never been one to hold your feelings back. Hunger or otherwise." He cracked a self-aware grin at the lame transition. "I'm trying to put myself in your shoes, and I just can't see how you think this is the right thing to do."

Their coffees arrived. Just in time to stave off the beginnings of Charlotte's caffeine-withdrawal headache.

"I could say the same about you. I'm surprised you didn't

blow your top last night." The bitterness was forward in Charlotte's voice, and despite her best intentions, she could feel herself letting deeper emotions into her words.

"We're not twenty-four anymore, Char."

"Yeah, exactly. When you're twenty-four you can chase your dreams with no consequences. Decisions don't matter 'cause you have all the time to move on. Nothing's hanging over your head like a guillotine."

"Is this about Bērziņš or about us?" His question pushed her back in the booth. She'd let the emotions out just a bit too far.

"It's about us, Evan. This feels just like it did six years ago. Like you don't respect the work I do, you think I'm just a silly girl who can't make decisions for herself. Well, that silly girl went off and earned her chops, and just because my work isn't combat or leadership or whatever, doesn't mean I'm not capable of making good decisions."

"Isn't that the whole point?!" Charlotte could hear a hint of exasperation in his voice. "You're worked up about how you think I'm judging you, but I *couldn't care less*. Maybe that's harsh, but there's a foreign agent on American soil, and you're more worried about your feelings than about the fact that you're abetting him right now."

"What, so I'm just an emotional woman?!" She dampened the quiet hiss in her voice to let the waiter refill their coffees. Evan took his time with the creamer.

"Look Evan," she continued. "Of course I agree with you. I'm fucking infuriated right now. I have a chance to make a difference, make a real difference. But I'm compromised. I'm stuck. Margaret has me in a vice — if I don't do her bidding, do you think I'll have any kind of future at all? Do you know how hard it is for someone with my background to get a clearance?"

"If you're worried about a clearance, how do you think the past twenty-four hours will make you look?" His words hung in the air as the sandwiches appeared in front of them. It was Charlotte's turn to take her time, squeezing every second out of a plastic Heinz bottle.

"Margaret sent my report to the FBI. She will let me know as soon as they've taken the lead. I'm going to the address," she continued between fries. Her hunger had been buried beneath their fight but now reared its head and demanded attention. "I don't know what Margaret expects me to see, anyway — it's not like I'm going to walk up and knock on the door." She realized that's exactly what she'd let Evan do on Ocracoke.

"And I'm going with you." Evan's unexpected support stopped Charlotte's club halfway to her mouth. "You're right. We aren't twenty-four. There's nothing to be gained by hanging each other out to dry on this one. I'm just as complicit as you, at this point. But Char" — he paused, poking his BLT with a fry — "I lived in Fayetteville. I know Bragg. I've heard the stories about Korean dry cleaners who know about Delta Force deployments before the Pentagon, and hairdressers who keep personnel files in the back room. That town is crawling with creepy business. If this is going where I think it is, the second we're done, we're going to the FBI. Margaret be damned."

Charlotte chewed and felt a piece of bacon wedge its way between her molars. "Fair enough. And Evan … thank you." She reached across the table and squeezed his arm. They finished in silence.

Leaving the restaurant, they pulled back onto NC-24, continuing west along the coast. The sunshine had finally burned through the mist, and they drove along listening to the local country station. Soon they were hitting the suburbs of Camp Lejeune, the Marine Corps' largest East Coast installation.

"Wherever you go, it's the exact same. Pawn shops, used car dealerships, tattoo parlors, payday loans, strip clubs. Could be any military town in America." Evan gazed, almost wistfully, at "A-1 Tailors," offering a high and tight and shoeshine for ten dollars. "God, I'm glad to be out." He ran his hand through his unkempt hair.

"So Evan," Charlotte chimed in, "where do you think this is going?" It was the first time Charlotte had let herself actually think about the case in twelve hours. "What is Bērziņš's plan?"

"I dunno. My gut tells me one thing but my brain another."

"Start from the top."

"Well, this is an extremely well-funded, well-planned, and well-executed little operation. In a matter of days, a man wanted by every police force in the developed world has slipped out of view, made his way across Europe, evaded detection, and snuck into the United States. That doesn't happen without months of planning and tens of thousands of dollars of cash.

"At the same time, the obvious candidate for sponsor — the Latvian government — doesn't seem to have much of a motive here. What do they care if this policeman escapes or not? Sure, it's embarrassing, but Latvia is a young democracy with obligations to the EU. It would be a point of pride to bring Bērziņš in and uphold the rule of law."

"Is the Latvian government the obvious candidate here?" Charlotte countered. "I did a lot of research on Latvian nationalist groups in the US. The numbers are small, but there are some real die-hards. 'Fascist' isn't an exaggeration. I could easily see this whole thing being a private endeavor, an informal chain of like-minded folks just doing their best to help a fellow Latvian in need."

"Reasonable enough. Like a crime syndicate — it's not like this doesn't happen every day on the southern border."

"Wait," Charlotte paused. "But then why is Bērziņš heading to Fayetteville, and not New York or somewhere with a bunch of Latvians?"

"Well, there's where my gut comes in."

"He's ..."

"Yup. Well-funded, well-planned, and getting evacuated to Fort Bragg as quickly as possible. He was working for the US, and this is his recovery plan."

Charlotte tried to run through the implications in her head as they passed through depressingly depressed towns surrounded by tobacco fields, but couldn't work it out. Why would the US want a Latvian agent to commit such a heinous act? To provoke outrage? Or had it been a mistake, but Bērziņš had to be protected? Her head spun. But Evan was right. Either Bērziņš was a foreign criminal, loose on American soil, or an American agent, fleeing for his life. Whichever, it wasn't their business — or Margaret's, or Natalya's, for that matter. Charlotte would follow through, but it was time for the FBI to take over.

"Ah, beautiful Fayetteville." They approached from the east, allowing them to cut through the downtown. Named for America's favorite fighting Frenchman, the town had little to distinguish itself aside from being home to the largest military installation in the world. Charlotte had only visited a few times while she was still in DC and Evan had started training, but she had always thought it would be quite a charming town of 10,000 if it weren't a sprawling mess of 250,000. The town's nickname said it all: Fayettenam.

Just west of downtown, they passed through an enclave of strip clubs and pawn shops and started to climb into Haymount, Fayetteville's historical neighborhood. They picked their way through charming, quiet streets lined with classic Victorians, amazed at how much difference just a few blocks made. They followed one last instruction from the GPS, and Charlotte pulled over a half block short of 119 Stanfield.

"Well, that's it," she said with finality. "What now?" The home was built in the Georgian style found across the upper South, with a large lawn framed by overgrown azaleas that thrived in the area's sandy soil. A driveway ran up to a two-car garage, but aside from a tricycle left by the front door, there was no sign of life.

"We wait. Came this far — let's at least see it through. It's nearly five anyhow; something or other should happen soon."

They sat and talked about nothing at all to distract themselves from the fact that they were, for all intents and purposes, doing a stake out. Illegally. A few cars came and went, as rush hour brought folks home to the quiet street. Charlotte was amazed: for how much tension there had been between them only hours before, for how insanely stressful their predicament was, she felt the air was clear between them. Maybe they'd just needed some conflict to make their friendship work.

At ten after five a grey Toyota RAV4 turned onto Stanfield Street, and somehow Charlotte knew it was the right one. Sure enough, it slowed as it approached them. Over the past two days, Charlotte had gotten used to North Carolina's lack of a front license plate. The RAV4 sported one.

"Did you catch what that plate was?" she asked as the SUV pulled into the driveway, passenger side toward them.

"Diplomatic."

Charlotte puzzled what that could mean as the engine noise ceased and someone got out of the far door. The man was tall enough that they could see his military haircut over the top of the vehicle, but it wasn't until he started walking toward the house that they could see he was wearing a splotchy, brown uniform. As he turned to put his key in the lock, she caught a glimpse of maroon and white on his right shoulder. The Latvian flag.

CHAPTER 13
FBI Headquarters, DC, December 31

"For the fourth time, no. We saw him go into his house and immediately drove here. We stopped twice for gas, and the only person I communicated with was my boss."

Charlotte was exhausted and didn't want to even imagine how frazzled she looked. It seemed like a year ago and thousands of miles away that they'd crawled out of bed on Ocracoke. *If this keeps up much longer*, she thought wryly, *I'll celebrate the New Year in this cell, and it really will be a year ago.* She glanced down at her watch. Nearly eight, and the weak FBI coffee wasn't helping her through the morning all that well. Her eyes rose back up to the suit sitting across the table from her in the spare, yellow-tinged interview room.

"That's all well and fine, Ms. Sorenson, but if you sent so much as a text to anyone else—anyone at all—I need to know." Special Agent Julia McCandless slowly tapped a yellow pencil against her legal pad. Charlotte had wondered how someone so heavyset could manage such a physical career, but Agent McCandless moved with a grace and control that belied her frame. Impeccably attired in a boring grey suit, she exuded the confidence Charlotte would expect of a woman with decades of experience in a field as male-dominated as the FBI. She even managed to alternate condescension and care in her tone, maintaining an unfaltering mask even through the sixth hour of Charlotte's debriefing.

"No." Charlotte was finished.

"Alright. I'll be back in a moment."

Charlotte's eyes fixed onto a dingy sound-absorbing panel on the wall above Agent McCandless's departing head as she tried to recall just how long it had been since she'd slept. *Let's see. Up before five, tiny nap in the car. Driving all day, got to Fayetteville around five in the evening. Left right after we saw the guy, came straight back to DC too excited to sleep. Stopped by the office around eleven, went to FBI headquarters straight away, then napped while waiting for them to decide what to do with two late-night walk-ins alleging a massive conspiracy. Pulled into separate interviews at what, around two in the morning.? Phew.*

What had seemed straightforward as they discussed it in the car, bolting up I-95 at eighty miles per hour, was growing increasingly muddled through the four rounds of retelling they'd put her through. McCandless had let her tell the story straight through the first time, keeping a perfect composure even as Charlotte described what she felt as her own complicity. She tried not to sugar-coat anything but was surprised that even the fourth time through, the agent's cross-examination didn't linger on Charlotte's own guilt.

Which had compounded itself several times over, by this point. It wasn't enough that Charlotte felt like she'd aided and abetted a foreign agent, all just for the sake of a signature on an NDA. No, it was that, in the end, she'd broken the NDA anyway.

Pulling out of Fayetteville, she'd immediately dialed Margaret. In the retelling, Charlotte realized how little there was to retell. The fact that Bērziņš had been smuggled to an official of the Latvian government certainly confused the picture, but the underlying story was the same: nationalist elements of the Latvian government were coordinating with

Latvians in the US, conspiring to support their brethren back home against increased Russian influence. Whether the US and Latvian governments were knowingly involved was irrelevant. After her brief report, Margaret had asked what her next step was.

"Well, head back to DC of course. Not much anyone can do from here without a search warrant. Did the FBI have anything to say about my write-up?" she responded without thinking.

There was a pause. "Oh, they took a look at it but didn't think it amounted to all that much, really" was Margaret's terse reply.

Charlotte's blood ran cold as she realized the magnitude of Margaret's manipulation. *She'd never intended to send the report in at all.* She fumbled through the end of the conversation, promising to write up a full report first thing in the morning, and pulled over.

"SHE FUCKING BETRAYED ME!" she raged at an undeserving Evan. "She used my own morality against me. That manipulative ... the whole time! She didn't let the right people at the FBI know. She didn't send in my report. She just dangled that in front of me so I wouldn't have qualms COMMITTING FUCKING TREASON to line her pocketbook!" The tears were streaming down her face.

"I'm ... there are no words." Evan shook with anger.

"Oh, there's a word. The word is traitor. I don't care if there's an NDA, or attorney-client privilege, or anything. Margaret has been acting as a paid agent of a foreign government. She's failed to report serious crimes on US soil because her loyalty is to a client's well-funded wishes, and not her own country. If she wants to play that game, fine. But then she made me her unwitting accomplice. And I'm not going to stand for it."

Even while stopped, Charlotte's knuckles clenched white on the steering wheel as a fine mist began to cloud the windshield. She reached over and turned the wipers on, but there wasn't enough moisture to prevent them from screeching across the glass on each swipe.

"Let's do something about it." Evan's simple response focused Charlotte's mind.

"We have to be very careful, and very fast. If Margaret suspects anything, she'll cut me off before we can ..." she trailed off.

"Can what?"

"We're heading straight back to my office. I'll copy every single document I have. And then I'm taking it straight to the FBI."

"And then?" A pause, as Charlotte realized Margaret's behavior if she suspected Charlotte would go to the FBI paled next to her retaliation if Charlotte actually went through with anything

"I'll stand on my own two feet and be proud of it. I'll text her before I go in. And if she wants to sue me, that's a small price to pay for doing the right thing. I'll survive." She cursed the squealing wipers and pulled back out into traffic.

Agent McCandless came back into the room a few moments later. "I think that just about wraps it up. Your boyfriend finished up a couple hours ago, so you're free to go."

Boyfriend? Charlotte's thoughts hung on the word choice even as a larger question loomed.

"That's it?" she replied. "What's next?"

"We will be in touch if we need to. But thanks to all the documentation and research you provided, and the consistency of your story, I think you've done just about all you can."

"But ... maybe I shouldn't ask this question. Aren't I ... in trouble?"

Her response was surprisingly humane. "Charlotte, it took a lot of courage to do what you did. There are thousands of people who don't have the nerve to speak up when they see something wrong, because they fear a reprisal. There's still a lot of work to do, but, all considered, you just exposed a serious counterintelligence breach. I don't think Margaret did anything illegal, either — she's just skirting the boundaries of ethical conduct. But regardless, we'll make sure you're covered as a whistleblower. That doesn't mean you won't face consequences within the terms of your employment, but it does mean that you're a witness now."

A surge of relief flooded Charlotte, exhausting her even further. She followed Agent McCandless out into a waiting room, where Evan was reading a well-thumbed issue of *People*. He looked up as they approached, and smiled.

"How long have you been out here?" Charlotte inquired.

"Oh, about five hours. I squealed right away." He smirked. Agent McCandless frowned and turned to Charlotte. "Here is my card. Please feel free to reach out at any time if you think of anything else, or if you have any trouble. I'll be in touch when we need you." She walked them to the desk where they'd checked in their belongings, and briskly spun away.

Charlotte knew, as the clerk returned her phone, that she was seconds away from a life-altering moment. Part of her wanted to just leave her work phone off and get back to her place to enjoy a New Year's Eve full of naps and a bath and wine and takeout. But the larger part of her, proud of the decision she'd made, wanted to follow through, to face what was surely to come. The phone booted up. For a moment, all that showed was Charlotte's last text to Margaret, one that she and Evan had excruciatingly carefully composed over the four-hour drive back to DC, and sent after she'd cleared her office:

"Margaret, I am submitting my report on this investigation to the FBI. I will be in touch tomorrow."

Then a new one popped up:

"Charlotte, your employment has been terminated, effective immediately. You may collect your possessions from the front desk. You will shortly receive communication from HR and our legal team."

Fired by text. She held back the tears until they reached the car.

CHAPTER 14
Northwest, DC, December 31

A ray of light splashed over Charlotte's face, half buried in a mass of pillows she'd burrowed into immediately upon getting home. She'd left the FBI in a daze, unsure where Evan was guiding her, vaguely remembering agreeing to a bite to eat and looking up to realize she was seated in a booth at the old 24-hour diner they'd once frequented. The warmth of the coffee cup between her hands had jolted her to the present, and before the first sip, she'd glanced up at Evan and started bawling.

They'd stayed there for close to an hour, a whole parade of early morning New Year's Eve customers filing through and scoping out the woman crying her eyes out and babbling and shoveling French Toast into her mouth. She felt like such a loser, such a failure. What did it even matter anymore? At one point she remembered Evan coming around to her side of the booth and putting his arm around her. Resigned, she let herself snuggle into his chest and sobbed snot onto his shirt.

"Evan I can't even. I was born with every opportunity, every advantage. But I keep on throwing it away. Working at the tiny nonprofit in DC instead of at an established NGO. Cutting ties and moving to Singapore. Jumping off and taking a wild job in India. Coming back here. Now this. Every time … there's been a path, a way to use the experience and the network I've earned to make a step forward … but I keep on spitting in the face of it, keep on throwing away that chance for … for what? What have I accomplished? Unemployed, unemployable, alone … fuck me."

"Charlotte …" Evan replied, holding her. "I'm here for you." Charlotte's heart sank even further. It was all she wanted.

After they settled the bill, Charlotte considered inviting herself over to Evan's. It felt so good to be held by him; that could be her entire day. *Crap. That could be my entire life.* A vision of Caitlin's unraised Botox eyebrows danced through her head, and she knew that a decision she was too vulnerable to make three days ago was certainly one she should avoid now.

"Evan, can you … can you just drive me home?" she resolved. "You can take my car with you. I'll come over later or tomorrow to pick it up."

"Sure thing, Char." It was so simple with him. He'd driven while she watched the grey, abandoned streets of a New Year's Eve DC pass by the window. She hated how easy the metaphor was for her future.

She'd somehow made it into her apartment, somehow made it into her bed, somehow made it asleep despite the overwhelming mix of anxiety and self-hatred and sadness and caffeine and adrenaline-dump churning through her.

She cracked her eyes open, enthusiastic since childhood at the chance to lounge, cat-like, in a sun-dappled bed. The light held the weak warmth of midwinter, yet for all her globetrotting there was still something so special about a frozen, sunny day in the Northeast. Her gaze explored the frozen boughs outside, the plumes of condensation rising from office buildings downtown, the hint of the Post Office building poking over it all, and came to rest on the bedside table, where the blinking light of her phone brought her momentary respite crashing down with the reminder that she was jobless. Having pissed off the gatekeeper to her dream career. The deepest sense of failure, of directionless wasted years, of pointless drudgery banished the last scrap of warm contentedness that had draped over her like the winter sun.

Refusing to mope, she threw off her covers and went to her closet. Pulling on her jeans and donning every layer she could, she glanced at the mirror as she left the apartment, unsure where she was headed. She pulled a thick beanie low across her forehead, knowing there was no way to cover up the defeat in her eyes.

A stiff breeze slammed into her as she stepped out of the lobby, but knowing a café was just around the corner, she turned upwind. Minutes later she reemerged, the warm brew tingling down to her toes. Where to next, she wasn't sure — she turned toward Rock Creek Park and started off at a brisk pace.

As a kid, she'd loved to go on walks with her dad on days like this in New York, hurrying along the west side of the wide boulevards near the Morningside Heights apartment she'd grown up in before her mother left academia, bracing each time they emerged from the lee of the towering buildings to brave the concentrated gusts that raged from the Hudson up the east-west running streets. Close to the river, where there was more of an incline, she'd liked to face downhill into the wind, leaning forward and hoping the blast would keep her from toppling over. Until she learned better, she always imagined the dim, red sun taking forever to slide behind the Palisades was doing the exact same thing, perched on the edge of what seemed to be the rest of the world.

She emerged from the southern end of Rock Creek Park, enjoying the lack of traffic and the cold biting wind as she picked her way between the Potomac and the Kennedy

Center. Once — was it the very first summer they were here, first out of college? — some work acquaintance of hers had given her and Evan ballet tickets. They'd dressed up best as they could, splurged on a cab in those pre-Uber days, and Evan had spilled his seven-dollar Heineken all over his crotch at the first sip. She smiled to remember.

Two years later she'd been relieved, even if she couldn't admit it then, to escape the city and the relationship and the routine and the job that seemed to be cutting her dreams off one early morning Metro ride at a time. She parried Evan's schemes to join the Army with her application to grad school in Singapore, both telling themselves they were making big career moves. Now she knew they'd just been stuck and needed a bold change to get on with their lives.

So what was different now? How could she tell if Evan was earnest, ready to commit, or if he'd just pick up and move again? He'd done it once before, after all, and maybe their loneliness was just driving them not to bring up any of the hard questions. And yet, look at what they'd been through the past four days. Maybe the roller coaster was clouding her judgment. Or maybe all they'd needed was to go off and prove to themselves they could make it in the real world, to live as individuals for a bit. After all, there hadn't been another person Charlotte had let see her cry in six years.

She passed the gilded statues capping the terminus of the Memorial Bridge, the cold forcing a brisk pace that left her breathless as she turned past the Lincoln Monument. In the distance, the Washington Monument, the Capitol dome, and hardly a soul on the entire Mall. Skirting the edge of the drained Reflecting Pool, she cut across to her favorite spot in the entire city: the DC War Memorial.

A simple Doric temple, its gleaming white marble stood out even amongst the frost-clad trees. The grand views of the Mall, the imposing majesty of national identity-forming, faded as Charlotte approached and the bare vegetation closed around her. Utterly alone, Charlotte allowed her thoughts, finally, to turn to her work.

If she was honest with herself, what she was angriest about was that a decade of work, striving toward finding a way to serve something bigger than herself, had been dashed against a silly NDA for a greedy boss. She'd put up with a crappy job for the sake of what came next. All she'd wanted was to contribute in her own way, and that was gone. It wasn't just failure. It cut her self-image to the core.

But the smaller question was easier. Whether she'd done the right thing or not, she was off the case. It hit hard to admit that, deep down, she'd enjoyed pursuing Bērziņš. There was the thrill of the chase, the sense of purpose. She'd miss that, whatever came next.

Sighing to herself, she ambled north past the World War II Memorial, out of the wind amongst the megaliths. What did come next? She had enough savings to last a few months. That would give her room to keep making friends, to find a new job. *Ha!* she laughed to herself. *What kind of job?* There would be no clearance for her, with what she'd just done.

No clearance. She'd never be a part of things that got monuments on the Mall. No chance to ever do the kind of work she'd fleetingly tasted over the past four days. She'd never find out how the Aleksandrs Bērziņš story ended.

She crossed Constitution Ave to head back home, and the wind almost knocked her flat. *Why not?*

She'd saved all the information. She had all the time in the world. She had enough savings. What was the difference between chasing Bērziņš as an employee of a private firm versus as a private citizen, except—except no one would tell her what to do.

She hailed a Yellow Cab that pulled around the corner just as she was pulling her phone out to call a Lyft, her mind racing as she fumbled over Evan's address. *Why not?* Well, however far behind Bērziņš she'd been in Fayetteville, she was a day and a half further behind now. So that trail was cold—and the Bureau was certainly all over whatever was left of it. She turned it over in her head and came away with only one thread left to pull.

Minutes later she was bounding up Evan's apartment's stairway, her cheeks burning from the sudden heat. She rapped on the door, realizing she hadn't warned him or even had to get buzzed in. He was probably asleep.

Evan unbolted the door, clad only in running tights, sipping on a protein shake. *Damn*, she thought.

"Uh, hi Char?" he inquired. Charlotte looked past him and realized he was unpacking a Whole Foods bag.

"You're not going to need those," she said, breathlessly.

"Hm?"

"How long is your winter break?"

"'Til the 27th ..."

"What do you say about spending it in Latvia?"

CHAPTER 15
Dulles Airport, Virginia, January 6

Try as they might, Charlotte and Evan couldn't convince the efficient Lufthansa representatives to seat them next to each other on the overbooked transatlantic flight, so after a heinously early morning and a hurried ride to Dulles and frenzied security checkpoint where a harried single mother kept jostling up against her, Charlotte was finally seated alone in a middle seat, watching the stream of fellow travelers nervously and wondering what lovely member of the species would share her bubble for the next ten hours.

Her spirits fell as a middle-aged man asked to slip by into the window seat, his legs immediately widening into what was clearly her space. Charlotte couldn't help but press her arm against him and was just starting to appreciate his unique odor when a tall, skinny German teenager plopped into the aisle seat and immediately ran his eyes down Charlotte's figure. She could almost taste his breath in the air between them and was sure she could feel his excited adolescent heart beating through his chest.

So she turned to a tried and true technique, one she'd learned from a long train ride with a female Indian professor at the University of Delhi. Working up a full head of steam, she delivered a convincingly cataclysmic sneeze into her hand, making sure that a little snot dripped out onto her fingers.

"I'm so sorry, oh my goodness, so embarrassing ..." she floundered about, wanting to raise the shadow of a doubt. "Don't worry, it's just allergies, nothing contagious ..." The boy handed her a napkin, and she wiped her hands off, crumpling it up and shoving it into the seatback pocket. "Thank you so much." She could feel the man in the window seat shifting his weight away from her, skeptical.

At that moment Evan approached from the aisle, a godsend. He assessed the situation and played to her advantage: "I'm just a few rows up, darling. Anything you need?" Charlotte watched the youth's confidence crumple under the towering figure over him.

"No thank you, I'll be fine. Enjoy your flight," she replied. Evan smiled and turned, and Charlotte pulled out the bridal magazine marked up with designs Caitlin had asked her to check out. *What a prop. I'm set now.*

Breaking the news about getting fired to her family had been hard, exceptionally hard, and was accompanied by her father's all-too-predictable comment that maybe this was a sign it was time to start working for him, her mother's unempathetic coo-cooing, and the unbearable feeling that the entire family was relieved her little ambitions to become a lowly bureaucrat had met an early death. Chuck was an ass, as always, saying he'd started looking forward to having a badass sister with a gun to scare his friends. Caitlin, again surprising Charlotte, was the only one who expressed empathy, inviting her over for dinner. Within ten minutes of her arrival, however, the old Caitlin was back, and the rest of the evening was spent on wedding gossip.

It was only toward the end of the evening that Charlotte felt she could get a word in about Latvia.

"So Caitlin … I'm going on a little trip. I just need some time away to think. It's not like I have any obligations."

Caitlin glared at her. "You slept with him, didn't you?!"

Charlotte made an exasperated frown at her little sister, truly wishing she actually had. Everything else was a complicated mess, why not that, too?

As Charlotte formed the words for an honest denial that she doubted Caitlin would ever believe, they heard the front door click open. "I'm home!" Ted, Caitlin's finance, crowed from the other room. Charlotte would never voice it aloud but instinctively felt that the combination of Ted's entitled boisterousness and Caitlin's embrace of the wedding identity spelled a certain future: in a handful of years, Ted would put his Mergers and Acquisitions experience to work at the Sorenson family firm, and Caitlin would decide to stay home at a new Upper East Side apartment with their perfect children. But for now that was all in the future, and for now Charlotte stifled her resentment of Caitlin and Ted's high-paying jobs with the smug observation that it was past nine and Ted was only just getting back to his faultless home.

Ted strode in, looking exhausted. "Charlotte!" he bellowed, "what a surprise. I hear you've taken back up with your ex?"

Charlotte drilled holes into Caitlin's eyes. *Fuck it.*

"Oh, we'll see. Just trying to enjoy life is all." Charlotte could see the verbal middle finger land on Caitlin's befuddled face. "We're actually about to go on a little trip together."

"Oh? Lucky you. Where to?"

"Latvia. We hear it's lovely this time of year." Charlotte was loving watching Caitlin writhe.

"Sounds cold. Well, have fun. Cait, darling, I'm going to

shower and hit the hay." Ted leaned over Caitlin, planting a kiss on that perfect forehead and caressing her neck. He turned and walked up the stairs.

Caitlin glared at Charlotte. "You lying little …"

"If I can't trust you not to gossip, Cait, why would I tell you the truth?" Caitlin was caught out. Charlotte loved to watch her realize she'd been outmaneuvered. "In any case, I'm not telling mom and dad or anyone else I'm going. I don't want to be talked about or pitied or anything right now. I just want to take a little time off and enjoy myself."

"In … eastern Europe … in winter." Caitlin was incredulous. "With a guy who broke your heart."

"That's right. So if anything comes up, let me know. I'm turning off my cell service, but you'll be able to reach me if you do a voice call on Zoom." Charlotte left it at that. Any further and she'd have to explain what she was up to, and Caitlin was the last person she trusted not to blab.

"Sorry … what's Zoom?" Caitlin asked. Charlotte grabbed Caitlin's phone and set up the obscure app on the device. It wasn't perfect, but it meant someone could reach her even if she wanted to cut off completely. Charlotte could feel Caitlin's judgment, curiosity, and, yes, jealousy as they finished their bottle of wine, and on the way home Charlotte couldn't help but smirk with pleasure.

The jet roared to life and they lifted off, immediately turning northeast for the nine-hour flight to Frankfurt. Charlotte tried to get lost in a bestseller she'd cadged off Caitlin, but kept getting distracted by the excitement of what was to come. She had no idea where even to start, but it would be thrilling to see where it all began, bringing her little part of the Bērziņš story to an appropriate close.

As the jet leveled off, the flight attendants made their way through the aisle, proffering warm towels. Dabbing her tired face, Charlotte felt the beginnings of something like relief, a giddiness of physically leaving the drama behind. The towel was scented, and breathing in deeply, Charlotte reveled in the warm touch of the moisture on her face. As she finished, the benighted teen to her left reached out in a pitiable gesture of puppy love, offering to take her towel on his lowered tray table. Charlotte smiled, genuinely.

Five minutes later, the next attendant poured Charlotte a glass of nameless red from a large carafe, and before it was halfway consumed, she could feel her eyelids droop. She quickly downed the second half, unable to keep her attention on the asinine whatever she'd pulled up on the screen before her.

Moments later she was shaken awake by the jolt of the wheels on pavement, confused. She looked around, trying to place herself, her two rowmates helping bring her back to reality. "You were really out, lady," the pudgy man to her right commented. "I really had to go but couldn't bring myself to wake you." Charlotte tried to look thankful while rolling her eyes on the inside, amazed that she'd slept so well.

She found Evan waiting for her outside the gate, and they made their way through the Frankfurt airport to the crowded passport control. Even jammed up against each other, the line of people stretched far out into the terminal. Charlotte braced herself for a long wait in the uncomfortable stench of hundreds of strangers straight off long flights while Evan went in search of a snack.

An hour and a half later Charlotte and Evan cheers-ed their waters *mit gas* in a dinky café at the furthest reaches of the Schengen terminal.

"Almost like the old days, right?" Evan asked, wistfully, referring to the six weeks they'd spent backpacking Europe together at the conclusion of college. Charlotte had started the trip—again, paid for by her family—apprehensive, unsure if their relationship could survive a heavy dose of adventure after two years of cloistered academia, just two months before they were set to move in together in DC. But it was Evan's first time outside the country, and his energy and enthusiasm had bulldozed through any fleeting disagreements.

"It certainly is. This time with more wrinkles." She breathed out, hard, appreciating the bubbly water. Definitely more wrinkles. But also, like then, free. Not an obligation in the world. And about to step into a new adventure with this man. Sure, there was tension. Buckets of it. But she was comfortable, and happy, and free, and that's all that mattered. She smiled back and took another swig.

CHAPTER 16
Outside Rīga, Latvia, January 8

SEE MAP "DAUGAVPILS AND THE BALTICS"

With every additional mile they drove through the snowy, pine-clad hills, Charlotte felt more and more like she was finally in Eastern Europe. She'd never actually spent time in this part of the world, her preconceptions instead shaped by the triumphalist American stereotypes of the post-Soviet 1990s: smoggy industrial wastescapes, velour-tracksuit-clad business moguls, unbearable techno, stringy blondes in tasteless heels.

Rīga, then, had come as a surprise. Charlotte had expected to arrive at a gloomy, polluted, destitute metropolis. But with half of the city's population celebrating Orthodox Christmas on January 7, they'd happily found themselves exploring a cheery city center decorated for the holiday, every square hosting a market, every building decked out for the season. Mulled wine greeted their initial wanderings around the picturesque cobblestone streets. As their guide Jānis — Evan had somehow convinced a graduate student in Latvian history to show them around for the day — was eager to point out, the capital was a city whose colorful art nouveau architecture made it the pearl of the Baltic.

The association was one Jānis emphasized, pointing out every detail that emphasized Latvia's western heritage. He himself seemed to be a poster child for a Latvia that faced the Baltic and Scandinavia as much as eastern Europe: looming a few inches over Evan's lanky frame, his piercing blue eyes and platinum-blonde hair, carefully coiffed into a neat crew-cut, were the only hints of color in a disgustingly trendy outfit of irregularly shaped grey woolen garments. And judging from the endless parade of almost offensively beautiful and hip men and women they passed, it was an identity many shared.

"You see, the 1990s were a terrible time of economic collapse and political uncertainty," he explained, leading them through a medieval square that hosted a Hanseatic trading office and a postmodern square of a building. "But it gave the three Baltic nations—Estonia, Latvia, and Lithuania—just enough breathing room from Eurasian hegemony to eke out our own characters and set out a path to reunify with Europe."

"But what do you mean by 'reunify,' Jānis?" Charlotte asked. "Aren't the Baltic nations kind of … their own thing?" She thought of the incomprehensible road signs, the combination of consonants and diacritical marks unlike anything she'd seen before.

"Absolutely," Jānis affirmed. "The Baltic languages are a distant cousin of Slavic and, therefore, the other European tongues, but they're utterly distinct. We trace our deepest roots to the pagan tribes who inhabited these forests and bogs, who celebrated nature and its cycles, holding out against the rising Slavic powers of the Kievan Rus' and Novgorod and Muscovy as much as the Teutonic Knights. Even today … see, look!"

Jānis pointed out a market stall peddling curious carved wooden insignia, rune-like designs Charlotte had noticed emblazoned on clothing, signs, even bumper stickers.

"These are ancient, pre-Christian symbols, each indicating a different Latvian concept," Jānis explained. "This one"—he pointed to a sunflower-like roundel—"is, obviously, the sun.

The triangle is *Dievs*, the pagan term coopted by missionaries to mean 'god.' And this one means strength, intuition, wisdom." Evan picked up the emblem, seemingly two overlapping but incomplete squares. "It's also just plain old *krupītis*," he explained. "The toad." Charlotte guffawed and picked out four of the handsome wooden objects.

"So there is something essentially Baltic," Charlotte summarized after paying. "But it doesn't clarify what it means to 'reunify' with Europe."

"Of course," Jānis replied, leading them through a low stone arch to the side of a large cathedral, where a simple bronze statue stood covered in ice and dark patina.

"Oh!" Evan exclaimed. "It's the musicians of Bremen!" Charlotte instantly recognized the image from her childhood, one of Grimm's fairytales about a merry band of neglected, aging domesticated animals. "But ... why is it here?"

"Exactly," Jānis concluded, as if in full explanation of Charlotte's question. "Rīga traces its modern history to a trading entrepot of the Hanseatic League, and a landfall of the Northern Crusades. Nearly a thousand years ago, German knights seeking to Christianize the pagan Baltic tribes eked out a foothold right here, building a tiny fort on the spot of the building you see before you. With centuries of continuous exchange, that cultural spark has never gone out. After the end of Communism, the city of Bremen — long Rīga's sister city — sent this statute as a gift, with the animals peeking their heads out from the Iron Curtain."

It was an apt metaphor, Charlotte thought.

"So we Latvians feel we are a distinct, unique nation, but one whose cultural ties are strongest with the Baltic, with the west. For it is only a geographic coincidence that the great powers of eastern Europe—first the Polish-Lithuanian Commonwealth, then the Russian Empire, and finally the USSR—have ruled Latvia for most of the past three hundred years. No matter our westward-facing coast, we are at the fringe of the great Eurasian steppe. And it is only through Eurasian dominance that you see the ... Slavic influence."

Charlotte wasn't as convinced by this nationalist interpretation. Maybe it was two generations, maybe it was three hundred years, maybe it was one thousand, but that didn't make the onion spires of Orthodox churches, Russian spoken on the street, or miserable Soviet-style high-rise suburbs any less a part of the Latvian cultural tapestry.

"But Jānis ..." Evan's slow lead told Charlotte he was measuring his words to minimize their ability to offend. "Didn't Latvians fight on both sides of World War II? And didn't the Latvian Communist Party enthusiastically welcome the Soviets?"

"Of course! All I am saying is that we Latvians are sick of being defined in relation to outside powers. Be honest, isn't you Americans' image of Latvia as some dreary, backwards 'eastern European' shithole? And it's the same the other way. Russians, like the Soviets before them, are always able to paint Latvian nationalists as 'Nazis' because many of our grandparents fought with the Germans in World War II. Their every action serves as a straw man for every effort we made, or make, to run our own country. But wouldn't you have welcomed the Germans as liberators if your country had been invaded by the Soviet Union? Let's not get caught up in old twentieth-century insults, or race-to-the-bottom analogies. For the first time in a century, Latvia is charting its own course.

We are proud to be our own nation. And we choose Europe."

It was a startling, powerful position, one that helped Charlotte understand the appeal of raw nationalism for the first time. Perhaps it was a bit unsubtle, but Jānis's simple plea for self-determination carried a weight she couldn't shrug off.

After bidding adieu to Jānis, Evan and Charlotte meandered their way through the city in the last moments of sunlight — the sun set before four — and then ambled to the city square for a few glasses of mulled wine and a solid plate of sausage and dumplings. It was there that she first saw an outward manifestation of the emotion Jānis had described. Evan was using his Russian to barter with vendors at the market when an older woman snapped at him in perfect English: "Why are you speaking Russian? You came to Latvia. Speak Latvian."

Reeling from the exchange, Evan shared his thoughts on Jānis's discourse. "It's just hard for me to see the contrast, Char. For all the rabid nationalism in the media, all the political grandstanding — there is no way to tell who's Russian and who's Latvian. Everyone's bundled up against the cold. Everyone's at the same markets."

"I know, right?!" Charlotte agreed. "I can't help but be reminded of something I read about Sarajevo before the Bosnian Civil War: no one had really cared they were Bosniaks, Croats, or Serbs until all of a sudden someone who did started pointing it out. And we all know how that ended."

They tramped about the markets, the warmth in their bellies helping them forget the freezing air. As they basked in the Christmas spirit, Charlotte didn't spare a second worrying about her job, or lack thereof. At American Christmas, she'd been alone, swiping on a dating app and hating where life had brought her. Now she was on an adventure in a new part of the world, hanging out with her ... whatever Evan was.

The door of a bar they walked past opened, and for a fleeting moment Charlotte heard the distinctive sounds of throbbing Russian pop. Her eyes met Evan's, which said the same thing she was thinking: We're here for a reason. If we go to bed now, we can leave for Daugavpils early.

So they spent the day after Christmas tracing the Daugava river as it wended its way eastward from Rīga. Charlotte shivered to imagine trying to traverse the bog-forest-hills they passed: the river was the only way through. And a string of historical monument signs pointed the way to castles that marked this geographic truth: hold the river and you hold the nation. At some point they passed into Latgale, Latvia's easternmost border region. Latgale had a history even more complex than Latvia's. The region featured Catholicism in contrast to the Lutheranism dominant on the coasts, and sported a distinctive dialect of Latvian — as well as a much higher proportion of non-Latvians.

All this came together as they entered Daugavpils, literally "castle on the Daugava." A Russian-majority town at the intersection of the major railways astride the Daugava river, in a region distinct from Latvia. No wonder there was trouble out here.

As they neared the city center, evidence of the protests was everywhere: wreckage in the street, new graffiti on the walls. They passed a brown concrete Greek Revival building, clearly a Stalinist effort at a theater, which was now draped in banners sporting the Russian flag. Evan piped up just as Charlotte started to imagine the question:

"I guess the protesting doesn't really get started 'til after lunch. Let's find a hotel and get something to eat."

They settled on a towering hotel in a plaza in the middle of town, the only building over ten stories, a testament to late-Soviet architecture overlaid with the sheen of capitalism. A massive parking and reception area sported enormous drifts of snow shoved up against the building, accentuating the moat-like feeling that this hotel stood apart from the rest of the city. They easily checked in; aside from reporters, the receptionist reported, who would come here at a time like now? After an awkward moment in which the receptionist had clearly assessed them as a couple, Evan spoke up, getting them two rooms on the eighth floor. As they turned toward the elevator, Charlotte reflexively checked her phone.

"Evan."

"Hmmm?" He was preoccupied with the jumble of paperwork and keys and had fallen behind.

"Evan. Stop. Look at this."

Evan came up even to her, and she showed him the *New York Times* splash page. He took a moment to comprehend.

"No shit. Do you think it was …?"

"I have no clue. But Margaret and the FBI are the only ones who know aside from us, and it sure as hell wasn't the FBI."

She scrolled to the bottom of the article, her heart starting to beat again after she was sure she was never mentioned. Satisfied, she went back to the top of the page, just to take in the headline once again: "Policeman suspected of murder smuggled into US, aided by Latvian officials."

CHAPTER 17
Daugavpils, Latvia, January 8

SEE MAP "DAUGAVPILS AND THE BALTICS"

"I've never seen anything like it," Charlotte puzzled, gazing up at a gracious building, constructed entirely of red bricks yet with all the intricate ornamentation of the Baroque Revival. Buildings like it were scattered throughout Daugavpils's downtown, holdouts against a sea of Soviet brutalist rectangles.

"So, Wikipedia says that the city was almost entirely leveled when 'liberated' by the Soviets at the end of World War II. They must be the only old buildings left." Evan read from the page. "But when I google 'red bricks Daugavpils'... got it. There's a brickworks outside town that supplied as far afield as Vilnius, back when Daugavpils was a stop on the St. Petersburg–Warsaw line ... so yeah, wealthy trading families wanted to get in on the Baroque Revival sweeping Europe in the late nineteenth century, but they adapted it to the local red bricks. Pretty cool."

"I wonder what the town looked like before Stalin renovated it," Charlotte speculated. "It's such a perfect grid, which you'd never expect from an older town. I wonder if that's a recent upgrade."

"Right? Except that the University and Central Square are also on the grid, as is ... yup, the synagogue, right over there. And given just how ... comprehensive the Holocaust was here ..."

"That means the city was on a grid before the Nazis showed up." Charlotte finished his thought. They'd read about how the entire Jewish population had been killed by death squads in just three days in summer 1941. The legacy of violence was coded into every street corner here, layer after layer of blood coloring the city as surely as the red bricks. Distrustful, rival identities at an economic crossroads: a dangerous combination that seemed destined to generate paroxysms of violence every couple of generations.

Their haphazard afternoon tour of town was getting more and more difficult as protestors started to fill the streets. Bundled against the bitter cold, groups were carrying signs, running into friends, even laughing. It was almost a festival atmosphere. Charlotte guided them past a crowd starting to form around a speaker on the steps of the University, toward the bust of Andrejs Pumpurs in the central square.

"Wikipedia," Charlotte read: "A poet who penned the Latvian epic *Lāčplēsis* (the Bear Slayer, first published in 1888) ... prominent figure in the 'Young Latvia' movement ... officer in the Imperial Russian Army and staunch promoter of Latvian culture." She paused and looked up at the bust, gesturing at the clumps of people assembling in the weak light. "Wonder how he feels about this."

Evan smiled and grabbed her hand. "I'm frozen. What do you say to a drink?"

They crossed over tram tracks, making their way toward a bar on the square in front of their imposing hotel. "Artilērijas." They read the sign as they approached a group of protestors crowding the entrance.

"*Izvinite.*" Evan led as the group barely parted, glaring them down. As she approached the door, Charlotte heard one spit behind her. Turning, she saw an old man, eyes full of hatred, staring after her. She retreated quickly into the warmth of the bar.

It was surprisingly empty for how many people were out and about—aside from one group at a table, Evan and Charlotte were the only ones in the place. They took their coats off and sidled up to the bar.

"*Dva piva, pozhalsta*," Evan said, holding up two fingers to the bartender, a tall, skinny young man with perfectly blonde, shoulder-length hair.

"Not in here, buddy," he responded with heavily accented English, posturing over them from across the bar.

"Excuse me?" Charlotte asked.

"This is a Latvian bar, in Latvia. Leave your Russian with the scum outside," he spat.

It took Charlotte a moment to process the clues they'd missed: the spelling of the bar's name, clearly not Russian; the aggressive protestors outside; the lack of clientele. Evan was quick on the uptake.

"Thank goodness. Getting tired of this mess. How about those beers?"

The bartender held Evan's gaze for a moment, then nodded and moved off.

"Jeez. I'd almost forgotten how serious this is," Evan whispered to Charlotte, fingering a napkin.

"What's wild is … it's almost a party outside. People excited to be a part of something, an outlet for emotion. Easy to lose track of the fact that it all started with a violent crime, and things like this could erupt into violence at any moment. If they start rioting ... this bar will be the first to burn."

"No kidding." Their beers arrived and they sipped away, scrolling through their phones. "Look at this." Evan tipped his phone toward Charlotte.

It was a *Slate* rollup of social media reactions: "The Bērziņš Leak: What the Media Are Saying." Up front the article summarized all the major news outlets and the predictable op-eds, then delved into who had tweeted what, what memes were trending, which talking heads staked out what position.

"Hm. What's interesting is" — Charlotte scrolled through the article — "yeah. Everyone is outraged. There just isn't much cross-aisle sniping going on ... normally these flashpoints trigger enormous cross-party conflagrations. But with this, conservatives are up in arms that some pissant so-called ally is violating our borders and plotting against us, and liberals are wondering if this will finally bring some attention to the plight of the protestors. It's almost as if — "

" — as if the outrage normally directed at each other has been redirected at Latvia, yet keeping its distinctive partisan flair?" Evan finished her sentence.

"Exactly. I wouldn't be surprised if the President starts putting pressure on little Latvia to make some concessions." She handed the phone back, watching the crowd grow on the square outside. Evan did his best to decipher some of the signs: "Bērziņš is a Nazi"; "Give us the Vote"; "I am Latvian" in Russian. The last piqued Evan's interest.

"Even the words are hard. Russian tends to have separate

words for ethnicities and citizenships ... *roosky* is ethnic Russians, while *rossissky* is a citizen of the Russian state. A Kazakh can be proud of being *rossissky* just like a Chinese immigrant can be proud of being American, but he'd never dream of calling himself *roosky*. But that sign says "*ya latishsky*" — I am a Lett — not '*ya latvisky*' — I am a Latvian citizen. It's a subtle word choice that almost makes no sense and would enrage any diehard Latvian nationalist, because it's claiming that you can speak Russian but still be a part of the Latvian ethnicity, not just a citizen. This place is totally messed up. I can't help but think of Yugoslavia again. The only meaningful difference between the Croat and Serbian languages is that you spell the former with Latin letters and the latter in Cyrillic. Same with Hindi in Devanagari, and Urdu in Arabic. It's almost like the smaller the difference, the more angry people get about it."

They paid for their beer, threading their way out into the main square. Groups were starting to chant, and there was a loudspeaker set up on the steps of the University, with a middle-aged woman taking the mic. They stopped to listen, with Evan translating under his breath:

"... uh ... and so this, yes, I will say it, Nazi regime leaves us no choice. We don't want to be *rossissky*. We want to be Europeans. But if this throwback regime, this puppet of the fascist invaders, who cares only for the descendants of their pure race, forces us to choose, then choose we will: we are *roosky*. And we will look to our mother state to save us from this ..."

Crack.

Screams broke out in the street past the University.

Crack. Crackcrackcrack. Crackcrack. Crack.

The screams spread as the entire crowd turned toward them and started running from the University. Evan pulled Charlotte into the awning of an apartment building, his voice surprisingly quiet for the din around them. "Here," he murmured, holding her close to avoid the flood of people. His eyes quickly scanned the street.

Moments later, the square was clear but for garbage and a few stragglers. Whatever had happened, had happened on the far side of the University — they could see no signs of violence on the square. Without the slightest sense of urgency, Evan unfurled them from the alcove, stepping into the sidewalk and glancing both ways. "This way," he uttered in the same quiet monotone as before, taking her hand and walking away from the University.

The streets had cleared before them, and they proceeded past Artilērijas — noticeably closed and locked up — to the next bar, a small café across from their hotel adorned with an enormous hedgehog sipping a cocktail. They stepped in, noticing an apprehensive silence reigning over everyone who hadn't gone straight home. Charlotte was surprised the crowd hadn't rioted.

They took their seats. "*Dva piva*," Evan said to the waitress, whose nerves showed as she kept glancing out the window. "*Yozhik v tumanie*," he said, glancing at Charlotte. "The name of the bar is 'Hedgehog in the Fog,' after a famous Soviet kid's cartoon." There was an intensity in his manner, a fire in his gaze that hadn't been there before. *The last time he heard gunshots was probably in Afghanistan*, Charlotte realized as their drinks arrived. *There is an entire side to this man that I do not know.*

A gasp went up from the next table over, with angry chattering in Russian.

"What are they saying, Evan?" He listened for a moment.

"Fuck." He pulled out his phone, tapped at it, and propped it up between them. The outrage in the room was escalating, with a woman starting to wail.

The clip, posted only minutes before, was a grainy cell-phone video shot from an upper story of an apartment building behind the University. The edge of the crowd could be seen overflowing into the street, with a small group of what were clearly teenagers messing around on the periphery. A Latvian police van slowly rolled into the frame. Suddenly, the back of the van opened and a handful of police in full riot gear stormed out, running at the teenagers, beating them to the ground, grabbing them by the collar and dragging them back toward the van. But they didn't stop there; they kept dragging them to the far side of the van, out of sight of the protestors. The policeman dumped their four prisoners against a small wall and, without a moment's hesitation, pulled out their pistols and shot them all. A female scream broke out and the video stopped.

Charlotte was beyond shocked. She'd just witnessed the Latvian police execute children! Evan had already restarted the clip, and on second viewing, she could see one of the teenagers had hurled a snowball at the police van. But that was hardly justification! The police must have been waiting, just waiting for any excuse …

"We've got to get out of here, Char." Evan was visibly upset. "This changes everything. We shouldn't be here." The fire in his eyes had intensified as they darted around, watching the restaurant and street. Charlotte wondered if hers betrayed the emotions coursing through her. She could taste the fear, even under the surge of outrage as she rewatched the clip. But cutting through it all … Charlotte forced herself to admit just how excited she was.

CHAPTER 18
Daugavpils, Latvia, January 9

Charlotte could hear Evan's low murmurs through the thin door, her hand pausing before she knocked. She couldn't make out anything specific, but maybe that was the haze of the deep slumber that had ended only with a misty gloaming that belied the alarm clock's blinking red 9:32 a.m. She'd slept ten hours.

Who was he talking to? Charlotte strained to eavesdrop, but try as she might, she couldn't pick out a word. Giving up the game, she knocked, hearing him end the phone call and come to the door.

"Good morning! Nice long sleep?" He guided her into the room, offering her a coffee.

"Mmmmmm. It's silly to say, with all this going on, but I think my body is finally starting to realize it's on vacation and relax. Who were you talking to?"

He looked at her, assessing. "Oh, just my ma. She was worried about the news."

Charlotte knew he was lying, and she plopped down in the armchair.

"Mmmmmm. What's the latest?"

"Well, Americans are going nuts. Both sides are crying bloody murder — which it pretty obviously was — and there's even talk of the President making an official condemnation. Nothing new on Bērziņš, though."

"Mmmmmmmm." Charlotte needed the coffee. They'd stayed up late, heading back to the hotel as night fell to discuss what to do. Evan was for leaving right away, at least back to Rīga. And his reasoning made sense: Things were about to get a lot more heated. Violence was far more likely after what Russian media was now calling *voynya v Dvinske* — "the massacre of Dvinsk," Dvinsk being the old, Russian name for Daugavpils. And now there was international attention, which would only force each side to dig in and escalate.

"On the other hand," Charlotte had countered, a big bowl of onion soup steaming before her, "this is the place to be. We're safe in the hotel, it's not like it's civil war." They'd decided to discuss their plans over dinner at the hotel. From the restaurant on the tenth floor, they also had a courtside view — totally safe — of the protestors starting to reemerge onto the streets. This time it wasn't clumps of people, disorganized groups listening to one speaker or another — it was a full-on crowd, seeming to expand and contract and move like a living, breathing beast.

"You say that now. But what if it goes that way? All it takes is one, two more events and all of a sudden this place goes up like the powder keg it is — gun battles in the street, burning barricades blocking us in, who knows. It happened in Sarajevo. It happened in countless cities during the Arab Spring. And there's no reason it couldn't happen here."

"And so what? Then we'd be here, with a front-row seat." She gestured to the crowd forming far below them, already easily twice the size of the one they'd seen that afternoon. She could taste Evan's reluctance. *This guy has two combat tours in Afghanistan. What's a little protest got him so worried?*

The jangle of Charlotte's phone interrupted their loggerheads, with a silly picture of Caitlin wearing a mustache popping up on the Zoom app. "Take it," Evan declared, and Charlotte swiped the phone.

"Hello?"

"Oh my god, Charlotte, thank goodness." Caitlin's voice was stressed, hurried. What could be wrong?

"Charlotte, Mommy and Daddy are freaking out. They don't know where you are, how to get a hold of you. They don't know I'm calling, but you should know … there is some FBI agent trying to get a hold of you. Apparently she's been calling you non-stop, but when you didn't answer she went and found Mommy and Daddy. So needless to say, they're out of their minds … they think you're missing, and apparently you're on the FBI wanted list …"

"I'm not on the FBI wanted list, Cait. Calm down," Charlotte interrupted. "Listen. Thank you for letting me know. Tell mom and dad you were able to reach me, that I'm fine, that I'll be in touch with Agent McCandless myself." *Eeek*! She realized too late what she'd just revealed.

"Wait, you know this person? What's this all about, Char?!"

Charlotte paused and took a breath, weighing her response. "Never mind, Cait. Everything is OK. Tell mom and dad I'm OK. I love you; everything is fine. We'll talk soon. Good night."

There was an awkward silence on the other end; Caitlin knew she was being hung up on.

"Good night, Char. Love you too."

Evan read her expression and made a sympathetic shake of the head.

"I'll have to contact Agent McCandless," Charlotte stated.

"Email her tonight. Set a time for tomorrow midafternoon when she's just waking up," Evan suggested.

Charlotte wrote the email carefully, arranging a Zoom call for three the following afternoon. That done, she tried to purge the whole drama from her mind and returned her gaze to the window. A few individuals had brought torches, and there were far fewer signs. The Latvian government had denied — completely denied — that they had anything to do with the murders. The tension had skyrocketed: she doubted the same festival atmosphere would be present.

Evan resumed the negotiation from before. "We don't go out at night. We watch from here, we read and relax and sleep in and … and if things start getting worse, we're out of here."

"Outta here," she confirmed.

They'd spent the rest of the evening getting progressively drunker, watching the protests unfold far below, teasing each other and following the latest on Twitter and Facebook and vKontakte — Evan had made a fake profile on the Russian social-networking site so he could see stories on the other side of things. At one point, when it felt well and late (it was only nine), Evan sloshed his beer on the table in a rush to put it down.

"Well … jeez."

"What?"

"BBC: Putin orders humanitarian convoy to Latvia."

"Huh?"

"In an unprecedented show of support for the ongoing anti-government protests in eastern Latvia, Russian President Vladimir Putin has announced he is dispatching a ten-vehicle humanitarian aid convoy to Daugavpils, the site of last week's tragic murder and the epicenter of the civic disturbance now … Blah blah blah background … The convoy will include medical personnel, a field kitchen, and a so-called "civil support element" … let's see … an expert in the UK Ministry of Defense theorized that the convoy could be cover for the infiltration of specialized propaganda teams like those that flooded the Crimea in the wake of 2014's Euromaidan protests … Yadda yadda … In response to the humanitarian convoy, local authorities have established checkpoints along major roads and bridges in and around Daugavpils. The Latvian government continues to deny any involvement in today's tragic murders, officially stating that it had no police presence in the area."

"Well, that's a good one." Charlotte hiccupped. Evan smirked. Charlotte's sodden mind was miles away from any geopolitical drama, and the elevator ride back to their floor didn't help.

"Well … this is me," Evan pointed out, unhelpfully.

Charlotte placed her hand on his chest, feeling him. She pushed him away. "Good night, Evan."

"Good night."

She rushed back to her room, trying to put as much distance as possible between her and a bad decision. She drifted off trying to unpuzzle how it could be wrong when she wanted it so badly.

The next morning, Charlotte finally heard the satisfying hiss of the coffee machine finishing its job, and gratefully accepted the warm cup. "Can we just … stay here all day?"

"Ha. What happened to Ms. Not-Wanting-To-Miss-Out?"

"We can go for a walk this afternoon. Let's just sit here and read. I need it."

By mid-morning Latvia had filed a formal petition with NATO, citing the infamous Article V mutual self-defense clause. But all Russia was doing was sending supplies and personnel—the two countries had a nearly open border, anyhow—and by the time the petition was filed, the trucks were already on their way back to Russia, with videos of Latvian police angrily flagging down humanitarian trucks painted white on a snowy bridge proliferating across the internet and further alienating the Latvian government. Some nations rushed to Latvia's defense; in Lithuania, Estonia, and Poland's eyes, the convoy had been a clear violation of Latvian sovereignty. But the rest of NATO waffled, weighing the scale of the action against the potential for escalation.

As Charlotte's anxiety about the upcoming call with Agent McCandless grew, they ordered room service, just a couple of sandwiches, watching the protestors outside in a brisk, flurry-filled winter breeze. Certainly no reason either could see to go outside.

At three on the dot Charlotte's phone buzzed, and she settled in for what was sure to be a very awkward call.

"This is Charlotte Sorenson."

"Ms. Sorenson. This is Agent McCandless. I am required to notify you that this call is being recorded."

"Um … OK. What can I help you with, Agent McCandless?"

"Ms. Sorenson, I need you to come in for questioning immediately. The disclosure of Bērziņš's presence in the United States has had a catastrophic impact on the progress of our investigation and is currently being investigated as a potential violation of confidentiality protocol in and of itself. While you are not currently a suspect, you are one of only two civilians with access to this information, and we need to review your custody of the information in question. When are you available?"

Charlotte gulped.

"I'm … uh … I'm actually out of the country." She squeezed the answer out.

"I'm sorry?!"

"I'm … on a vacation with my … boyfriend." Charlotte glanced at Evan's smirk. "After losing my job I just needed to take time. I'm sorry."

"We can arrange an interview at the US Embassy wherever you are. Where are you, Ms. Sorenson?"

Charlotte paused.

"Agent McCandless, is there a warrant for my arrest?"

"No …"

"Is there any other legal reason I would be obliged to make a statement?"

"Um ... not at this time ..."

"Then in that case, Agent McCandless, I will reserve my right as a private citizen not to conduct an interview at this time. Here is my statement. I did not leak that information. I possess the information on a USB drive that has been in my possession since my interview. I know nothing about the leak. I hope that helps."

Evan's wide eyes told Charlotte just how audacious her action was.

"Well ... um ... Ms. Sorenson ... how about this. You're part of an ongoing investigation. Two, now. I need to be able to get a hold of you. If anything else comes up, I will reach out by email. Will you be able to respond within twenty-four hours?"

"I will."

"Ms. Sorenson, while you are completely within your rights, I do have to advise you how suspicious your actions appear. Are you sure—"

"Agent McCandless, I am. I assure you: I have nothing further to contribute to your investigation. If you have nothing further ..."

"I don't. Please monitor your email."

"I will. Good day."

Charlotte hung up. The pressure of the call suddenly burst through her professional mask, and she rushed to Evan, hugging him.

"OK Evan. OK. That was hard. Let's go do something. I'm starting to feel cooped up."

"Vacation over, then?"

"I won't say no to a few more ten-hour nights of sleep, but I need to stretch my legs."

They bundled up in the obligatory layers upon layers, wrapping their heads in scarves and emerging from the hotel as the last slivers of daylight cut across the city. With the coming of night the protest took a palpable pause, as even the diehards went home for a hot supper before the evening's prime events. Yet even so, they could *feel* the difference, the chants rippling across the collected thousands, the anger right below the surface. Charlotte knew they'd always stood out as Americans, or at least western Europeans, but now there were far more stares, glances held a moment too long. She no longer felt like a tourist in an out-of-the-way backwater, but instead an unwelcome observer to inside business.

"Let's wander past where the kids got shot," Evan suggested. They skirted the University and cut around the back of the imposing building, turning onto the fateful lane. Even at 150 meters in the dark, they could pick out the enormous pile of flowers, wreaths, and notes arrayed around the wall where the shooting had occurred. There was a steady stream of visitors, some crying, some laying flowers, some simply observing as they moved back to the protest. They paused briefly but, aware of the crowd noticing their difference, kept moving along the street.

"I remember reading about this place." Evan gestured at a sign reading "Gubernators" and leading down some stairs. They entered, and it was just right: a cozy, warm, bright basement adorned with all sorts of knickknacks and permeated by the smell of pork and beer. Charlotte could almost forget the stirring memorial she'd just seen.

"What do you say we just forget it all and have a carefree eastern European feast?" she jested, the waitress arriving to take Evan's order. It was less than a minute before a small bottle of vodka surrounded by an assortment of snacks appeared before them. "Perfect," she concluded.

They cheers-ed, the frozen drink and pickled chasers fitting perfectly with the warm surroundings. Charlotte felt herself start to relax. All of this was exciting, sure. And it was neat to feel in the middle of things. She could worry about the consequences later.

She picked up a piece of something grey and slimy, unsure exactly its provenance, and threw it to the back of her mouth. Too late; the intense taste of pickled fish flooded her sinuses and she squinted in surprise. Stifling herself, she turned to the side as Evan snorted in laughter. Looking away, she saw a couple seated on the other side of the restaurant. There was no mistaking the short, ramrod-straight figure with cropped brown hair facing her: it was Natalya.

CHAPTER 19
Daugavpils, Latvia, January 9

The possibilities flew through Charlotte's head faster than she could stop to consider them. Over the previous days, she'd somehow managed to forget that their Latvian vacation had all started because she had betrayed that woman. There was no telling how she'd react. For all that was happening here in Daugavpils, Charlotte could only surmise she'd be furious: Natalya had entrusted Charlotte with a delicate investigation, only to be betrayed to the FBI. And now Russians were dying on the streets of Daugavpils. Could she be jailed in Latvia for breaking the NDA? Natalya was a lawyer for the police ... *oh god, what was I thinking coming here?!*

"Evan," she whisper-yelled, hunching toward him. "Don't look now. Over your right shoulder, in the corner, sitting with the large man. It's Natalya." Evan's eyes went wide. "Shit," he responded.

Charlotte did her best to keep her eyes away, but they kept on being drawn back. Natalya was instantly recognizable, but there was something subtly different about her. Her clothes were less stereotypical, maybe, or she held herself with even more authority, if that was possible. Charlotte was reminded how much she'd just *liked* Natalya when they'd met.

Natalya's companion, on the other hand, didn't look like someone Charlotte would particularly care to meet. He was burly, easily over 200 pounds, crammed into a stocky frame. He wore tight jeans and a simple tee shirt, with biceps and traces of tattoos disappearing up his sleeve. His bald head was pointed intently at Natalya, and though Charlotte couldn't see his face, she was sure his eyes held hers intensely. Natalya's arms were crossed and she was nearly staring him down, and her body language didn't hold a hint of affection. *I'd pick up their tab if that's anything but a business dinner.*

"Do you want to try to slip out?" Evan asked.

"I think that would be best. I have no clue if she—" Natalya looked up and met Charlotte's gaze. For the briefest moment there shown in Natalya's eyes a look of absolute terror, but just an instant later Charlotte was unsure if that's what she'd really seen, replaced as it was with a rictus of composed dominance. Natalya quickly stood and muttered something to her companion, who twisted toward them wearing a look of absolute shock.

"Well, game's up," Evan added as Natalya walked toward them sporting a broad smile.

"Charlotte! What a surprise to see you here! Won't you come join us?"

"Natalya, we, uh"—Charlotte nervously glanced at Evan—"we'd be overjoyed." They collected their drinks, while Natalya harangued the waitress, and went to join the burly man.

Seated, Natalya continued, happy to hold the upper hand. "Charlotte, please meet my friend Misha—we went to University together. I am sorry to say he speaks very little English." Misha grunted out a hello of some kind. "And who is this?" She gestured to Evan.

"My name is Evan, pleased to meet you." *In English*, Charlotte noted, *smart*. They exchanged handshakes all around.

"Now Charlotte, I must know: What on earth are you doing here in Daugavpils?"

Careful, Char. Never volunteer information. "Oh, well ... I guess you could say my interest was piqued. I had to see the protests for myself."

"And? Have they met your expectations?" Natalya's question was dripping with implied contempt. Charlotte paused.

"We seem to have arrived at quite a critical moment. Yesterday's violence was tragic."

"Indeed. So you see just how badly we needed to find Bērziņš." Silence. Here it came. "I can't blame you for what you did, Charlotte. If it were my country, I would have done the same." It took every ounce of Charlotte's willpower to hold Natalya's gaze and keep a stone mask. "And as far as I'm concerned, all's well that ends well, as they say. The American people care about Mr. Bērziņš now like they never did before, which means your government cares, which means Latvia is starting to care. What else could I have asked for?"

They were interrupted by the arrival of four plates and a massive steaming platter of roast pork in a bed of vegetables, followed shortly by a full-sized bottle of vodka.

"I hope you do not mind," Natalya explained. "I took the liberty of changing your order. You are our guests."

Charlotte looked at Evan, both of them skeptical and somewhat confused by the turn events had taken. He made a half shrug and turned back to Natalya. "It's very kind of you, Natalya. Let us toast to your hospitality."

The raising of glasses woke Misha from his scowling remove,

and he enthusiastically joined in with a resounding *nazdrovie*. After a practiced shot, he muttered something in Russian to Natalya before carving the roast and putting a hefty portion of meat, potatoes, and vegetables on each of their plates.

As they ate, the conversation turned to the protests. Natalya's composure loosened just a hair as the alcohol flowed. According to Natalya, the police had already identified and disciplined the perpetrators of the murders, though not a word of it had been released publicly. They were trying to be as hands-off as possible, she relayed, not wanting to provoke in the least.

"You can't imagine how difficult it is to see both sides. How much I'd like to join the protestors out on the streets, demanding justice … and yet, at the same time, the Latvians I work with in the police are good people. They are trying their best and honestly want nothing more than peace. I'm not sure if it is possible to have both."

She paused, considering the half-eaten pork slab before her. "I imagine your situation was much the same, as you chased Bērziņš across North Carolina. How is our friend Margaret doing? What does she think of your vacation?"

Ah, so this is it, Charlotte deduced through the haze of her buzz. She may be mad as hell, even murderous, but she's enough of a master to play this one for as much info as possible. Don't volunteer information.

"Margaret? Oh, she could care less, I imagine. I'd been planning a trip with Evan for a while … we just changed the destination is all." Too late, Charlotte realized she may have been tested. Either Natalya had seen the headlines in the US and called Margaret demanding an explanation … or

Margaret had told Natalya about Charlotte's betrayal, and together they'd leaked the story. Either way, Natalya would know Charlotte had been fired ... which meant her answer was dangerously, dangerously close to a lie.

"Oh, so are you two ... together then?" *She got the info she wanted and moved on. A pro.* Evan cut in.

"Oh, we've known each other for ages." The conversation was slowing down.

"Well," Natalya replied, "it is very nice to see two young Americans so interested in the plight of our little corner of the world. I truly hope you enjoy yourselves here. Where are you staying?"

"The hotel in the Central Square." The answer was out of her mouth before Charlotte could wonder about the question's purpose.

"A wonderful view, the best possible choice." Charlotte gulped. Another card played.

Ten minutes later they were out on the frigid street saying their farewells, the imposing Misha bumbling through something resembling a "goodbye" before they parted. Without a moment's hesitation Evan and Charlotte linked arms and turned to skirt the square, once again full of protestors, heading to the hotel.

"What. Was. That." Evan gasped.

"I am so confused."

"So confused."

"She handled the entire thing like a game. Everything she said was perfectly constructed to be innocent yet probing. I feel ... used. And yet, when we first made eye contact, when she first recognized me, I could swear she was scared. I mean, her eyes were enormous! For a second she was petrified. And then took charge."

"She's up to something, that's for sure. What did you think of Misha?"

"He's a brute, just seems like a typical Russian guy to me. Why? What did you notice?"

"That guy is Russian military through and through. Not some pencil pusher with a uniform, not a Russian in Latvian service ... a combat soldier in the Russian Army. The way he held himself, the tattoos, the haircut, the scowl—it's all of a mold, a certain ... archetype they all go for. Like plaid and ballcaps and tactical pants and beards for Americans wanting to look like 'operators.'"

"Well, all the better that you didn't let them know you spoke Russian. Did he say anything interesting?"

"That's the thing, Char. Right after we cheers-ed, right at the beginning—"

"Yeah?"

"He said, 'be careful, Natalya. They could be anyone.'"

CHAPTER 20
Daugavpils, Latvia, January 10

The bleating of the hotel phone banished the last remnants of Charlotte's slumber, pushing away strident traces of the alluring dream that had followed their return to the hotel. She flung her arm out to the receiver, groggily answering with just enough brain working to form words.

"Room 804, this is reception. You have a visitor. May I send her up, or would you like me to hold her here?"

A visitor? Bits of Charlotte's brain were starting to come online.

"I ... um ... sorry ... who is it?"

"It is Ms. Natalya Lubachevsky. She has a delivery for you."

Charlotte closed her eyes, hard, willing herself to think.

"Yes, um ... I will be right down." *Shit.* Her eyes picked out the digital clock after hanging up: 8:30. And not even light out yet.

She jumped out of bed and threw on a pair of jeans, a simple flannel shirt, and the hotel slippers, pulling her hair back into a quick bun. She glanced in the mirror, horrified, and forced herself out the door. The same door she'd exited at one in the morning, half awake, desperate for Evan, yearning for him after a goodnight hug that had lingered a shade too long. She'd come to as her hand reached for his doorknob; the electric excitement of knowing he was on the other side of the door, hers for the having, was doused only by the shock at her juvenile behavior. *What am I, thirteen? If I'm going to do this, I'll do it on purpose.* She'd slinked back to her room, full of desire, slipping back into a slumber tormented by what could have been.

Charlotte made her way to the elevator, composing herself even as she wished she were able to indulge her groggy memories lying in bed. *What was Natalya doing here? What's her move?*

The elevator doors sprung open and Charlotte emerged into the lobby, immediately picking out Natalya's short frame thanks to an absurd black fur cap perched on her head. In her hands was a small package.

"Charlotte!" she exclaimed, moving quickly toward her. "I am so sorry to come by without warning. But last night I felt I had not properly welcomed you." They kissed three times in the Slavic manner. "Please, take this."

Charlotte took the package, seemingly a shoebox wrapped in brown recycled paper. She stumbled out a response. "My goodness ... um ... thank you. So sorry to make you wait ... just woke up ... what is this?"

"But of course, no worries at all. This is just part of good Russian hospitality. In the package you will find some of my family's *samogon*—I believe the word in English is moonshine—as well as some local foods. I could not have you visit my city without a proper welcome!"

Charlotte was honestly taken aback—suspicious as she was, she just *liked* Natalya, and this display of polite generosity spoke to her southern inclinations.

"Wow ... um ... thank you so much. You really didn't have

to."

"It's nothing. If we weren't completely tied up with this whole situation, I would take the day to show you around. There really are some wonderful out-of-the-way spots you must visit. I've included a list of a few in the box—if you hire a car, you can take a day or two to visit them. And you simply must spend a day at a Russian *banya*—I have given you the number of a man who can arrange one for you. This is the best time of year for a hot steam and plunge in a frozen lake! But Charlotte"—she still swallowed the 'r,' despite her fluency—"would you and Evan be able to join us for coffee tomorrow morning?"

"Um ... well ... yes, of course."

"Good. I will see you at ten at my office—the address is in the box. Good day, Charlotte—stay safe out there!"

With that Natalya abruptly turned and left, even as Charlotte voiced an "and to you."

Dazed, she turned back into the elevator. *What?!?!*

Returning to their floor, she proceeded to Evan's room, visions of the night before crossing her mind. He answered the door half-dressed, post-shower. She had been happy to see that a few years in the Army hadn't completely erased his slightly messy habits, even if it was clear he was packed to leave at a moment's notice. Now, the bed was sloppily made, coffee was brewing, and she admired his strong back as he bent over, clad only in jeans, to dry his hair.

"So, what did she want?" he asked without looking up.

"She ... brought us a gift package and invited us to coffee

tomorrow."

"So ... she checked to see if we were staying where we claimed?"

"That or ... maybe she is just being hospitable."

"Yeah, OK. Sure. What's in the package?"

Charlotte didn't appreciate his dismissiveness but didn't want to make anything of it. She pulled apart the paper wrapping.

"Let's see ... moonshine, some jam, a cured sausage, and a note with a bunch of recommendations on what to do, and her contact information."

Evan came over, hair tousled, his scent reaching Charlotte's nostrils and sending her back to the night she'd just spent painfully alone. She pulled herself back. "Oh, a *banya* recommendation. We need to do that. Do you know how relaxing it is to have someone beat you with birch boughs in 180 degree heat?"

"What?"

"It's what makes a Russian bath Russian. You get all heated up in the sauna, then your friend beats you with dried birch branches. It's very refreshing. Then you go plunge into an ice lake and repeat. A few hours later and you feel reborn."

"Sounds ... unique?"

He observed the page. "And a bit of a commitment ... notice a pattern?"

"Hmm?"

"All of her recommendations are outside of town."

"Of course they are," she retorted. "Daugavpils is clogged with protestors. Why would she recommend places you can't even get to thanks to the crowds, not to mention whether they're open or not?"

"That or she wants us away from the city, out of her hair." He turned and looked directly at her. She could feel the warmth from his bare chest. "Just being hospitable, eh?"

"I'm just saying …"

"Mmm." He turned and finished dressing.

An hour later the sun had finally splashed onto the streets, lighting up the ice and drawing all the more attention to the piles of detritus left from the night's protests. The city was shut down, so no one was cleaning up, and each day the streets got a bit dirtier, with random graffiti adding to the impression of neglect. *Broken windows mean a broken community*, Charlotte thought as they bundled up to head out for lunch.

It was noticeably colder, and they quickly made their way to a café for bowls of delicious hot stew. Charlotte pulled a pad of paper from her bag.

"Let's start with what we know." She needed to organize her thoughts if she wasn't going to feel like she'd lost all control.

"OK. One: Aleksandrs Bērziņš, a Latvian policeman, murdered two innocent Russians in Daugavpils on December 18."

Charlotte picked it up from there. "Two: with well-organized outside help, he immediately fled to the US by way of Germany, arriving in Ocracoke on the evening of December 28th."

"Where he was met by Thomas the smuggler and taken to Fayetteville early on the 29th."

"Where he was received by a member of the Latvian military working at Fort Bragg." Charlotte scribbled the note and put a definitive dot at its end. "Separate from all that, Natalya gets me spun up following Bērziņš on the 26th. By two days later we're hot on his trail, and by the 30th we've turned it over to the FBI. A week later, someone leaks it to the press."

"So that means that Natalya, who works for the Latvian police, was here from the 18th to the 25th, then flew to DC to meet you. You said she had a flight that same day, so she was back here on the 27th and found out about you going to the FBI … no later than the 8th. The day of the massacre. Then the very next day we scare the bejesus out of her when she is meeting with a sketchy Russian military dude who knows who we are and is worried about talking to us."

"The same day a Russian 'humanitarian' convoy crosses into Latvia to help the protestors, who've already been on the streets for almost three weeks."

Evan paused, looking at his phone. "Apparently several large groups of motorcyclists have been spotted crossing the border into Latvia from Belarus and Russia."

"And?"

"Biker gangs are one of Putin's favorite, easily-deniable surrogates. A perfect recon unit … it was a biker gang, the Night Wolves, that started the uprisings in Donetsk in April

2014."

"So … Russia is escalating. They're making a play for eastern Latvia."

"And it makes ours the million-dollar question. Is Natalya working with the Russian military?"

Charlotte tapped her fingers nervously, finding an outlet in beckoning the waiter over and paying their bill.

"I need to walk and think."

They re-bundled and walked through a thickening crowd toward the bazaar, the only place they'd be free to wander out of the cold.

"Well at the minimum we have to assume that we're being watched," Evan stated as they sized up a booth full of fake leather jackets. "If not constantly, then at least the hotel reception and others are keeping tabs on us. I know it's paranoid, but if something is going on here, we've got to be high on the list of who they're watching. But Natalya …"

"I think we are being overly suspicious of her," Charlotte stated definitively. "The only reason we're thinking this way at all is because we happened to see her with Misha out to dinner. Misha could be anyone — a retiree, a Spetsnaz officer who got smuggled in yesterday morning, a nobody … anyone. Of course Natalya hangs out with Russians. By going to Margaret, Natalya did something very, very risky to her own job and safety, and the reason she is scared of me is because I am the one person who could tie her to the leak. I look at it this way. If Natalya were some criminal mastermind with control over the Latvian police and connections to the Parliament and ties to the Russian … whatever Misha is, we'd have way bigger problems than having her drop by and leave us a gift box."

"But what about what Misha said in the restaurant, that we 'could be anyone?'"

"Normal Russian paranoia. He's absolutely right—we could be anyone. From what little I've seen, Russians aren't outgoing by nature, and I bet they assume that Americans' friendly disposition has an ulterior motive. It was a harmless comment."

"I'm not buying it," Evan disagreed. "Maybe it makes *me* the paranoid one. But if it's all innocent, then why check in on us, why give us an activity list that—oh, shit!"

He pulled Charlotte into a booth full of household electronics.

"Evan, what the—?"

"Shh. Not twenty meters behind you: Misha. He just walked by."

CHAPTER 21
Daugavpils, Latvia, January 10

The shopkeeper looked up, surprised, until Charlotte caught on and acted excited about an egg boiler (it wasn't hard; at thirty she was getting tired of boiling water just to make eggs each morning) while Evan stood out of the way, able to watch Misha through the corner of his eye.

"He's in the shoe booth across the hall and three down."

"Why exactly are we hiding, Evan?" she inquired while sizing up two different models.

"Maybe you're right. Our excitement is getting the better of us, and we're seeing something in Natalya that isn't there. But she's right on the line. And it's Misha that puts her there—so with everything we know, I assume he's dangerous."

"Is he following us?"

"I don't think so, he knows we know his face. If he wanted us followed, he'd send someone we didn't know."

"So ..."

"Wanna follow him?" He looked back at her with an insolent smirk. It was irresistible.

"One condition."

"Mm?"

"Buy me this egg boiler." He glanced at it, disbelieving.

"It's a European plug."

"It's dual voltage."

He spat a few words at the shopkeeper, handed him twenty euros, rolled his eyes, and turned his attention back to the bazaar.

"Here's how we'll do this. You'll be his tail. Always stay behind him, at least thirty to forty meters—enough that, if he decides to turn around, you can do something normal to keep him from seeing you. Don't do anything silly or outrageous. It would be better for him to recognize you acting innocent than get the idea you're following him. I'll post up well ahead of the direction he is walking, and when it is safe for you to keep going, I'll text you. If he ever makes a stop, at a store or something, just keep walking by and note where he is, and we'll swap roles. Got it?"

Was this part of his training? He was clearly engaged, clearly knew exactly what he was doing, and clearly had tapped into the same efficient-but-calm place that had led them away from the running crowd after the massacre.

"Uh, yeah … got it." Evan looked at her, nodded, mumbled "OK, watch your phone," and headed out of the shop.

Charlotte was left standing, bag with an egg boiler in one hand and cell phone in the other. The shopkeeper had returned to his Sudoku.

A few moments later her phone buzzed. "Go out turn right."

She walked out of the shop as normally as she could, self-conscious and convinced that everyone around her could see right through her. She snuggled down behind her scarf and bulky coat. What was it the receptionist had said after greeting her in Russian? "Pardon me, Ms. Sorenson! You blend right in." She could do this. She looked right, and sure enough there was Misha, about forty meters ahead, steps from the bazaar exit. Even through a crowd of a couple dozen shoppers, his bulk and upright, hip-forward gait stood out. He wore a ridiculous padded jacket and a cloth cap, making the mark all the easier.

Misha pushed through the exit doors, and seconds later her phone buzzed again. "Took a right out the exit."

A few seconds later she exited into the bitter cold, glancing in time to see Misha cutting across the tram tracks on the street to her right. She decided to act normal and just jaywalk straight away, turning right as she reached the other side, a good fifty meters behind Misha.

"Nice move," Evan's text read. Misha continued straight, passing an Orthodox shrine on the edge of a pedestrian-only street churning with people heading to the protests after lunch. *This is going to get tricky.* Misha cut through the crowd, entering a liquor store. She stopped short, huddling behind the glass cover of a tram stop and pulling up her phone to call Evan.

"I'm at the tram station, he just went in that liquor store. I can see the entrance from here and wait for him to exit. Where are you?"

"You're a natural. You'll see me in a second. I think he is going to come out going left from your point of view and continue down the pedestrian street away from the central square. I'll go further down that way."

"Got it." She saw Evan cross in front of the liquor store, pushing his way against the flow of the crowd. He must have been out across the street, kitty corner, able to watch the whole thing unfold. *He certainly knows what he is doing.* She was starting to enjoy this.

A gust of wind edged its way around the tram shelter, biting Charlotte's cheeks and making her urge Misha on with all her ability.

A tram started to clank toward her. *It would be awfully weird if it stopped and I didn't get on …*

Luckily Misha exited the liquor store, wrapped package in hand, just as the tram pulled up. Charlotte joined the flood of people disembarking as she noted Misha turning, sure enough, to her left, moving against the crowd away from the Central Square. *How had Evan guessed that?*

So far, all Misha was doing was routine errands, but that didn't diminish how much fun she was having. Charlotte paralleled the pedestrian street, keeping an eye on Misha, then cut into the throng behind him. She didn't like it, but she had to stay a mere fifteen steps behind him to not lose him in the masses. She wouldn't have long to react from here. Not to mention all the stores were closed — there was nowhere she could hide and look "normal."

Misha abruptly paused in the middle of the street, pulling out his phone. *Fuck.*

Charlotte cut toward the opposite side of the street — it was all she could do — and walked past him. *Fuck fuck fuck.* She kept striding, heart pounding through her chest, sure Misha had seen her. She took a right turn to get out of his sight as quickly as possible and pulled her phone up.

Even had texted: "Good. He didn't see you. I have him. He's using an ATM." Then: "Find somewhere good near that ugly theater we saw on the way in and watch for him." She looked up and glanced over in time to see Evan, barely recognizable under a bulky scarf he hadn't owned ten minutes before, smoking a cigarette and shooting the shit with a protestor on the far corner.

She pulled up Google, realizing it was only a block and a half to the theater, and headed off. As she approached, she noted a small café across the street; she stepped in, bought a Diet Coke, plopped her egg boiler onto the counter, and stood watching out the window pretending to read her phone. She had a perfect view of the theater, a squat, brown, temple-style building built in the neoclassical style she was starting to associate with the era of Stalin. Massive columns stood atop broad steps, with a placard hung from the pediment indicating the building had been converted into a nightclub. Appropriate to the moment, enormous Russian flag banners hung from the cornice, their bright colors lighting up the otherwise drab facade and obscuring Charlotte's view of the stylobate.

After a moment a new text popped up: "Moving toward you." Misha walked into her view, seemingly unconcerned with the world, his shoulders hunched into the wind and eyes on the ground in front of him. At a crosswalk he paused, looking around and behind him. *If this guy is up to something, he's certainly just going about his day.*

The light turned green and he continued, crossing in front of the theater. Charlotte saw Evan approach the intersection, crossing just as the light turned red. Glancing back, she saw

Misha head up the steps of the theater. She had a perfect view.

Unable to stop innocuously, Evan kept walking past the theater. *It's all me now.*

Misha reached the top of the stairs, pulling a piece of paper out of his pocket. He turned behind one of the large brown concrete columns, passing from her view. She knew he hadn't gone inside — she could see the doors — but the flag banners prevented her from seeing what he was doing. She called Evan and told him what was up.

"OK, this one is tricky. We need to know if he's doing anything up there, but then pick up the tail again once he leaves. As soon as he is out and turns, text me what way he goes, and I'll try to lead him. But then get up there and see if you can figure out what he did."

As Evan finished his last sentence, Misha came back into view, looking all around much more assertively than before. Charlotte hid herself in her phone, putting a window frame between them. Through the corner of her eye she saw him head back the way he came, catching the light and crossing back over the street. Charlotte stepped quickly out of the café.

She jaywalked and hurried to the steps, glancing to her right in time to see Misha's bulk take a left back on to the pedestrian street, blending in with the flow of protestors. She pulled up her phone.

"He went back the way he came."

"Yup, I've got him. Stay on the phone and let me know what you find."

She tucked the phone in her pocket as she reached the top of the stairs, glancing around the shady spaces among the columns. He'd turned to the left: right there in front of her was a bulletin board. Approaching, she glanced over the layers of postings, unable to read their Cyrillic announcements.

"Evan ... it's a bulletin board. He must have posted the paper I saw him pull out of his pocket."

"I'm on the way."

At first Charlotte was shocked that Evan was giving up the chase. When he came loping up the stairs, she had to ask, even in her excitement: "Evan, why let him go?"

"He came here to post something. All his other stops were just to confuse and confound a tail. But this is what he was trying to do."

"Is that how you knew where he was going?" They moved over to the bulletin board, assessing its messy contents.

"Not where, but how. At each stop he changed direction a bit so he could see someone following him. First southeast from the bazaar, then northeast from the liquor store. So it was logical he'd go southeast from the ATM." It made sense. She turned her attention to the board.

"OK, I've been looking at it, and only these three" — she pointed them out — "are recently posted, based on how unweathered they are."

"OK ..." Evan started deciphering. "This first one is an official announcement of a government hearing on a zoning change for a restaurant down the road. This one ... this one is an advertisement for farm-raised eggs with a farmer's contact number. And this one ... is an announcement for the 'Old

Believers' Literary Society.' Hmmm ... all three totally innocuous, and all three could have hidden messages."

"It's the third one." Charlotte was sure.

"Um ... why do you say that?"

"I did a short stint as a guest lecturer at a technical school in southern India. The campus was tucked in a rural backwater—I couldn't leave without a pass, and to all my male colleagues I was either a spy or a conquest. Besides a few brave female students, the only women there were cooks and maids who came in from the village each day. But I wasn't allowed to 'fraternize' with students. So I'd set up official group meeting times by posting on the bulletin board. Announcements about cooking classes, sewing circles— anything so stereotypically feminine no man would even pay attention. And then we'd just meet in plain sight.

"If there's a message hidden in the official announcement, there's no way we'll ever decipher it. And the egg ad has to be at least part real, because anyone could see the ad and look for eggs, which would bring a lot of extra attention. So even if we called the number, we'd get nowhere. But the third one—I don't know what the 'Old Believers' Literary Society' is, but you have to know what it is to care at all."

Evan looked her up and down, impressed. He turned to the posting and continued reading.

"Members: the annotated copies of *The Life of Alexander Nevsky* have arrived. They can be picked up in the basement of the Old Believers' Church of Resurrection, Birth of Mother of God and St. Nicholas."

"That's it?"

"That's it."

"What is an 'Old Believer?'"

"It's a sect of the Russian Orthodox church that rejects reforms of the seventeenth century. Think of them like Hasidic Jews or Mennonites."

"And Alexander Nevsky?"

"A medieval Russian folk hero who defended the realm against invaders from the West."

Charlotte's phone was up as quickly as her eyebrows. "The church is a half mile away." She looked up and met his eyes. They started down the stairs.

CHAPTER 22
Daugavpils, Latvia, January 10

The spires of Daugavpils's Church Hill loomed above them, taunting them on as they trudged up the icy slope. A half mile as the crow flies, perhaps, but thanks to a detour around the train tracks the walk was more like a mile, the last half of which was a long uphill slog into the biting wind. Their destination was clear enough: a cluster of four churches, one from each of Latgale's major Christian sects, huddled around the city's only high ground. A Germanic spire ascended from a red brick neo-Gothic Lutheran Cathedral, while two squat Baroque towers marked a Roman Catholic Church. Ornate, gold-sheathed onion domes rising from the Orthodox Cathedral reflected the last rays of the afternoon sun.

"The Old Believers' Prayer House is just beyond the onion domes," Charlotte encouraged Evan, and herself. "Just a bit further." Her eyes and nose were running from the cold wind, but she didn't dare pull her scarf up: she was breathing so hard she knew the moisture would just freeze. Nothing to do but hunch over and soldier on.

At long last they reached the crest, turning left around the Orthodox Cathedral and, thankfully, out of the wind.

"Two blocks more," Charlotte guided them. "What's the plan?" After Evan's wizardry following Misha, she was happy to let him lead this one as well.

"The Old Believers are a traditional sect. I don't think they allow just anyone to wander into their Church. You'll hate to hear this, but I'd say we need to wait outside and watch how someone gets in so we're not sitting at the door fumbling. Once we enter, we need to find the stairs before anyone can ask us why we're there. If they do, same as in Ocracoke: we're cold and lost. But then the game's up."

"Reasonable enough."

"Oh, and Charlotte?"

"Mm?"

"Head covering." He glanced over to see her reaction. She rolled her eyes and tilted her head in acknowledgement.

They rounded the corner, the single low golden onion dome indicating the church was at the end of the block. As the building came into sight, they could see it was a simple, square structure that melded the Latgalian style with the Byzantine traditions of Orthodoxy. Behind the main structure was a smaller annex. Evan guided them into an apartment entryway just close enough that they could see the entrance, and pulled out a pack of cigarettes.

"Ew," Charlotte commented.

"Only way not to look suspicious, hanging out in front of an apartment building after dark. Here." He handed her one. "I won't even light yours. Just pretend." He lit his.

"The way I see it," he continued between awkward puffs, "Misha posted the announcement thirty minutes ago. The very earliest someone would be reading it would be now — if there really is something shady going on, the whole point of using an anonymous posting board is to avoid a connection between the poster and the reader. So I'd say we have fifteen minutes before anyone else goes to pick up their copy of *The*

Life of Alexander Nevsky. If no one enters the church in the next five minutes, we'll have to just give it a try."

Charlotte nodded her agreement, stamping for warmth as the effort of the trudge quickly faded. The bare hand "smoking" didn't help.

Luckily, the front door of the church opened, and an older man and woman walked out. "Good enough?" Charlotte asked.

"Well at least we know that's the way folks go in. Let's do it." Evan stepped on his cigarette butt and walked off, adopting a humble gait. "Just follow my lead. Orthodox naves are standing room only—no pews—and this one may be segregated by gender so we will stay at the back until we can scope the whole place out."

They passed through a gate, walking up the short path to the large wooden door. It was closed with a simple metal hasp. "If I can't get it open, we turn and walk." He reached for the handle, pressing the hasp. The satisfying *clunk* of the latch matched the creaking of the hinges as the door opened. Evan glanced at Charlotte and stepped into the narthex.

It was the first time Charlotte had been inside an Orthodox church of any kind, and her first impression was just how gloomy it was. Even coming in from the growing darkness outside, it was dimly lit, with mysterious shadows obscuring the *sanctum sanctorum* and an interior space defined by how closed it felt. The entirety was permeated with a thick cloud of incense, almost visible even in the low light. An airy Gothic cathedral or light-filled megachurch it was not.

Evan immediately pulled her to the right, toward a bank of

small candles. He stood before them and slowly pulled out his wallet, deliberately depositing some coins and choosing candles to light at an almost absurdly glacial pace.

"Do you see anyone," he whispered.

"Not a soul."

"Me neither. Any basement doors?"

"No. Just the wooden stairs up to the gallery."

"Fuck. Er, darn." Charlotte smiled at his transgression.

"OK. The only place a door could be is behind the altar. But you have to stay on the women's aisle, on the left. Just walk up there holding this candle and don't engage anyone. If either of us finds the stairs, the other will just have to risk it and hop over." Charlotte was amused that Evan would feel bad about swearing in a church but was suggesting to just "hop over" the ornate altar.

They split ways, and as she crossed behind a column, Charlotte was aware of Evan watching her. Like *that*. *It must be my demure headscarf*, she thought, glancing at him in time to see someone emerge from a door behind the altar before him. She held her breath. Evan nodded his head, looking down, and they passed each other. *Phew*.

Drawing close to the altar, she saw a door on her side as well. She hesitated a moment, looking back to make sure the stranger had exited the building, and cracked it open. Evan's smiling face greeted her.

"It's an ambulatory," he whispered. There was a single door leading further back; Evan turned the knob soundlessly and peeked through. He nodded. "Stairwell down, with another door to the annex out back. No light. Let's go."

They quickly passed through the door, eyes fixed on the passage to the annex. Turning onto the stairs, they had to slow due to the dark; only the slightest light passed through the cracks of the doorways to show the way down. "Should I risk it?" asked Evan, pulling out his phone. Charlotte nodded.

The blueish tint of the phone's flashlight lit up stairs ending in a large, open, space; as they stepped down, they could see it was a plain, square, featureless storage room. A jumble of church accoutrement met their eyes: nice chairs and tables, presumably for special occasions; a rack jam-packed with assorted robes and vestments; a large stack of what, even to Charlotte's non-Russian-speaking eyes, were clearly Bibles; a pile of broken furniture and assorted wood scraps.

"Not a likely place to be handing out literature, I'd say," she observed, turning her phone's flashlight on as well.

"I'll say. I don't even know what we'd be looking for. There was nothing else on the paper. Maybe we got the wrong church."

"No. Look." Charlotte pointed to a far corner, where an improvised shelf cast a dark shadow over a stack of boxes, seemingly the only orderly part of the whole room. They picked their way through the mess.

Laid out on the floor were three wooden crates, each about a meter long with a rope handle on each end. "Ammo crates," Evan whispered. He quickly kneeled down, feeling for a hasp. The tops were held down only by gravity; he lifted the lid and shined his light on the contents.

Charlotte's stomach went into her throat. The crate was packed with ammunition.

Evan snapped into action and started taking pictures while describing what he saw: "five four five by thirty-nine, that's pistol ammo, three spam cans of 1080 rounds each ... ten kgs of plastic explosive ... det cord, blasting caps, initiators ... HF radio with antenna materials and hand mic ... smoke grenades ... Jesus."

"Evan." Charlotte spotted something in the corner she didn't want to recognize. She moved over to the large pile of jumbled cloth and started pulling at an edge. Sure enough, it was as she thought: Latvian Police uniforms.

"There are probably ten complete uniforms here: tops, bottoms, boots ... oh god."

Charlotte stared at the pair of blue trousers in her hands. Even under the dim cellphone light, her eyes could confirm the distinctive smell: dried bloodstains.

"It's ..."

The sound of a door opening and footsteps above them shocked them into action. Evan quickly closed up the box and Charlotte dropped the uniform, both rushing to the only place in the room that offered even the slightest concealment: the rack of clothing and drapery. They stepped behind a voluminous black priest's robe just as a flashlight shown at the bottom of the stairway. Their eyes locked, terrified. All it would take is an offhand glance for them to be discovered.

"Togda skazal, poprobuy, prosto propobuy! Y ugaday...ana eta sdelala, kakaya shluha! Klyanus ... zarubezhnye russkiye ... oni vse hotyat ... vkus rodiny!!!" The one gruff man's voice was

augmented by the vulgar laughter of a second as the two reached the basement floor. "*horosho ... gde knigi?*"

The second one answered. "*Tam, v uglu.*" The two walked to the corner, just feet from their faces. Charlotte couldn't have taken a breath if she'd wanted to.

The two grabbed one of the ammo crates, lifted it, and proceeded straight out of the basement.

"Now. We go *now*," Charlotte demanded.

"Yup" was Evan's terse reply. "We need to stay close to them. If they are coming back for the other crates, we'll need to come back and hide."

"They won't," Charlotte assured him, already moving up the stairs. "The crates were labelled one, two, and three, and they took number two. That announcement was for three different groups to come pick up their stuff. And I'm sure their pickup times are staggered."

"If I didn't know better, I'd say this wasn't your first rodeo." They split up in the ambulatory, exiting to their respective aisles and instinctively resuming their hunched walks. The nave was thankfully empty, and they soon rejoined in the narthex. Charlotte pulled the front door ajar and peeked through the crevice. "They just put the crate in the back of a sprinter van. They're getting in ... and ... moving."

She opened the door and they slinked out, getting away from the church as quickly as they could. Reaching the main street, they turned back down the hill, steeling themselves for the long, cold walk back to the hotel.

"Evan, you know what the worst part is?"

"Mm?"

"I left the egg boiler back at the café by the theater."

CHAPTER 23
Daugavpils, Latvia, January 10

"Phew." Charlotte exhaled, the middling warmth of the hotel lobby rushing through her lungs and causing her nose to tingle. She couldn't wait to get upstairs and get toasty. They had barely spoken a word the entire walk home, dedicating each painfully cold breath to making the fastest possible pace. Charlotte had told Evan about the bloodstained uniforms, and Evan had translated the soldiers' vulgar joke-telling, but if she was honest with herself, she had been thankful for a chance to think.

They stepped into the elevator, unwinding the scarves from their faces and removing their gloves. "Dinner?" Evan asked. Charlotte was famished. "Can we just get it in one of our rooms?" she asked, nodding.

"We have to assume the room is bugged, Char. Let's talk this over upstairs while it's still fresh, then we'll crash."

"I hate it when you're right. If that's the case, where have we been all afternoon?"

"Out in the protests?"

"Fine with me. Just poking around the central square, talking to folks. Got it."

The elevator opened on their floor, and they quickly entered their rooms, doffed their winter garb, and started for the restaurant, pens and paper in hand. At the threshold, Evan stopped short. "Char, I've just got to use the restroom real quick. I'll join you in a moment."

Well known to the wait staff by this point, Charlotte quickly had a window-side table and a hot tea in front of her. The warmth flowed down to her toes, and she knew she had no more than two hours before the bed would be her place of duty. She gazed out the window, amazed at the increase in protesting. A few intersections featured bonfires, and the din of mass movement reached her ears as a dull roar. Even compared with just two nights before, the protest had assumed a new character. It was noisy, messy, angry ... alive. As far as Charlotte could tell, there was still no large police presence, but she knew from her college days that all it took was a little spark for a protest like this to explode out of control, police or not.

Evan sat down in front of her, looking thankful for the hefeweizen she'd ordered him. "So, let's start with the facts," he started off. Charlotte turned over a fresh sheet in her notebook and started narrating as quietly as possible.

"A man we assess as Russian military left a surreptitious posting on a public board. It led to a stash of Russian weapons, radios, and explosives. There were also blood-stained Latvian police uniforms piled in the corner. While there, two men speaking Russian came in and recovered one of the three crates."

"Here's the military side of it." Evan jumped in. "First off let's assume each of the crates has the same contents as the one I opened. All of the ammunition is Russian pistol ammo — useless for outright combat, but just the thing for concealed weapons, submachine guns ... you get the drift. There were 3240 rounds in each crate. That's enough for something like ten people to have a concealed weapon for self-defense, and another five with submachine guns to be able to do a whole lot of mischief like drive-bys, assassinations, or whatever for about a week. Say a fifteen-person action element."

"So ... three fifteen-man teams? Total of fifty guys? That's probably the size of the Daugavpils police force. What's that going to accomplish?"

An excited flash ran through Evan's eyes. "Oh, the fun of guerilla warfare. Did you ever read *For Whom the Bell Tolls?* You know, Hemingway's novel about an American explosives expert in the Spanish Civil War?" Charlotte made an exaggerated eyebrow raise to communicate how patronizing he was being. "OK, then you remember. There were only five or six of them left to blow the bridge at the end. The strength of a guerilla band isn't in its numbers — it's in its ability to move undetected amongst the people. And with the right equipment, training, leadership, communication ... that fifteen-man element could tie up an entire Latvian battalion."

"Battalion?"

"A few hundred soldiers. It doesn't matter if you have a highly-trained unit ready to go ... if they get stuck behind a blown bridge, or lose comms with their headquarters, or all their fuel is tainted — you get the idea."

They both went silent as giant bowls of a clear vegetable soup appeared steaming before them, a dill aroma filling the air.

Charlotte continued. "And I can't imagine the Latvian military is that large."

"Oh no. Three small elements, their actions coordinated through a headquarters, equipped to sabotage, harass, disrupt ... I don't think it's unreasonable to estimate they could throw this entire area into chaos at just the right moment."

"But why distribute the equipment now? We're less than sixty miles from the Russian border, even closer to Belarus. Why not preposition the equipment earlier, so it's ready to go?"

Too excited to eat, Evan was gesticulating with his utensils as he thought aloud. "Risk. Think about Afghanistan. Who do you think has spent the past twenty years selling the Taliban and anyone else weapons? Russia, China, Iran … it's not just a question of dollars; it's good geopolitical logic to bleed us. But what don't they do? Sell anything that isn't deniable … surface-to-air missiles, advanced warheads, fancy stuff. Because those things carry a signature that could escalate into a political crisis. And it's just not worth it to them. Same thing here. If someone took a video of a few Russian nationalists playing around with plastic explosives in the woods, it would cause an enormous outrage. So … get them organized. Send a Spetsnaz guy out for a while to get them trained. Set up the capabilities you need to make sure everything works when you need it. And now, at a moment when the entire ethnic Russian populace is out on the streets, starting to boil—"

"—at a moment when you've stoked the fire and salted the water and done everything you could to get it to boil…"

"Go on …"

Charlotte had pieced it together on the long walk back. "Evan, the Russians want eastern Latvia. It's majority Russian and right on their border. It would be a propaganda coup back home. They've invaded it twice in the last century. So clearly there's a well-laid plan. And it's just like you said about Crimea. In a world with Instagram, they're not going to do it with tanks. It's going to look like an irrepressible, grass-roots movement."

Evan's eyes went wide over a mouth full of soup. "The protests ..."

"So you lay the groundwork and wait for the spark. Bērziņš was that spark. The temperature rises. You test the waters, to see if conditions are right. You release propaganda. You get everything set. And if it feels right, you escalate ..."

"You mean that—"

"Those bloodstained uniforms can mean only one thing, Evan." She glanced around and reduced her voice to an intense whisper. "Latvian policemen didn't carry out those murders."

Evan chewed slowly. She continued.

"Maybe it was guerillas, maybe it was a special unit—it doesn't matter. It was a setup. The cameraperson was a setup. They staged the event to generate the perfect video to go viral and turn up the heat."

"And then ..."

"It gave them an excuse to send the convoy, which brought in agitators, organizers ... and supplies."

"And the next day, the 'civilian' biker gangs showed up, ostensibly to show support for the protestors ..."

"But really to serve as a reconnaissance element for whoever is coordinating the guerilla bands."

They stopped, silent, staring at their bowls.

"So Natalya," Evan declared, emotionlessly.

"A patsy" was Charlotte's verdict. "Well, no. Not a patsy. A willing ally unaware of the big picture. A patriot, an ethnic Russian with conflicted loyalties, someone who had access to some important information and wanted to do her part for her cause without giving up her station. But more importantly, in doing so she led us to Misha."

"Who can be nothing other than GRU, or one of the other Russian alphabet agencies, responsible for knitting together all the elements: meeting the mole inside the police department, distributing supplies to the guerilla bands, coordinating the biker gang's patrols—"

"—which makes him the number-two man, the fixer," Charlotte concluded. "But if he is number two, then who is number one?"

CHAPTER 24
Daugavpils, Latvia, January 11

Natalya's office was in a run-down office building across the street from the Daugavpils Police Headquarters, itself a gorgeously restored neo-baroque structure hideously protected against potential rioters. Its windows boarded up and front door barricaded, the building sent the exact same message as the Latvian government as a whole: this thing was beautiful before all these unnecessary protests kicked off, so circle the wagons, ride it out, neither acknowledge nor engage, and minimize how much we have to deal with it.

Inside, Natalya's building looked like any other Spartan government annex — it seemed to be government, at least, with offices scattered throughout handling overflow from all manner of different organs of municipal power. It certainly was Spartan, although even after several days in eastern Latvia, most buildings still seemed that way to Charlotte.

They went up a flight of stairs, seeking the office number on the sheet Charlotte held. Arriving, they knocked and were welcomed by an effusive Natalya.

"Charlotte! Evan! So wonderful to see you! Please, come in." She kissed them both three times and led them through a waiting room of sorts with a couple of chairs, a low coffee table, and some Daugavpils tourism posters in Latvian. "Please, come into my office. Oh!" She turned. "I nearly forgot. As this is a government facility, we allow no personal electronic devices. Would you mind leaving them in the little boxes here?" She gestured to a purpose-built shelf. "Completely routine; I'm sure you are used to it in your line of work."

It was nearly automatic for Charlotte to place her phone in the top cubby; indeed, it was a normal practice entering any sensitive meeting. But glancing at Evan, she saw him hesitate, giving her a subtle yet clarion glance of distress that took her back to their conversation the night before.

"So, who do we need to tell?" she'd asked Evan, enjoying every bit of her *syrniki*, small dessert pancakes lathered in cream and raspberry jam. Evan took a deep breath in, contemplating.

"No one." Charlotte's eyebrows went up. "Not yet."

"Explain," she countered.

"If we try to report this now, what do we do? Walk into the embassy in Rīga? With a cell phone photo of some pistol ammo and a wild tale of chasing GRU operatives around a city writhing in protests? Then they'll check you out, call around … and the first thing they'll find is that you're the same person who reported Bērziņš to the FBI. Without hard evidence, you and I are just excited kids looking for an adventure. Our story won't change a whit of what anyone already knows about what's going on here, and we'll spend the rest of our vacation sitting in an interrogation room at the embassy."

"But Evan … we *do* have direct evidence. We know numbers, plans, personalities—all important info for whoever at the embassy is in charge of watching this."

"Two tourists, credibility and reliability unknown, walk in with a fantastic tale. They're as likely to write us off as whackos—or as a Russian red herring—as they are to listen to us."

"But how can we not do something? It's … our duty as Americans!"

"If we want to be of use, the best thing we can do is stay safe, stay clean, and stay here—if something really big goes down, we may be the only Americans around to see it."

Charlotte contemplated the last half of her last *syrniki*. "I don't like it. For the record, I think we should go to the authorities. But we have coffee with Natalya tomorrow—no matter how loosely she's tied to this, if we blow that off, then we'll really be targets."

"And from here out, we'll be extra careful. We need to destroy any paper notes or record that we're snooping, and at the first sign of danger we'll split."

In the office, Evan fingered his phone, the tension in his eyes speaking volumes. He placed his phone next to Charlotte's and followed Natalya into her office.

Inside, there was an imposing wooden desk with a laptop half-covered in scattered paperwork. A small Latvian flag stood on one corner and the concentric rings of years of careless coffee drinking stood out through the mess. Natalya beckoned them to sit in two overstuffed chairs facing the desk, and as she rounded it to take her seat, she introduced them to a small, fat man sitting in a cheap sofa against the far wall. "My assistant and paralegal, Yuri." He shook their hands. "May I offer you some coffee?"

They both accepted, and Natalya turned to a trolley behind her desk and started fixing their drinks. An assistant Yuri may have been, but Slavic patriarchal traditions clearly didn't bend quite that far.

"So, how has your visit been? Have you seen any good sights?"

"Oh yes," Charlotte started off. "Yesterday we spent all afternoon out. We headed up to Church Hill — what a remarkable spot!"

"And the view from the spire of the Lutheran church is just unmatched." Evan picked it up, improvising.

"I'm so glad," Natalya replied.

Charlotte continued. "We passed through the protests a bit, and while it's tremendously exciting ... I think the energy is starting to get a bit out of hand. Have you noticed anything?"

Natalya answered with her back turned, fixing their coffees. "Well, to be honest, the Police are keeping quite a hands-off posture, as I'm sure you've noticed. I think they are right that any presence at all, at this point, would only pour gasoline on the fire. That said ... I have felt the same energy. There are many, many more people out, and I would guess that most of them aren't even from Daugavpils anymore. I would not be surprised if the good behavior that has characterized this disturbance so far begins to wear away as fewer and fewer people have a vested interest in not destroying the city. Only time will tell." She placed small, strong black coffees on the desk in front of them.

"Has there been any progress into finding Bērziņš?" Charlotte asked.

"This is perhaps a question better directed at your own police, Charlotte." Natalya smiled.

"In any case, we are all praying for a safe and quick resolution," Evan diverted, sipping at his coffee.

The phone rang, and Natalya looked to Yuri to answer it. "*Yuri Bogdanovich, slushayoo.*" He listened for a moment and handed the receiver to Natalya, who pardoned herself. She listened then answered: "*esli Sasha gotov, me vstretimsya sevodnia vecherom.*" It was gobbledygook to Charlotte, but at least she could pick out the name "Sasha." Natalya hung up. "Please excuse me, terribly rude. Where were we?"

The conversation continued, turning around inanities and irrelevancies of life in general and the sights of Daugavpils in particular. On the latter topic Yuri weighed in—apparently he was a member of a Russian historical organization, with a passion for preservation work.

"My absolute favorite spot is the St. Alexander Nevsky Orthodox Church, just out of town over by the Heroes' Cemetery. It is built in the old, wooden, northern 'Archangelsk' style—very evocative."

"Isn't it a bit … odd that everything around here is named after Nevsky? Isn't that a bit … inflammatory?" Charlotte asked.

"Inflammatory? Not in the least!" Yuri answered. "St. Alexander is one of Russia's greatest folk heroes, like you Americans' George Washington. And here we are, just a few kilometers from the battlegrounds where he rose to prominence. What better figure to celebrate Russia's pride?"

Charlotte weighed her options. "But … we aren't in Russia."

Yuri puffed up. "Not ye—"

"It is a delicate question, as you so astutely observed, Charlotte," Natalya interjected. "I can't speak for whether Latvians care one way or another about our folk hero, but I do know that the stories of Nevsky fighting off the Germans are told to every Russian child. He is an indelible part of our heritage, and I suppose we may sometimes forget what he might mean to others." Yuri looked on, incensed. He may not make coffee, but Natalya was certainly his boss.

The phone interrupted the awkward silence, Natalya picking it up this time with a simple "*Allo*" followed by a simpler "*da*." She hung up and continued addressing Charlotte and Evan. "Unfortunately it seems I must be going. Thank you so much for coming to see us. If there is anything you need, anything at all, please do not hesitate to reach out."

She stood up, shook their hands, and led them to the door, where they collected their phones. Charlotte could see a bleating notification telling her she had a new email from her parents. "Farewell," she said, closing the door behind them.

They stood in the dingy hallway. "Well, that was abrupt," Evan observed.

"Figure that call was for real?" They started down the stairs and back out onto the street. It had started to snow, a low cloud ceiling casting a darker tint to the limited midday light. Charlotte checked her phone, ignoring her parents' message, too caught up in the here and now to worry about the back home.

Evan put a finger to his mouth, walking another block or two toward the hotel. He stopped, pulled out his phone, placed it on the hood of a car parked next to them, and gestured for her to do the same. He grabbed her hand and walked her a few meters away, whispering.

"Who knows. At this point ... Natalya may just be a pawn, but she's definitely being played. Played to play us. And our phones — we now have to assume that all the data on those phones has been compromised, that they are recording everything we say, that they're tracking our location."

"Oh, come on, don't be paranoid!"

"I did it to every Afghan I met. Why wouldn't they do the same to the only Americans here? It may be that the sole purpose of that meeting was to get into our phones." Charlotte looked at him, astounded. They went back, grabbed their phones, and kept walking.

They were approaching their hotel through the city park, trying to have a normal conversation about where to have lunch while passing by the somber stones of the Memorial to Soviet Soldiers and assuming every word was monitored. Charlotte remembered something she'd wanted to ask, and took her phone out, again placing it on the ground. Evan followed suit and met her a few meters away.

"They still don't know you speak Russian, and I don't want to ruin the surprise," she explained. "What was it she was saying about some chick named 'Sasha' in the first conversation? Anything interesting?"

"Oh, nothing much at all. Something like 'now that Sasha is ready, we will meet tonight.' But Sasha isn't necessarily a woman. Usually it's a man's name."

"Huh?"

"Sasha. In Russian it's short for Alexander, or Alexandra. I know it makes no sense, but it's like… Dick and Richard."

Charlotte stood, stunned. She took in the granite obelisks of the Memorial, the snow falling thickly on Evan's shoulders, a pack of protestors making their way across the park to the Central Square. It was all so straightforward.

"Bērziņš is a Russian spy."

"What?!"

"Sasha. Aleksandrs Bērziņš is Sasha."

CHAPTER 25
Daugavpils, Latvia, January 11

Evan was flabbergasted, thinking. "Aleksandrs Bērziņš ... Sasha."

Charlotte continued. "Natalya isn't a pawn, a patsy, a willing participant ... she's—"

"She's Bērziņš's handler."

"She set the whole thing up. The incident that started it all—a setup. Chasing Sasha across Europe and the US—"

"—a red herring. Its sole purpose to infiltrate Latvian groups in the US and turn Americans against them. Holy shit. Charlotte... you're a genius."

"Evan ... Natalya *wanted* me to go to the FBI. That was the only way the Bērziņš story would get any attention in the US. She's probably the one who leaked it to the press. When we showed up here, Natalya wasn't scared because we threatened her position. She was scared because we were the only people on earth who could find both halves of the puzzle. Which means—"

"Which means we need to get the fuck out of here, now." She nodded, and they raced back to their phones.

"Can we just ditch them?" Charlotte asked, holding back.

"No. They know where we are. If we ditch them, they'll know we're onto something. We'll ditch them the second we're moving."

They moved back, grabbed the phones, and started off toward the hotel.

Charlotte's senses were completely attuned as they entered the building. Was that just a taxi out front, or was it someone watching them? Had there always been three receptionists? She thought she remembered only the two. Where were the security cameras? They hurried into the elevator.

"Get in, pack, get out," Charlotte said. Evan nodded.

Even as they hurried down the corridor, Charlotte knew something was wrong. Sure enough, their doors were ajar. Evan put his hand up, stopping short. Gesturing for Charlotte to stay put, he crouched down facing his doorjamb, and soundlessly nudged the door open. Charlotte watched him inch his way across the floor, gaining a better and better picture of what was inside with each movement. He stood up and beckoned her to wait, entering the door.

A moment later he returned, holding his hand out for her phone. He walked down the hall and placed them on a table. "No one's inside. It's been ransacked."

Charlotte's stomach dropped. She walked up to the threshold and looked in.

The room was a complete mess. Every part had been torn up: the bed was ripped apart, the upholstery destroyed, furniture upended. Evan's belongings were strewn everywhere. She was dreading to see what they'd done to hers. She pulled him back into the hall.

"We need to report this," Charlotte whispered.

"No. We need to find out what they took."

"But ... if we don't report it, we'll have to pay for all the damages."

"Would you rather have to pay a few hundred dollars, or have our room turn into a crime scene?"

She knew he was right. "Well, now we know what the meeting was for. I assume they've added full video and audio in the room, too. Time to act like a shocked tourist." Evan nodded, then returned for their phones. Charlotte inched toward her door, unsurprised at the exact same outcome.

Evan showed up a few minutes later and made a few loud, obvious comments about how they must have left the doors unlocked, how they'd have to call reception and report it just as soon as they made sure their passports weren't stolen. Charlotte made herself cry, started a pile on the bed of anything ruined, and began separating all of her possessions in a corner.

Evan found Charlotte's passport laid out neatly on the bathroom counter, as if to say "the last thing we'd want is for you to have any delay in leaving."

When they were done, Evan had brought his completely repacked bag to Charlotte's room, and Charlotte had neatly arranged her belongings on the floor. She looked up at him, fear in her eyes, and then did one last sweep of the room.

"What did they take?" Evan asked.

"Well ... all of my backup cash — three hundred euros — and my nice DSLR camera. And my laptop."

"Mine too. Two hundred and my GPS. Let's go report it to reception." He winked, and they turned to leave the room, leaving their phones. Evan led them right, away from the elevator.

"Evan, I had everything on that laptop. All the Bērziņš stuff from before, but also ... I retyped and saved all my notes from while we were here."

"Me too."

"The hard drive is encrypted, but even so, we have to assume that they'll know everything within a few hours."

"If they don't already. It's time to leave." He turned the handle on a door marked "Privāts" and pulled her into a maintenance closet.

"Charlotte ... it's time for a little honesty on my part." From beneath a shelf, he pulled a small bag, unzipping an outer pouch and pulling out a rubber sleeve. "First things first: here is a few hundred euros to replenish your emergency fund. Now ..." He pocketed a few bills, closed the pouch, and slung the bag over his shoulder.

"What the ...?" Charlotte was perplexed.

"I need to get to the roof." He left the closet, heading to the end of the hall and entering the stairway. "Evan, what are you doing?" Charlotte asked, trailing him.

One floor up, he mounted the ladder. Charlotte could see the emergency hatch had been propped slightly open by a tiny shim; Evan pushed it up and climbed out. Charlotte followed. The snowfall had intensified; the wind was still gentle, but visibility was down to just a few dozen meters, and their movements were dulled as if by a soft blanket.

"Evan, you owe me an explanation." Evan sat down and started rooting around in the bag.

"No, Charlotte, I owe you an apology." He pulled out a ruggedized cell phone and a small beer can–sized pouch. "I lied to you. I had to. I'm technically still in the Army, scruffy hair notwithstanding. After my first stint as an intelligence officer down at Fort Bragg, I was selected for a more ... specialized program a few years back." Charlotte reeled at the magnitude of the lie. Evan had booted up the cell phone and opened the pouch, pulling out a spider-like contraption that he was unfolding into what had to be an antenna. "I finished my training last spring. Attending Georgetown is my cover for the work I do now." He stopped, looking at her. Charlotte was speechless.

"Everything between us has been honest, Char. But cover is cover: nothing more, nothing less. I want to be back in your life. I'm sorry." He plugged the phone into the antenna. Charlotte felt a perfect rage of betrayal rising up. To think that the past two weeks, this whole time, he'd been looking at the problem as an agent — a *something*? — was a direct insult to her dignity.

"I had to report what happened in Fayetteville to my unit. So when you asked me to come to Latvia with you—"

She glared and finished his sentence: "You saw the opportunity to use me to do whatever shady shit you're up to. Oh, I get it, Evan." She couldn't begin to reevaluate every interaction they'd had in light of his new role. Those quiet conversations she'd walked in on; the skills he'd brought to bear. Caitlin's all-too-insightful observations came back to her. Evan typed something into the phone, then turned back to her.

"I've been reporting back everything we've found over an encrypted app on my phone." Charlotte's eyebrows went up. "Don't worry, it's safe. There's no way they could have accessed it in the time we were in there." He continued. "Two days ago they told me to stay put and keep observing until I felt unsafe. I was lying to you yesterday—everything we found is extremely important. But it's already in the right hands. It was best for you not to know. But now everything's changed. I'm sending up my abort signal. We'll pack and leave. It's not safe for us anymore."

The phone lit back up with a sent message confirmation, and Evan started packing up.

"You're kidding me." Charlotte fumed.

"Char ... I'm sorry. I ..."

"Here we are traipsing around a warzone. You're a ... a fucking *spy* and you wouldn't tell me? And you have the nerve to tell me you're ... you're ... being honest?!"

"I do. I would have told you about the program ... in time. But then all this happened."

"And it was too fucking exciting to tell the truth. Dammit, is that all I mean to you? That being honest with me isn't as important as getting to come along for the ride?" She stood and opened the hatch, starting down the ladder.

"Charlotte, you don't have a clearance. I couldn't tell you," he pleaded after her as she descended.

"*Fuck* you, Evan." She glared at him and turned down the stairs.

She heard him descending behind her. She pivoted. "Yeah, we need to get the fuck out of here. And we're stuck together 'til we're back in DC. But first I need to get the hell away from you." She shook her head at the wall. "I'm going for a walk. Get everything ready and I'll meet you at reception at one thirty. One hour." She left.

CHAPTER 26
Daugavpils, Latvia, January 11

The streets had cleared of protestors thanks to the strengthening snowfall, which had already accumulated a good three inches since they'd gotten back from Natalya's. Tense it may have been, but no one wanted to get caught out in what her phone—stupid traitorous phone—was saying would soon be another nine to sixteen inches, if she was doing her metric conversions right. So she cut right across the plaza to Artilērijas, realizing as she stepped inside that she hadn't eaten lunch.

She sat at the bar and ordered immediately. "Soup and a beer, please." The bartender, remembering her, poured a large dark brew. She downed half in the first gulp.

Stupid Evan. Stupid, stupid, stupid Evan. It was all too easy to see it from his perspective—it's not like she hadn't lied to him about Bērziņš at the very beginning, and even if it hurt, his comment about the clearance was right. Of *course* he shouldn't have told her. But that didn't change how much danger he'd put her in, how used she felt. How much it hurt to feel betrayed, again.

The snow piled on outside; she could barely see across the tram tracks. A man hustled past the window, hunched from the weather, and Charlotte's thoughts turned to Bērziņš making his way through a North Carolina storm to land in Ocracoke. *There is a Russian spy loose in the United States.*

It raised an interesting question. Was Aleksandrs Bērziņš a Russian mole all along, someone Natalya had recruited inside the Latvian Police and slowly cultivated for this one act? Or had Bērziņš been a real person, someone as expendable as the family they'd killed in staging the murders that started it all, who was then replaced with a loyal agent who followed the smuggling route through Europe to the US?

In either case, it was an inconceivably bold and masterful plan: Spark protests in Latvia. Spin the protests into something of a wedge issue in Europe and the US by pushing out the right propaganda. Wreck Latvian support elements in the US by infiltrating them from the inside. And turn US opinion against Latvia just as you escalate pressure and invade. It was genius.

Her soup came and she finished her beer, burping with not a care in the world and slurping it down. The worst part was just how much she'd been a pawn in all of it. First, Margaret: pulling the wool over her idealistic eyes so she'd stay on Bērziņš's trail. Then, Natalya: knowing all along just what Charlotte would find, wanting her to find it, using her to publicize it. And now Evan: using her to do—whatever it was he was doing. Charlotte paid her bill, glanced at her watch, and decided to take a walk. If they were heading back, she may as well get one last good look at the city.

Her thoughts returned to Evan as she passed a small Orthodox shrine. Wasn't she using him, too? She'd used him to escape the pain of facing her family, to distract from feeling stuck, to feel connected and excited while shutting down his advances. Even in Ocracoke, she'd felt more confident with him along. He was a good teammate. And there was no one else on earth she could have gone through the past two weeks with. He may have lied to her, but at least she understood why. It didn't reduce the hurt, and it would take a lot of work to heal. But if she was honest with herself, it was still worth it.

She approached a zebra intersection, and looming through the thick snow was the ugly Soviet theater where Misha had posted his notice. *What the hell, let's just see.*

She ascended the stairs, treacherous with ice, and reached the bulletin board. Misha's first posting was weathered, hanging from a single staple. There was a new flyer with a picture of a Peugeot. And below it ...

Charlotte's eyes went wide. A fresh sheet of paper had the exact same logo as Misha's first posting, and upon closer inspection, the title text matched. It was another announcement for the Old Believers' Literary Society.

But how to decipher it? Charlotte couldn't read Cyrillic, let alone understand Russian. Her phone was still stashed back at the hotel—and was monitored, in any case. She didn't dare take the entire posting with her. And a quick fumble in her purse told her she didn't have a pencil.

Screw it. She looked behind her, suddenly aware that, were the wrong person to see her here, she'd be in big trouble. She grabbed the posting and walked to the other side of the dais, finding an ensconced spot hidden by columns and the Russian flag banner.

She stripped, first her hat and scarf and gloves, then her heavy wool jacket, then her sweater, and finally her white undershirt. The cold wind biting at her exposed torso, she shoved the undershirt into her purse to keep it dry and redressed as quickly as she could.

Decent again, she pulled the undershirt and her lipstick out of her purse, pinning the shirt against a column. She held up the announcement next to it. *Here goes.*

The lipstick left broad smudges on the shirt that made it difficult to copy the precise details of letters whose form and function were a mystery to her; she painstakingly concentrated on each flourish and serif, unsure what was important. *Like a medieval monk*, she thought, *hunched over a desk in some monastery, copying the Bible by sight.*

She stepped back, finished. Her scrawls covered the shirt, which looked like the leftovers of either a really good or really bad night on the town. Carefully folding the shirt and placing it in her purse, she returned to the board, reposted the message, wobbled down the icy stairs, and hurried back to the hotel as quickly as she could.

She burst into her hotel room at 1:15. A shape surged out of the corner of her eye; she raised her hand in defense, but nothing happened. She opened her eyes to look and saw Evan with a piece of broken furniture drawing down. Surveying the room, she saw the bags neatly packed, Evan dressed. Clearly he'd been poised, assuming that anyone coming through the door was there to get him.

"Phew," Charlotte breathed out. "Sorry about that, didn't think that one through."

"I hope I didn't scare you," Evan replied, in monotone.

"Evan, no. Look. I'm really, really hurt, and feel betrayed, and there is a lot of healing and honesty we should have done before coming here. But right now …" She paused, pulling the shirt out of her purse. Evan looked on, puzzled. "I went back to the posting board. There was" — Evan stopped her and gestured to the hallway. She continued outside the threshold — "a new announcement. This was the only way to copy it." She held up the shirt. Evan looked at her, impressed.

"The monthly meeting will be held at the Levitskaya Bath House at six o'clock tonight. Non-members prohibited."

Charlotte looked at him. "Evan, we have to be there."

Evan looked down. He was clearly conflicted. "We have to get out of here before they try to hurt us. This is madness. Do we have any clue where this place is? Or what we'd do when we got there?"

"We need to find a computer that isn't monitored."

"The business center, downstairs." Evan popped back in the room, returning with another waterproof pouch. "A map, from the kit," he responded to Charlotte's quizzical gaze. "If we're going to do this … we can't take phones, they stole my GPS, my emergency phone doesn't have location services — we'd have to do it the old way."

They hurried downstairs, signing out the key to the business center and logging on to a beat-up old computer in an out-of-the-way room. Charlotte pulled up Maps, searching "Levitskaya Banya."

"Nothing," she said, dejected.

"Wait." Evan thought for a second. "Go to Translate. Put Levitskaya baths in and get it in Cyrillic and try again." Charlotte quickly Ctrl-V'd through the process, and the location popped up. It was a single, small structure huddled against a small pond in the woods north of the city.

"OK, so it's a tiny little bathhouse, probably just the sauna building itself," Evan observed. "It may be guarded, but if not, it would be too easy to get next to the wall and listen in. Let's do it."

Charlotte grabbed Evan's hand and gave it a hard squeeze. "Yes. Evan, I need this. I need to … own this thing. To fix this problem." Evan smiled, approvingly, as she continued. "We'll go listen in, then continue straight on to Rīga. We'll have to drive and park somewhere."

"We can't do that. If we leave here driving, they'll tail us, and then we're finished. We have to leave the car here."

"Along with the phones, and our stuff, and sneak out. They've got to think we were here the whole time. So how do we get there?"

"How far is it?" Evan asked.

"Let's see … seven miles, straight line." They both paused with their thoughts.

Evan stated the obvious. "Seven miles, through a forest in a blizzard, to a single building in the middle of nowhere …"

"Can you do it?" Charlotte pictured Evan's confident stride through the Shenandoah foothills, requiring neither a map nor a compass to arrive at the waterfall spot-on.

"Huh?"

"If we walk, can you get us there?"

A smile crossed over Evan's face. The glint in his eye told Charlotte that the allure of the challenge had just catalyzed his enthusiasm for the mischief.

Evan spread his map out over the table next to the computer. "No GPS, my crappy survival compass, and a 1:50,000 map from the Cold War? No problem. Now, where is this place?"

He carefully correlated the location from the screen onto his map, glancing up only once to confirm the spot before staring intently.

"It will be about eight miles of walking to get there. We could easily do that in two hours if it were easy terrain, but it's through snow and a blizzard and I'll need to be stopping to navigate. Say ... four hours."

They both looked at the computer clock: 1:40. Four hours and twenty minutes until the meeting.

"Let's go. We have two and a half miles to walk through the city, then we can stop for a break and I can plan the rest of the route." Evan stood up and collected everything, then paused. "Charlotte, are you sure—"

"Screw you Evan. Yes, I'm sure I'm up for it. Four hours out, four hours back. Let's go."

CHAPTER 27
Outskirts of Daugavpils, Latvia, January 11

SEE MAP "DAUGAVPILS AND ENVIRONS"

Charlotte surveyed the meager offerings of the suburban gas station and hesitantly pointed at a folded confection she hoped was filled with cheese and spinach. She paid for it, some drinks, and Evan's sweaty pierogi while he hunched furtively over the map at a table in the corner.

They'd made excellent time, taking just minutes to put on every piece of winter gear they had and pack up a day bag before returning to the roof and picking their way down the fire escape. On the way out, Charlotte had the inspiration to order room service, to be delivered inside the room, as a decoy. The snow fell heavily, but thankfully the air was still; they could hardly see across the street as they reached the ground and got away from the hotel as quickly as possible. From there they'd headed north, passing the ominous forms of long rows of Soviet apartment blocks looming out of the mist like sentinels picketing their escape. As the developments turned to detached homes and the road became more and more pockmarked, they reached a gas station at the edge of a large tract of homes.

"We're getting close to the woods—this may be our last chance to stock up. Let's grab a bite to eat at this place and I'll check the map."

She returned to the table, snacks in hand, having also purchased bottles of water and candy bars for the coming trek. Evan gestured her toward the map, using a plastic fork to point.

"So. We're somewhere around here — it looks like we're in the woods because all of these buildings are newer than the map. The bathhouse is here, on the north side of an unmarked pond. It's a four- or five-mile trip, off-road through snow. So we don't have time for mistakes. That means I can only rely on the largest features to pick the route — if we follow the wrong dirt road, for example, we won't have a clue when we started to go wrong."

Evan was thinking aloud; Charlotte let him work it through.

"So, I'll start from the end and work my way back. We don't want to approach the pond from the north, cause that's where the main road is — too risky. But we also don't want to approach from the south — the pond is so close to the large open area around the stream, they may be able to see us walking there. So we have to approach the pond from either the east or west.

"For all we know this area may be entirely built up. But if it's still just a forest, then the only reference point I can find at all is this building — see the little black dot? — south of the stream and a few hundred meters east of the pond. From there, we can cross the stream out of view, then head west along the woodline until we hit the pond.

"Getting to that building is the crux of the entire trip. It's 1500 meters — almost a mile and a half — from the nearest landmark to the south, this small pond. Which is itself 1200 meters from this larger pond, which is 800 meters from the intersection of the high-power lines and this paved east-west road. For each of those legs, we've got to stay on azimuth — on the right compass heading—almost perfectly, or else we'll miss the landmark and wander off. If we're off by just five degrees over 1500 meters, we'll miss the building by ... 130 meters. Visibility is 50 meters, tops. We have to be perfect."

He paused, tilting his head and examining the map. Charlotte noticed the attendant was watching them. There was no helping it; if they were successful, it didn't matter who saw them. If they failed ...

Evan stood and replaced the map in his bag. "Ready?"

"Let's go."

They bundled back out into the snow. Charlotte's boots were ankle-high and waterproof, so her feet were still nice and toasty. But in a couple of hours the snow would be deeper than her ankles—and they still had at least twelve miles of walking.

Evan glanced at his compass and took off. Moments later they reached the end of a cul-de-sac and passed into the woods. At first Charlotte was incredulous; branches clawed at her from all sides, and brambles caught her every step. There was no way they could make time in this mess! But after a few meters, it cleared out, and she realized that the underbrush grew only along the edge of woods. Inside, it was a sparse pine forest whose tall, thin, red trunks shown out brilliantly from the bright green boughs and drifting snow. It was gorgeous. Charlotte shook herself back to reality, with Evan already taking off.

"I thought you said slow and steady?" she asked, doing her best to step only where he'd already broken the snow.

"For those three middle legs. This first leg we've got about two, two and a half miles with a nice backstop. We just head north-northeast until we hit a high-power line running northwest to southeast. We cross over, then follow it northwest to the intersection. Then the fun starts." He glanced back and smiled.

They walked along, mainly in silence, enjoying the woods. The snow wasn't yet deep enough to really slow them, but even so, Charlotte appreciated Evan breaking trail. She decided she should take a turn and hurried to join him. He turned to her. "I've got it."

"You sure?"

"Yup. I can keep us on azimuth and lead pretty quickly during this part. Don't worry—you'll have your chance."

"Well, in that case, let me at least offer some help." She held up a small bottle of vodka she'd bought at the gas station. Evan smiled and took a swig. Charlotte followed suit.

"Oh, that's warm," Evan purred, smiling.

"You could almost forget we're in a warzone, trudging through no man's land to try to eavesdrop on the enemy commanders," she said playfully, gazing up at the silent trees. In saying it she accidentally forced herself to face the reality of what they were doing. They were spies now, through and through. If caught, the best they could hope for was being the focus of a massive international incident. At worst ... she drove the thought out of her mind with another swig of vodka. Evan acknowledged her with an "mm" and kept walking, glancing at his compass every couple dozen steps.

The distance whiled away, and though Charlotte didn't feel particularly cold, thanks to their pace and her clothes, she could note the snow getting thicker and the light getting dimmer as they progressed. Soon, it would be dark—just as they hit the most difficult portion.

It was a mere thirty minutes before they hit the power lines, and after a brief pause to be sure no one was watching the open space, they hurried across, turned to their left, and continued.

"This is the easiest part. We just need to follow the power lines as quickly as possible until we hit the paved road."

Charlotte took the lead and left nothing back. Another swig of vodka and "The Eye of the Tiger" playing in her mind drove her on. She had to fight the constant urge to peer through the gloom, hoping to see a landmark or something to tell her she was on the right path, or something to at least distinguish one direction from another. She tried to focus on watching the ground in front of her, as the snow piled up and each step became more of an effort.

And just like that, it was dark. With the thick snow and mist, it had been hard to tell as the light grew lower and lower, but once it was night there was no question. Charlotte looked at her watch: 3:40. She suppressed a note of panic, knowing they'd covered at least a good six miles. But who knew how long the last few would take.

She started to pick her way only by the unearthly white glow to her left, a feeling of openness rather than actual knowledge that the power lines were there. It somehow grew before her, and all of a sudden, they were staring at the road.

Evan came up beside her. It was closing into the darkest of dark nights, but even through the snow they could see the road was about twenty meters wide. Evan led them thirty meters farther away from the power lines, then poked his head out of the tree line. He waited a moment, then beckoned Charlotte over.

"I'm going to run across. If you don't hear me yell, come over after one minute."

A minute later she followed his trail, and they cut back to the intersection of the power lines.

"Why didn't we just cross here?" she asked.

"We had to leave tracks across the road. But if we left them near the power lines, the most likely place for there to be traffic — it's just that much more likely that a casual observer might see them. Plus, on the road there were only two directions to watch for trouble, not four." He shrugged. "Long years of training, I guess. Old dog."

Evan took off his backpack. "We're on schedule, but it's way darker than I thought. I'm not going to be able to keep us on azimuth using just the compass."

"So …?"

"So we'll have to take a risk and use a flashlight. Here's how it will work. I'll stand sighting through the compass. You'll head out about fifty meters in the direction we're heading. Then you'll shine the flashlight back toward me. I'll call out which direction you have to move to be exactly on azimuth. When I shout 'mark,' you'll take a stick" — he wrestled with a dying bough, pulling it off the tree — "and mark the exact point. Then I'll come up to that point, and we'll repeat."

"Sounds slow."

"Very. The farther you go each time, the more accurate and the faster. Since we're using light and shouting anyway, we'll both just use flashlights so we can move faster. But that means we'll be totally unaware of our surroundings." Charlotte looked at him, appraising. He handed her a flashlight. "Ready?"

"Ready."

"OK. First leg ... 800 meters at 54 degrees magnetic. That's ... that way." Charlotte got up and started off. "Oh, Char!" She turned. "Don't forget we're heading to a pond. Watch your step." She smiled and walked into the darkness.

After walking what seemed a reasonable distance, she turned. "FARTHER" was the word from Evan. After a few more steps, she tried again, facing back his way—he was completely out of sight—with the flashlight. "GOOD, RIGHT ... RIGHT ... RIGHT ... MARK!" she planted the stick under the light. A few moments later Evan came walking up. "Straightforward, right?" Charlotte headed off.

They fell into an easy rhythm. If Charlotte was going 50 meters each repetition and it was 800 meters to the first lake, she figured it would be sixteen reps. At rep nine she started to feel disoriented. There was no way, in the darkness and snow, to have the remotest clue where they were. Their only link to reality was Evan's compass.

At rep fourteen she started peering into the gloom, hoping for a pond. At rep fifteen she hit it.

"EVAN! POND." So it worked after all.

"COMING!" He loped up.

"It works!" She exuded relief.

"Of course it works. We're spot on, good. Now let's head around. Our next leg is 1200 meters at 23 degrees, so we want the pond immediately behind us at 203 magnetic." They cut around the pond, reaching the far side. After the short pause, Charlotte could tell just how much deeper the snow was. It had started to seep in the top of her boots, and soon her socks would be sodden. Nothing to do but continue.

"We're moving too slowly," Evan declared. "We won't make it. We need to start running."

"Running?"

"You have to run every time you head out, and I have to run up to you. It's where we're losing time. Right now we're doing less than half of walking speed."

Charlotte looked at her watch: 4:40. It had taken them forty minutes to go a half mile. They did need to hurry.

She took off into the woods, and they fell into the same rhythm as before. But this time her socks quickly soaked with icy water, the sweat started to cling to her long johns, and she barely caught her breath between each fifty-meter sprint. The snow was deeper, so each step was a struggle against the weight of the ice accumulating on her boots. She lost track of how many rounds she'd gone, her life reducing to an endless repetition: run, turn, move, plant, wait, repeat. She knew that every step was misery, but that every step carried her closer to their goal. *If I didn't feel so much like I'd been used, that I'd messed up, I would never care enough to put up with this crap,* she thought. *Evan just enjoys it for its own sake. Or does he? Is what I'm feeling now — this need to prove myself, to redeem myself —*

maybe something just as strong as what's been driving him this whole time, since losing Kyle.? The next time he bounded up to her, she saw him with new eyes, no longer remotely angry. The same hunger that had separated them six years ago was what would bring them together.

"Should be getting close." He panted, bringing the compass to his cheek. She turned and headed off.

Two rounds later they hit the second lake, dead on. She glanced at her watch as they jogged around to the far side: 5:05. They had made far better time but could make no mistakes on the final leg. And then they still had to cross the stream and find the pond.

Run, move, wait. Run, move, wait. Run, move, wait. Charlotte's body was an ecstasy of pain, of cold, of sweat, of misery. She couldn't go on but she did, couldn't bear it another second but had to. Just turned her brain off and …

… WHOOMP. Her leg plunged through the snow and she nearly reversed her knee. She grimaced in pain, but for a moment, she thought, it was nice for her brain to have something other than the sweaty cold to focus on. Evan rushed up.

"Charlotte, are you—"

"I'm fine. Just help me up." He grasped her under the arms and pulled her up. She was thankful he wouldn't be able to see the frozen tears in the dark. "Go back to the last spot. I'm fine. Let's go." She could countenance no sympathy at this moment. There was a job to do.

They fell back into the rhythm. Same misery, just a bit slower. Her brain just filled up the extra time with extra misery.

Then she saw it. Ten meters to her left, halfway through a round. A small woodsmen's hut, just an open shelter. Evan ran up.

"Ten meters off. Not bad." Charlotte said.

"OK. Let's take a second and have something to eat."

The chocolate hit Charlotte's bloodstream and lit her world up. She couldn't care how painful her knee was, how cold her feet were, how nasty the freezing sweat on her neck was. She was famished.

"Ten meters off over 1500 … that's 6.6 mils. A third of a degree."

Charlotte looked at her watch: 5:40. "Let's go."

They picked up and headed north. In just a couple of minutes, the forest thinned out. They couldn't see the other side, but it had to be the stream.

"Well," Evan observed, "at least we know no one can see us. No light, no sound?" Charlotte nodded.

They soon came upon the stream, picking their way across. Evan's right foot plunged into a slushy puddle on the far side, and he muffled the clear desire to yell an expletive. A minute later they were in the woods on the far side. They took a left, picking their way gingerly and silently.

Charlotte saw the glow of an artificial light through the gloom and checked her watch: 5:55. They'd made it.

"OK, so we'll just walk toward it until we see more," Evan planned. "We already decided the east was the safest way. We have to chance it. But Char—"

"Hmm?"

"I have to go alone."

"Huh?"

"You don't speak Russian, and two people is twice the noise, twice the chance they'll find us. It makes no sense. I'll go up to the window alone." Evan looked her in the eye, searching.

"What the fuck, Evan. You think I trudged all this way just to … to sit in the woods waiting for you?"

"Yes. I need you to keep a lookout. I'm leaving now."

He turned and moved off toward the light. Charlotte leaped after him, grabbing his hand.

"You're a dick, Evan. I'm not some silly girl you just boss around. I came all this way with you; I'm going to see this through."

"No, you're not. You'll come with me to the edge of the clearing, then work around the edge to find a good place to keep a lookout. If anyone sees my tracks, you can distract them so I can get out. We'll meet up back at the other building." He turned and kept moving. She knew he was right.

At the last tree, they could just pick out the outline of the bathhouse through the snow and gloom, backlit by an exterior light just twenty meters away. Evan turned and met her gaze, his eyes open and honest, clear in his purpose. He slunk off into the fog.

CHAPTER 28
Outskirts of Daugavpils, Latvia, January 11

Charlotte creeped around the clearing, keeping the ethereal glowing form of the bathhouse just in view. When she'd gone far enough west, the front of the building came into view, and the exterior light illuminated far more detail: a small, covered porch with a bench big enough for six or so to sit, a single door into the bathhouse, a secondary glow from what must be a window facing the pond on the south side of the structure, and a parking lot with the forms of three vehicles — and not a sign of a sentry. She continued circling, verifying that there was a single road serving the place from the northwest, worked her way back to where she could see the porch, and settled in, leaning against the trunk of a pine tree.

The moment she stopped moving was the moment the misery returned. Without the mad rush of an impossible time goal to meet, without the constant threat of detection as she prowled the perimeter, her mind was free to turn to its most pressing concerns: numb feet, sodden clothing, frozen sweat, terrible fatigue, and an aching knee. If her minded transcended her physical ailments, the throbbing, uncertain pain of whatever was happening with Evan was lying waiting alongside the dire question of what the heck she was doing with her life.

She did her best to think only of the stress Evan was under; he was right there, only a stone's throw away, but out of sight, likely tucked beneath the window on the far side. After hours of mental and physical toil, foot frozen through, he was now trying to eavesdrop on and memorize a technical conversation in Russian under the constant threat of discovery. Yet it felt as if he was a world away and she was alone in the woods with her numb feet and heavy eyelids.

She had to think of ways to keep herself awake. First, her socks. She'd brought a dry pair, but they'd only be dry once. Her thoughts turned to the seven-mile trudge that awaited her, and she convinced herself this was the moment. She quickly stripped her boots off, amazed at how much ice was clinging to them. She'd been dragging that along this entire time! She quietly hacked off as much as she could, then pulled the wet socks off her poor feet. She was thankful for the darkness so she couldn't see what they must look like; even as she rubbed the blood back into them, she could tell she'd have hell to pay for days.

But the dry socks felt like she'd been dipped in a warm bath. *Dangerous*, she thought, pulling her boots on. *Might get comfortable.*

Next: vodka. She pulled out the flask and took a mighty swig. It burned but prolonged her warm-bath feeling. She was about to down it when she remembered Evan and tucked it away in her jacket.

Then: chocolate. She had half a bar left. Two squares now, and two squares when we're halfway back. She savored the chunks.

And finally she was out of distractions. She glanced at her watch: 6:25. Her entire being sank as she realized they could be here for hours.

Unbidden, her thoughts turned to the future. When they made it home—*if* they made it home—what was next? Her chance at a clearance was shot. She was a pariah to anyone connected to

Margaret. And she'd burned enough bridges to be unsure if she could ever return to microfinance. Evan had certainly made it clear he wanted her to be with him, but regardless of chemistry, they just had so much baggage, not to mention the uncertainties of this new career he'd chosen. She could give it all up, just move in and move on with him. She could find some entry-level job in another field. She could retreat to NYC and the family business. None of these sounded particularly appealing.

Her thoughts returned to the present with a spine-deep, unnerving shudder of cold. She noticed she'd been shivering without realizing it, stamping her feet to stay warm. 6:30.

The seconds ticked by with agonizing slowness. She tried doing word puzzles in her head, practicing old Chinese phrases she'd learned in Singapore and Hindi students' slang. She tried to fantasize about a particularly steamy night she'd once had in Mumbai, but thinking about her body only led her back to the pain, and the fire didn't kindle. It was still cold. It was 6:40.

She noted that the snow had ceased. It was still foggy, but if it started to clear up ... Evan needed to get back soon.

She stamped her feet, worked her fingers in her gloves, flexed and reflexed her muscles from toes to eyebrows—anything to stave off the boredom and cold and exhaustion.

His hunched shape appeared out of the gloom, moving from the bathhouse back to woodline. Charlotte hustled to meet him.

"I am frozen solid," he gasped, hugging her. "We have to go, now. They are coming for us."

She handed him the vodka. He downed it in one swig, then hurried on. "They are going to have a few more drinks, then head back. They think we're up to something. They want to check in on us, to make sure we're leaving. If we're not there, we're finished. We've got to move; we'll never make it in time." He put the empty vodka bottle in the backpack and wolfed down the rest of his candy bar.

"Evan, they already think we're up to something. Let's get up to something." She smiled mischievously and moved off around the clearing toward the cars.

"Char?" Evan was dumbfounded but followed her.

"They can't follow us if their cars don't start." She pulled her pocket knife from the outside pouch of the backpack. "You don't spend months doing fieldwork in rural India and not learn a thing or two about broken-down vehicles."

Glancing at the front door, she soundlessly moved through the snow to the first car, just yards from the porch. It was an old model Skoda. She pried the hood open, fiddled around to find the battery terminal, and slashed the wires. One down.

She moved to the next vehicle, an ancient Soviet Lada SUV. *A great car*, she thought, reaching under the hood for the same operation. Two.

She instantly knew the third one would cause a problem. It was a new BMW, with a hood release in the cabin of the car. *Fuck*. She'd have to go for the tires. Puncture too hard, though, and it would blow. She started scraping the knife into the sidewall of the front left tire. She felt the tube give way, and soon heard the hiss of a good break.

But what good would that do? They'd mount the spare in

minutes and head straight to the hotel to confront the prime suspects. She needed to do a second tire.

She pried the knife into the same spot, beginning a slow sawing motion. But this one wasn't going as easily. It started to hiss, the high whine of air escaping. Time to go.

She bolted back to Evan, her heart pumping. "Go, go go," she hissed.

They took off, following their tracks back into the woods. The snow and mist were fading into the darkness of night, and they could pick out the trail three or four meters to their front.

Far behind them, they heard the loud "BANG" of the tire exploding, followed by the slamming of a door and yelling. They picked up their pace as they broke out of the woods, turning south to retrace their steps over the stream.

Reaching the woodsmen's hut, they paused, panting.

"They're going to follow us. Fuck. Charlotte, we can't let them catch us."

"They won't. We'll run the whole way back." Her voice pulsed with confidence.

"At least we won't be cold. Look … it will be much shorter to go straight south instead of following our tracks, but there are no landmarks to help us stay on azimuth and we'd have to stop all the time to correct. So let's just follow our tracks and move as fast as we can. Every once in a while, we'll double back or circle around to slow them down." Charlotte nodded and took the lead in a slow jog through the snow.

After a few hundred meters the effort was getting to her, and she felt the sweat starting again. But this time, she didn't remotely care. They had seven miles to cover. It would be the most painful seven miles of her life, but if they kept a good pace, they'd be back in under two hours. She slowed to a walk. "I'm going to do twenty paces walk, twenty jog. Just to break it up. Want to tell me what happened, keep me distracted?"

"I'll tell you while we jog. That way we can listen for trouble during the walking parts. After I left you, I went straight to the side of the building. It was a blank wall, so I poked around the left side—the south, next to the pond—where there was a window. The drapes were drawn, but there was a tiny crack. I poked my head up just enough to see I was looking into a dressing room, with the actual sauna behind. I picked up the top of someone's head standing on the far side of the room, and ducked back down. The window was a new design, newer than the rest of the building—a normal double pane number, with horizontal sliders. At first I thought I was out of luck—I could hear muffled voices but knew I wouldn't be able to decipher a thing unless I got it open. Luckily it was unlocked—it must be used all the time for getting humidity out—so I was able to slide it, soundlessly, just the tiniest bit open so I could hear.

"So by the end I picked up seven voices. I knew Natalya's, Misha's, and Yuri's. I am ninety percent sure another was one of the guys we heard in the church basement. Of the other three, two were mostly quiet, but the last one everyone called 'sir.' He was clearly in charge, there to make a decision."

Charlotte was panting, hard. But by listening closely for followers during the walking breaks, and listening to Evan's narrations during the jogs, she was able to keep her mind off how heavy her legs had become.

"It started off with a bit of idle chit-chat and small talk, jokes about the stupidity of the Latvians and such. Then the business started off. First Yuri spoke. He may be subordinate to Natalya, but he is certainly not her assistant. He was sort of the 'civilian relations' guy for the whole plot. He seemed to be in touch with a whole mess of organizations in the area, lots of them like the historical society he told us about: cultural heritage groups, student organizations, some unions, musical groups, prayer circles. He went through a whole list of groups, twenty or thirty of them. The first fifteen or twenty he just rattled off, saying 'these are the ones that are ready,' and finishing by saying 'with a total membership of over eight hundred patriots.' Then he named five or ten more, describing them as 'willing but unorganized, will have to be developed as we go.' Those totaled one hundred and fifty patriots. Finally he named three — one was a musical group, one the postal union, one other I can't remember — that were 'unwilling.' He said he had to assume they would support the occupiers.

"The man in charge told him 'good report,' and Misha went next. He turned it over to his 'three brave partisan commanders.' The first one set the tone, saying 'we have received and handed out the books, and are in position. The bridges in sectors A, B, and C are already rigged and our drop zone is clear.' The second, whose voice I thought I knew, made a similar report but referred instead to ambush locations. Oh — here's the second pond. You follow our tracks; I'll go the other way and meet you on the far side."

Five minutes later they had rejoined on the far side. Neither had a breath to lose on niceties, and they set off directly. Evan resumed his narration.

"Where was I ... right, the first two partisans had just spoken.

The third one, whose box I think we opened, identified seven targets by code name—there was 'harbor,' 'elephant,' 'leopard,' 'monk,' and three other words I didn't know—and said they would be neutralized within twenty-four hours of the signal. In sum, it's pretty clear—a sabotage team to target infrastructure, a disruption team to cause chaos behind the lines, and an assassination team to take out leadership."

"Serious stuff," Charlotte chimed in, instantly regretting the waste of breath. By now, she was pouring sweat inside her long johns, feeling it freeze where it met the cold air on the back of her neck. No matter. Keep moving. No time.

"At this point," Evan continued, "Misha cut back in, his voice also growing louder. I realized he was walking toward the window, and I quickly hugged as closely as I could to the wall. He slapped the window open, throwing a cigarette butt out. I am very lucky he didn't peer out, plus he left the window completely open after this. He went on narrating. 'As you can see, sir, the partisans are ready. In addition, our friends from the wolves'—I think he is referring to the Night Wolves, one of the most famous Russian biker gangs—'are in critical locations across the region, ready to report.' The man in charge cut in for the first time, asking 'how are they reporting?' Misha answered—'by WhatsApp, of course. Everyone here is in the group, so everyone gets the latest information right away. Just like in Syria, but here we can be sure the Americans aren't listening in.' The man in charge grunted.

"The last part of Misha's report was a description of his instigators, people inside the crowd who would carry out extreme acts to try to elicit a reprisal or escalate violence. He drew praise from the man in charge for their performance with 'those teenagers.' I don't think there is any misinterpreting that one."

Charlotte could see they were approaching the first pond. It was amazing how much faster they were going, not having to navigate. She caught her breath for a moment, noticing for the first time as she gazed across the pond just how much the visibility had improved. They'd have to be careful. "Same plan?"

"Same plan." Two minutes later they reunited on the far side and kept jogging.

Evan picked right back up. "Almost done. Natalya was the last to brief. 'Sasha will require another twenty-four hours,' she said. 'The house is prepared, it is a perfect position. 13th and Avenue U, in Brooklyn—"

"Brooklyn?" Charlotte was as incredulous as she could be through her panting. "You mean to say they're plotting something back in the US?!"

"Yes. Brooklyn. She said, '13th and Avenue U in Brooklyn, across the street from a Latvian grocery.'"

"Holy crap. Holy crap! Evan, why haven't you used your little radio doodad and called this up?!"

"Can't. It sends pre-coordinated codewords only."

Charlotte picked up the pace. "I guess we really do have to hurry. What did she say next?"

"Uh ... then 'Boris is not yet in position. He will initiate the signal when he is ready.'"

"Boris?!"

"Yes."

"So there must be someone on the ground helping Sasha/Bērziņš."

"Yes. After Natalya finished, Misha snorted — there is clearly no love lost between those two. 'Typical SVR,' he said — SVR is like the Russian CIA — 'At least in the military we can hold to a timeline,' he jabbed. Natalya answered, 'I make no pretense of micromanaging my men in the field. Sasha will be ready when Sasha is ready.' The man in charge cut in. 'As well you shouldn't. We will be fine as long as Sasha initiates in the next forty-eight hours. But tell me, what of these two young Americans? They are your loose ends to tie up.'"

Charlotte's blood went cold, as Evan continued. "My blood went cold as Natalya answered. 'They are a couple of children on an exciting winter vacation.' Then she said some … uh … mean things and —"

"What did she say, Evan?"

"It's not important."

"Tell me."

"She said, 'The girl has thrown away her life on undisciplined, impulsive decisions just like the one we relied on her to make. She is simply adrift. And the boy is a shaggy nobody, a typical American hippie student.'"

"Undisciplined and impulsive?! That …" Charlotte fumed at the insult. Evan would clearly have been red-faced had there been light enough to see his embarrassment at having shared, but then again they were both red-faced from the journey. She stayed silent. "Wait a moment, how didn't they figure out you were in the military? They had your whole identity from the passports."

"I never was. At least ever since all record of it was deleted. According to anything public, I've spent the last six years traveling, volunteering, freelance writing. There's even an embarrassingly naïve blog all about how worldly my travels made me."

"Neat. Maybe you should have told me that, too."

"And have to explain?"

"Fair. Go on."

"Well ... long story short, Natalya didn't assess us as a threat, or at least didn't report that to the group. I think she's just hedging, hoping we're just a coincidence so it's not her piece that's holding the whole thing up. But in any case, Natalya said she would follow up on this morning's 'message' tonight, and if we weren't at least planning to leave in the morning, she'd take 'active measures.'"

"Well. At least we are making the best time we can. Here is the intersection."

They approached in silence, knowing that if their adversaries had put two and two together, they'd have sent someone to find where they crossed the road. Evan jerked his head, so they backtracked and crossed the power lines first. Emerging into the open, Charlotte could see almost a hundred meters. They were losing their concealment.

They turned south, jogging out to the west to put distance between them and the intersection, then carefully crossed the road as before. They got into the woods, returned to the power lines, and turned southward.

"We'll pick up our tracks when they cross back from the other side." Evan took the lead and picked up the staggered pace.

"Did they say anything else?"

"There's one last part. The man in charge finished up by saying how satisfied he was with each of the parts being in place, then he reviewed the course of upcoming events. He said 'from here, we wait for Sasha. That will ensure the Americans and NATO will have no hand here. Then we amplify the protests, and I will send in the polite men' — that's their code for Spetsnaz. 'If the Latvians react, the partisans take action and I'll reinforce with army units. Then we hold the referendum, and it is all finished before anyone knows anything happened. Now, I must head back to my post. But first, let us enjoy a few drinks together. To our health!' They echoed his *nazdrovie*, and I slunk back to you."

"Jesus. Evan. They're planning something in the US as part of an invasion of Latvia. Holy—"

"Yeah."

They continued on in silence, an endless alternation of walk-run-walk-run, the fatigue in their limbs drowning out any desire they had for conversation.

CHAPTER 29
Daugavpils, Latvia, January 11

Every step was a universe of agony. Her feet were utterly numb from the cold, but every time she lifted them, a swath of blisters screamed out in pain. Her legs had long gone sore and tight, the distance and deep snow and layers of ice up to her calves weighing her down, yet her knee wouldn't stop throbbing. A solid layer of sweat covered her entire body, accumulating in what her Shenandoah cousins would call swamp ass, but at her wrists and neck and lower back and anywhere else her skin met the air, it had frozen into a band of prickly ice. And she could hardly keep her eyes open, but fear drove her on.

The air had cleared enough for them to see the lights of the suburb where they'd entered the woods from almost a quarter of a mile away. She checked her watch: 8:15. They'd made phenomenal time. Even better, with any luck the gas station would be open and they could stop, even just for a second, for something to quell her rebellious stomach.

Ten minutes later they entered the warmth of the store, her cheeks instantly prickling in pain. She headed straight toward the tables, but Evan held her back. "Don't sit down. It will be too hard to keep going. Food and drink, and we go."

It was a different attendant, luckily, one who saw them only as two tourists in from a long walk in the cold. Odd, but not "gone for five hours in a blizzard" odd. They quickly paid for hot coffees, bottles of Gatorade, and a menagerie of snacks and candies. Charlotte thought she could eat the whole store.

They set off back onto the street, munching as they went. Two and a half miles to go.

After the coffee poured a new warmth into her soul, Charlotte felt ready to give voice to the thoughts that had been forming as they'd rushed through the forest.

"I'm still trying to wrap my head around this, Evan. Sasha and Boris are Natalya's agents in the US. They are almost done with a long scheme to turn American opinion against Latvia, one that will culminate in … something they're preparing in Brooklyn. As soon as that happens, they'll escalate over here, knowing they've got a free hand. Russia is trying to conquer eastern Latvia. But what can we do to stop it? How can we get the right information to the right people, knowing that everything's already in motion, that the US public is pretty much already deceived?"

Evan's head hung from exhaustion, but she could see he was hearing her. She continued.

"I've been thinking about it. I think you need to head straight to the Embassy, so you can do whatever you can to get this information in the right hands. But me … I think I should fly back to NYC. Get there as quickly as possible. Get in touch with Agent McCandless as soon as I can; if that doesn't work, tell the NYPD; if that doesn't work, just go there myself. I'm our hedge against the worst-case-scenario—that the bureaucracy somehow messes this one up—and if needed, I'll try to stop this myself, there."

"I think you're right, Char. But I think the situation is even worse than that."

"Worse? How so?"

"In Ukraine in 2014, Russia's interest was clear. Whether we like to acknowledge it or not, at least in Crimea there is a whiff of a legitimate historical precedent for the Russian annexation. It may have been totally illegal, but at least there was some sense. And was a massive domestic win, and a great way to test out new techniques."

"So …?"

"Wait. In Donbass, though, the techniques didn't work so well. It was another laboratory, but the conditions just weren't quite right. So it turned into a quagmire, a stinking stalemate the Russian media talk about as little as possible. But even so — Ukraine has an almost mythical role in the Russian psyche, the birthplace of their culture and all. So even then it at least had some other … justification."

"You're starting to lose me, Evan."

"Well, that's just the thing. In Ukraine — Crimea successfully, and the Donbass unsuccessfully — Russia had a chance to test out new techniques, in a place where no matter the outcome, the Russian people would generally approve. And, more importantly, where the sovereign power wasn't a member of NATO."

"You're saying …"

"Yes. What we've found isn't the opening moves in an invasion of eastern Latvia. It's the opening moves in a ploy to split NATO."

"No!"

"It's Russia's single, overarching strategic imperative: faced with the most powerful alliance the world has ever seen, sow division. As long as NATO stands, Russia faces a stone wall."

"But if you can break NATO …"

"In a single action, have the core purpose of the entire treaty — mutual self-defense — thrown out the window — "

" — NATO will cease to exist. And Latvia's already requested NATO support …" Charlotte exhaled deeply, her mind racing once again, jumping ahead. "So they've placed NATO on the horns of a terrible dilemma."

"Either support an ally whose actions appear to be oppressive, fascistic, and against everything the alliance stands for — "

" — or hold to their principles and watch the alliance drift away in the wind." Charlotte finished his thought, shaken to the core.

"And here's the thing," Evan continued. "Just like in Crimea, in Donbass, in Syria, in the rise of nationalists across Europe, in the 2016 election … it doesn't matter what the 'truth' is. Russia understands, has always understood this. Make sure the right people see the right things, read the right things, react to the right things, like and share the right things, think about the right things, *argue* about the right things … and they won't notice what's really going on. Even if it is naked aggression, we dither, too caught up in how we feel about the online debate to keep the faith."

The audacity of the scheme made Charlotte's head spin. She'd returned to the US wanting to be a good guy, believing that the faithful application of consistent, fair laws could bend history toward justice. But this felt like the ground had shifted and everyone else was playing by a new set of rules. It was an entirely different level. It was a whole new way of waging war, the culmination of decades of technological progress and postmodern relativism, a whole new battlefield: the battlefield of the mind. *And the US wasn't just unprepared,* she thought. *We are already losing battles we don't even realize are being fought.*

They turned a corner onto a main road and could see the lights of downtown Daugavpils through the haze. "I don't know if we'll be able to sneak back in with visibility like this, Char," Evan observed.

"I've got an idea." She moved to the edge of the sidewalk, continuing to walk while trying to flag down a cab.

"How will a cab help?" Evan asked. "They'll be watching the entrance."

"You'll see." A cab finally stopped. "Give him five euros and tell him to wait in front of the hotel with his blinkers on. If anyone asks him what he's doing, he had a request to pick up two Americans at nine." Evan smiled and spoke with the driver.

"You're a genius. They take everyone off the perimeter and get them ready to tail us."

They continued their trudge, their pace slowing as they neared the end of the trek. Charlotte didn't look forward to the ten-story climb up the fire escape.

"OK, so let's think this through," Evan began. "First, if they catch us outside the room we're toast. So we've got to get inside undetected as quickly as possible."

"And once we're inside, we've got to make it look as if we're trying to get ready to leave—we called a taxi 'cause we don't want to drive through the snow, but we're running late."

"There's a chance they've already decided we're a threat and sent someone to the room," Evan speculated.

"If that is the case, then we're screwed—they're waiting for us. We'll just have to take each step as deliberately as possible. No, we'll have to do one better. I'm going in first."

"Huh?"

"Forget it, Evan. You're the one in the most danger. With the highest consequences. I'm unemployed. You're a government asset. You need to hang back somewhere you can see our room. I'll climb on the roof, go to the room, make sure it's clear. If it's safe to come in, I'll flick the lights three times. Exactly three if it's safe."

"Charlotte, but—"

"I won't hear it. If you don't see the signal in ten minutes, you need to leave, and report."

Evan acquiesced. "You're right. OK." Charlotte felt like she was back on the team.

They turned a final corner and the hotel was before them. Charlotte turned to Evan, sizing him up, wondering if this was the image she'd daydream about from a Siberian prison. *Fuck it.*

She grabbed his neck and pulled him into a deep, hard kiss. She felt his muscles, tense at the surprise, relax as he gave in to her. She opened herself to him, his energy flowing through her, filling her with purpose and confidence. This was right.

She pushed him away, looking him in the eye and patted his chest. "Evan, I forgive you. I … see you in fifteen minutes."

She reached up and kissed him on the cheek, looked at his wide eyes, and turned.

She walked quickly toward the fire escape, feeling completely in charge of herself. She knew full well anything could happen at any moment, but that didn't stop the wonderful feeling of power, of sheets of anxiety just avalanching off her. She knew that she'd never see the trap coming—so why even worry?

She reached the metal stairway and began to climb. It was exhausting; she could barely lift her legs. *How do you eat an elephant?* she asked herself. *One bite at a time.*

An eternity later she was on the roof. No sign of trouble. *It's all downhill from here.* Next the hatch. She wrenched it open and clambered down. The stairwell was empty. Two floors down.

She cracked the door onto the eighth-floor hallway, opening it fully when she saw it was clear straight to the elevator. The overheated hotel instantly made every cell in her body cry out for bed. She paused in front of her door. The "Do not disturb" sign was right where they'd left it, slightly catawampus in a distinct way. *Here goes.*

She opened the door and strode in confidently. Nothing. She took her boots off—no reason to leave a sign they'd been outside—then checked the closet, the bathroom, under the bed ... nothing. She exhaled, flicked the lights three times, and went to run the bath.

She was out of her sodden, disgusting clothes in thirty seconds, leaving them in a pile in the closet so as to keep them out of sight, and plopped down on the bed naked to inspect her broken body. Her toes were white and her entire feet were pickled, with pieces of skin starting to peel off the soles and wide blisters on the heels. Her knee was an ugly shade of blue and her inner thighs were chafed bright red. The rest of her had fared a bit better, but every ounce felt like it had been sent through an industrial washer with a couple of boulders, then left out wet. She slunk into the bathroom and lowered herself into the hot bath, an extended "oooooooooo" being the highest praise she could ever imagine to confer upon anything, ever.

She lost track of time in the water, but it couldn't have been more than a couple minutes before she heard Evan come in. Charlotte answered his call with a splish-splash, and he laughed a full laugh. "Good move." She heard him remove his boots and clothes, then knock softly on the bathroom door. A hand appeared through the crack, offering a flask of whiskey.

"I couldn't bear the tension and made a quick visit to the pharmacy."

"Ohhhhh. How thoughtful. You must be freezing. I'll be out in just a moment."

"You take your time. Let's talk this through. They're still on the way."

"Indeed. Well, we are pretty much packed and ready. Let's throw the wet clothes into a garbage bag and shove it in a suitcase, and just leave in street clothes. We can be gone in fifteen minutes." She could have slept for three days, but thinking about the three-hour drive ahead of them gave her new resolve.

"And if they come before then?"

She stood and started toweling off. Her skin was warm and

relaxed. "I'll be decent in one minute. If they want to arrest us, fine. But we can relax. As far as anyone can tell, we've been here all day and are just getting ready to leave. We're innocent. Your turn!" She wrapped a towel around her torso and strode into the room.

Evan, towel around his waist, raised his eyebrows, running his eyes up her legs to her eyes. She felt undressed. She was ready.

Charlotte moved toward Evan, his arms wrapping around her as she drew close. She felt his freezing chest press against her, the pressure of his thighs on hers. She dove into his kiss, losing herself, and reached up to undo her towel.

There was a knock on the door. Evan's entire body tensed.

"Who is it?" Charlotte sang as sweetly as possible.

"Charlotte, it is Natalya. Please, open the door. You are in danger."

Evan nodded. If they were here to arrest them, there was nothing they could do. Best to play innocent. Charlotte tightened her towel and opened the door.

Natalya was there, with Misha. Charlotte could swear she saw a look of profound confusion cross Natalya's face. Misha wore a grim mask. "Oh! Excuse me," Charlotte exclaimed, feigning modesty in her towel. "I just got out of the shower. If I had known—"

"Not to worry." Natalya didn't miss a beat. "Charlotte, I am here because you are in trouble. It is no longer safe for you here. You must leave." Evan came wandering out from the bathroom, clad in a bathrobe. It looked, Charlotte thought, like they'd just been walked in on. Perfect.

"How are you, Natalya?" Evan chimed in. "Thank you for the *samogon. Ochen vkustni.*" Natalya's eyes went up in surprise.

"Charlotte, Evan." Natalya sounded like she was actually pleading. *Maybe she is pleading with herself, doing her best to believe that we really are harmless.* "Truly I must insist. It is not safe for you here. After what happened to your room today … there is a police car here at your disposal …"

"Oh, you're so kind," Charlotte interrupted. They'd never called in the burglary; Natalya had tipped her hand. Charlotte felt like she was playing with four aces. "But there's no need. We've arranged to leave our rental here and ordered a taxi to take us to Rīga through the storm. We came to much the same conclusions."

"Well … this is for the best. Charlotte, have a safe journey home." Natalya held out her hand for Charlotte's while Misha turned back toward the elevator. "Evan, best of luck." They shook hands and exchanged farewells, and Charlotte closed the door as Natalya turned away.

"Charlotte …" Evan looked at her, his eyes wide with fear. "They know."

CHAPTER 30
Daugavpils, Latvia, January 11

"They know? How. Natalya played every card she had. She was expecting to catch us red-handed and didn't; she just wants to see us on our way," Charlotte asserted, sure of herself.

"Red-handed, no," Evan explained. "But Char, I shook her hand. I hadn't showered yet. I saw it in her eyes. She knows."

The implication dawned on Charlotte. Evan's hand must have been cold as ice.

"We—"

"Get dressed. Only take the essentials. They may already be on the way up."

In a frenzy of activity, they both stripped naked — *this isn't exactly how it was supposed to go, and poor Evan hasn't even showered yet*, Charlotte thought, *he must be freezing* — and quickly dressed. It was misery to put her wet boots back on, but there was no way she was leaving them behind. Evan was even worse off, pulling his sodden pants right back on. In a flash they were dressed, divvying up essentials between their day packs. No room for toiletries, clothes — just the essentials. Evan started blasting music from his phone and drew Charlotte close.

"They're watching the foyer," Evan whispered. "And Natalya has already made the call to cover all the exits. So we need to find a different way out. The stairwell is too risky, so is the roof. Fuck."

"The maintenance room."

"Huh?"

"The maintenance room where you hid your bag. It had a drop ceiling, with the foam squares. We can head there, then go through the crawlspace into another room and lay low 'til we figure something out."

He nodded and turned to the door. "You're amazing. Ready?" She nodded. "Phones off."

He opened the door and looked out. Empty. They hurried out and cut quickly into the maintenance room. Just seconds after the door closed, they heard the elevator doors open.

"We have to hurry!" Charlotte hissed, as Evan stood on a pile of dirty laundry to test the roof squares. They were loose.

"Wait …" She stopped, pointing. Behind the laundry pile was an opening: a laundry chute. "It must have an opening at every level. I'm not dumb enough to say we should try to fall to the basement. But if we can shimmy down just one floor—"

"—we'll be more than one unlocked door away." Evan got down and stuck his head through the hole. Returning, he nodded. "It will be miserable with our legs in the condition they're in, but it should be no issue. It's small enough that, once we're in, it should be easy to control your slide. One at a time." He put his head through the hole, facing up, then wormed his way into the duct. He sat on the threshold, upper body upright, then slowly his legs disappeared as he braced himself upward. Charlotte saw his body then face pass the opening, with a broad smile. "Easy," he said. She heard footsteps in the hall and looked nervously at the door. "Hurry!" she rasped.

At that moment she felt rather than heard the doorknob behind her start to move, and turning, saw a crack open in the door. Without thinking she rushed to the corner behind the door jamb as it swung open; she just caught the interior doorknob in time to hold the door open and stay hidden as she heard a body step into the room.

From sound alone she couldn't tell much, only that it was a largish person wearing heavy boots. But then again, it was hard to hear much of anything over the pounding of her heart. Charlotte realized she hadn't warned Evan, and prayed he could sense the need to stay quiet as their visitor made their way to the laundry pile, lifting it up and grunting in a masculine tone.

Charlotte reacted almost automatically to Evan's call of "made it!" from the floor below. Letting the door swing shut, she closed the short distance to the thuggish-looking man now hunched over the laundry chute in an instant, slamming into him just as he began to react to the new sound behind him. He easily had sixty pounds on her, but she had momentum, and surprise, and as her mass shoved him forward, her right hand found the back of his neck, pushing his face into the metal edge of the laundry chute. She heard something crunch. She grasped his neck, hard, pulling his head back to repeat the move, when she felt her left ribs crack under an oppressively hard jab from the man's elbow. Clenching her teeth with the pain, she put everything she had into forcing him forward again, looking up in time to see his cheekbone collapse as it made contact with the metal.

Charlotte felt the man go limp under her and, unsure what to do, stepped back from him, letting him crumple to the ground. Evan chimed in as she looked down at his bloody, disfigured face.

"Uh, Char … what was that?"

Charlotte was at first horrified by the man's appearance, at what she'd done, and was waiting for feelings of disgust or self-hatred or regret to well up. But none came, instead just a calmness, a puissance. An awareness that they only had moments on their pursuers, and now she had a few cracked ribs to add to her problems.

"Keep going, Evan. They are right behind us. I'm getting in now."

She checked the man's pulse, satisfied but somehow unemotional that he was certainly still alive, then quickly rummaged through his equipment, shoving his pistol into her beltline. *Sorry, dude*, she thought as she slipped into the laundry chute like Evan had. Clambering in revealed every sore and tender fiber in her body, the pain in her ribs shooting through her body as soon as she was tensed against the chute walls. She moved down inch by inch until her feet met the lip of the seventh floor opening. Evan touched her leg from below. "Keep going?"

"Yup. We need to move," she answered. Inch by inch they shimmied downward.

Halfway between the fourth and third floors a sound resonated through the shaft, and with Evan's quick "sh" they both froze. Yelling Russian voices reverberated through the duct; the searchers had reached the eighth floor utility room and found the body.

Charlotte kicked Evan from above. "Get the eff in." Evan reacted instantly, awkwardly but soundlessly inserting himself into the opening to the third floor maintenance room.

In a moment he was through, and Charlotte began to skootch down. Evan's arms appeared through the opening, and she placed her feet on the edge of the duct and reached out for his hands. She slid forward, shifting her weight onto her hamstrings, sliding forward ... too late, feeling the pistol squeezing out of her beltline. Unable to let go to grab it, she felt it pop out and collide with the chute wall. *Shit.*

The loud metal CLANGs as the pistol careened down the chute brought a yelling Russian voice to the duct far above them; unable to look up, it was all Charlotte could do to hurry through the opening.

"Someday you'll have to tell me what the hell happened up there. Where next?" Evan asked, brushing dust off his coat.

"Let's stick with the original plan. Through the crawlspace to the next room over. It will only be a thirty-foot drop to the snowbank on the side of the hotel; we can open the window and hop out when we're sure no one is looking."

"And if the window can't open?"

"We're in eastern Europe, Evan. Smokers?"

Evan laughed and mounted the laundry pile to lift a ceiling tile. He grasped a joist and pulled himself up into the crawlspace. Once set, he turned to help Charlotte up.

She cursed her lanky form and broken bones and the entire half pullup she'd ever been able to do, but luckily the adrenaline of the chase and Evan's grip helped her up, with assistance from a few well-aimed kicks at the wall, and soon they were in the crawlspace. She slithered a few feet over and lifted a tile. "Light is off down here, and it faces the backside of the hotel."

They lowered themselves into the empty hotel room, with a wide vista onto the abandoned square. Inspecting the window, Charlotte found it would open. "Hold up," Evan declared.

The sounds of running feet echoed through the hallway, Russian voices yelling as they hurried to the maintenance room. They didn't have long.

Evan picked up the phone and dialed a long number from memory.

"Yup, we're ready. Drive around to the back side of the hotel, but stay on the far side of the plaza. Let me know when you're there … OK. Flash your lights twice … got you. In exactly two minutes, pull up to dead center of the back of the hotel, as close as you can to the snow bank. If it is safe, roll down your window and put your hand on the roof. Make sure the doors are unlocked."

Charlotte could hear the Russian voices starting to knock on every door; it wouldn't be long before they were breaking down theirs.

Evan hung up, then dialed 804, her old room number. He mumbled Russian into the handset, then hung up.

"Time to go."

Charlotte moved to the window, cranking it open, then mounting the sill, feeling her ribs shudder with every movement of her torso. Even fully open, the window was barely wide enough for Charlotte to squeeze through; perched on the edge, the thirty feet was a lot more intimidating staring it in the face. Evan held her from behind; she turned and kissed him. *Better not to think.* She pushed herself off.

She certainly felt the landing, having rotated midair in the least beneficial way, landing left chest down so all the force channeled through her ribs straight to her soul. It was all she could do to stifle a scream, but when she realized she had plowed down at least six feet into the snow, she permitted herself to let out a whimper. A loud THUMP of Evan landing next to her foreshadowed his hand slamming into her face; while at first she was indignant, she quickly realized it was about the best they could hope for.

"You OK?" Evan murmured through the snow.

"Close enough," Charlotte answered.

"Come with me. Stay in the snow," he dictated, swimming through the snow bank toward the plaza.

They reached the edge of the snow, where they could look out on the plaza. "Thirty seconds," Evan declared.

"What did you say when you called the room?" Charlotte asked.

"I told them I'd been on the fifth-floor stairwell, that the two Americans surprised me and took my gun and radio and kept going up. It was a long shot, but hopefully they're focused on the roof now."

"Good move."

"Thanks. Here he is. You'll take the back seat."

Two headlights moved toward them, fast. It was only now that Charlotte realized there was no road on the backside of the hotel; the vehicle was just driving across the plaza. It pulled up directly in front of them, sputtering and belching disgusting fumes, a beat-up sedan that couldn't have been younger than forty years. A hand appeared on the roof.

"Let's go," Evan ordered, and they wormed out of the snowbank. Charlotte opened the back door to realize that the diminutive vehicle would be even more uncomfortable than the laundry chute.

They were moving before their doors were even closed, Evan exchanging some cryptic words with the driver. Charlotte couldn't place it but was certain she knew the voice …

"Ms. Charlotte, it is good to see you again!" The vehicle crested the curb onto the main road and turned north.

"Jānis?!" Charlotte was shocked. What was their shaggy nationalist graduate student tour guide doing in Daugavpils at this time of night?

Evan filled her in. "Jānis has been working with some of my friends for years now, Charlotte. So when we started to talk about walking through the woods, leaving our rental … I figured it might be nice to have a backup plan. Even if it means being stuck in a shitty old Trabant with this smelly dude for three hours."

Charlotte realized it all fit together. If Evan had needed permission to come with her, if he was very much on the clock, then of course he would have wanted to take extra precautions. How else had he so easily found someone to show them around Rīga? Now, it would have been a lot nicer if his extra precautions had driven a fancy Mercedes with seat warmers instead of a 1980s East German rolling coffin whose heaters blew exhaust fumes, but hey, she wasn't going to complain.

"Evan …" Jānis chimed in. "I think we are being followed. BMW from the lights."

"OK," Evan replied.

"Wait, why are you guys so calm?" Charlotte demanded. "There is no way we can outrun a BMW in this thing."

"Who said anything about outrunning?" Jānis answered, smiling. "There is one thing a shitty Trabant driven by a Latvian student can do that a fancy BMW full of Russian thugs can't."

"And that is?"

"Get through a Latvian police checkpoint." Jānis grinned as he rounded a traffic circle, exiting onto the bridge made famous by the video of Latvian police harassing the Russian humanitarian convoy.

"Easy peasy." Evan laughed as they pulled up to the barricade, the policeman hardly checking Jānis's ID as their attention shifted to the BMW behind them.

CHAPTER 31
JFK International, New York City, January 12

The moment the wheels touched down at JFK, Charlotte hit the airplane icon on the phone she'd bought in the Frankfurt airport, willing it to connect even as she hated cutting off the last lines of *Hamilton* piping through her headphones. The stupid little bars had filled in, but she wasn't registered on the network ...

The fourth time she hit "call" the phone started to connect. Roaming, long distance ... whatever. She put it to her ear, impatient.

"FBI Counterintelligence, this is Agent McCandless." Relief stopped the impatient tapping of Charlotte's fingers on the seat.

"Agent McCandless, this is Charlotte Sorenson."

"Ms. Sorenson! Are you safe? We need to get you in right away."

"I know ... but look. I just landed at JFK. I have crucial information I have to get to you right away—"

"Go ahead, tell me."

"Aleksandrs Bērziņš. He's planning something big in Brooklyn, at 13th and Avenue—"

"U. Yes. I know. Is there anything else?"

Frustrated, Charlotte tried again. "Well that's not all of it. You see, Bērziņš ..."

"Ms. Sorenson. We've been searching for Bērziņš for the past two weeks. We've got this. But now that you're back in the US, I strongly advise you to come in to the DC field office right away for debriefing."

"What?! No, you're not hearing me ..."

"Ms. Sorenson, we were able to trace the metadata on the documents you gave us to the leak. If you don't come in willingly, I'll be forced to ask the judge for a warrant. So please. Go in right away. When can they expect you?"

Charlotte weighed her options. They weren't good.

"Agent McCandless, I can meet you in DC tomorrow morning."

"Tomorrow morning it is. But I won't be there—I am in the field at the moment."

"Where are you?"

"Ms. Sorenson, I'm not going to tell you that."

"Are you in New York? I can meet you in three hours."

"Ms. Sorenson, that is not possible. We are in the middle of a very delicate—"

Charlotte ended the call. If Agent McCandless didn't want to listen, Charlotte would have to make her.

It didn't take her a moment to get off the plane; after twenty-four hours of nonstop excitement the flight was her first chance to rest, and she'd sprung for a first-class ticket at only a few hundred dollars more than the exorbitant last-minute fare Lufthansa had demanded. Sinking into its enormous, welcoming warmth, she'd reviewed her travails as she drifted off. They'd met Natalya at her office what seemed like a year ago. Then returned to a trashed room. Then a huge fight. Then the second-worst walk through a blizzard of her life, followed by the first-worst. Sneaking into the hotel, fighting their way out, into Jānis' car …

Evan had woken her up as they entered the snowy outskirts of Rīga. She'd somehow drifted off, despite her ribs and knee and the exhaust fumes and the contortions she had to pull to fit in the back seat, but the adrenaline cascading off her must have pulled her down.

Evan turned around in his seat. "Charlotte, I have to go. You know what you have to do. Jānis will take you to the airport. I'll reach out once I'm back in the States."

She had so many questions, but one of them wasn't her faith in this man or in herself. She knew what they'd just accomplished, knew exactly what her next move had to be.

They shared a passionate farewell kiss on the threshold of the embassy before a group of serious-looking men came out and enveloped Evan. She watched him go, then returned to Jānis and the Trabant. They went straight to the airport and she bought a ticket on the last flight of the night; arriving at Frankfurt she said goodbye to a month's paycheck to get on the Lufthansa redeye to JFK.

It was nine o'clock before she cleared customs, thankful she had no baggage whatsoever, and hailed a cab. Sunday morning traffic wasn't too bad, but it still took them nearly forty minutes to cover the distance. It was always a shock for Charlotte to return to the US, even after short trips like this one. So much space, even in NYC. So many cheap ugly buildings. So many cars. So many people just going about their lives, free to live however they chose. She was glad to be home. Maybe later she could swing by her parents' for dinner.

The cab pulled off Belt Parkway onto 13th Street into a mess of traffic. "I don't know, miss, but there's a big detour sign up ahead," stated the cabbie. They sat on 13th, inching forward until they reached the intersection leading off onto Gravesend Road. Charlotte noted with a smile that there was a Russian Bath on the corner, next to a Chinese restaurant. Very good to be home.

As they turned, she saw down 13th and realized it was blocked off by the police. *Oh god I'm too late.* She shoved a 100-euro bill at the driver and yelled for him to stop, jumping out and starting to run up 13th.

The road was blocked off halfway past Avenue V, with press vans and spectators crowding the barrier. A handsome NYPD officer stopped her.

"Sorry miss, police only."

"Sir. My name is Charlotte Sorenson. I have information crucial to the conduct of this investigation. The Special Agent in Charge is Julia McCandless. It is imperative that I speak to her immediately."

The officer sized her up, skeptical, and reached for his radio. He turned and spoke into it.

He looked back after a moment. "Sorry ma'am. No access."

"You don't understand! There are officers in danger up there! I know something that can help. It's—"

She saw Agent McCandless's distinctive form step out of a building down the block. She waved and jumped up and down, yelling. "JULIA!! JULIA MCCANDLESS! IT'S ME! CHARLOTTE SORENSON! IT'S CHARLOTTE!"

Agent McCandless turned, acknowledging her presence. Charlotte passed the barrier and started running toward her. "AGENT MCCANDLESS! YOU HAVE TO HEAR ME OUT! THERE'S—"

The wind left her lungs entirely and her vision went starry with pain as the handsome officer tackled her from behind. "Ma'am, stop—no, ma'am … fuck … you have the right—"

"Ms. Sorenson. What in the name of—what do you think you're doing!?" McCandless stood over them.

"Agent McCandless. Give me five minutes. Just five minutes. Your men are in danger. I have information that can help."

"And charging a police barrier is the way to help?" She stood over them, considering. "Let her up. Ms. Sorenson, come with me. If this isn't pertinent, I'm having them book you. Sergeant, thank you."

Charlotte stood, every muscle in her body reminding her that a few hours' sleep in an airplane chair, first-class or not, does not equal recovery.

McCandless led her into the building she'd emerged from, where there was a hasty command post set up in the foyer of a grocery store. "We picked up Bērziņš's trail two days ago, heading here," she explained. "We know he's dangerous. He's in that building. And we're sending in a SWAT team to arrest him. I've got everyone from the President on down breathing down my neck, eighty officers from four different agencies to manage, and the press biting my heels at every turn wanting to know what we're doing about the Latvian threat. Now, what could possibly be so important?"

The room had gone silent, as the dozen or so men and women hunched over radios and shuffling papers and bustling about heard the authority in McCandless's voice. Charlotte gulped, taking in their defensive gazes, feeling waves of pain course through her body. Clearly Evan's message hadn't gotten through. There was no telling how they'd figured out how to be here. There was no telling how much danger they were in. She took a deep breath and started to talk.

CHAPTER 32
Brooklyn, New York City, January 12

The SWAT team emerged from the storefront kitty corner from the target building, eight armored figures bunched up behind steel plates. They moved slowly, careful not to expose themselves, under the protective gaze of a bevy of snipers overwatching them from the surrounding rooftops. The NYPD had pushed the cordon even further back, and a bomb team with a dog waited, out of sight behind a large police van.

Charlotte watched from the roof of the grocery, giving her a front-row seat to the team's approach and all the surrounding buildings but no view at all of the storefront they were approaching. If the FBI's intel was right, Bērziņš would be in apartment B, 1302 Avenue U: the corner apartment over a nail salon. They'd done their best to evacuate the area, hedging against him putting up a stand.

Everything seemed to be going right when the SWAT team leader, just a few meters from the building, put up a clenched fist. The entire team took a knee, covering the building, while the leader seemed to mess with his radio.

Charlotte scanned the windows opposite the nail salon. The NYPD had gone door to door, telling everyone who answered to evacuate the area. Most of the windows were dark; all were empty. Except for … there! Charlotte spotted it: five buildings down—with just the perfect angle to take in the SWAT team, the target building, and some of the police in the background—the slightest movement of the drapes. Charlotte checked Maps on her phone and leaned over to Agent

McCandless. "1311. Above the Chinese restaurant." McCandless made a brief call on the radio, and a second SWAT team flooded that building. The first team withdrew from the street as the bomb team moved in on the original target building.

"What I don't get is how you figured it out, Charlotte," McCandless stated, waiting for the second team's report. "You pulled on a thread and found out Bērziņš was Russian, and the lynchpin of this massive operation in Latvia. But how did you figure out he didn't exist at all?"

Charlotte nodded, feeling vindicated and thankful for the short gasp of reflection the transatlantic flight had given her. She'd liked to have admitted it was the result of careful consideration, but really she had the nameless person next to her to thank. She'd just gotten settled in the capacious chair and was fiddling with her new phone, trying to get it up and running so it would be ready the second she arrived. So she hardly noticed when the flight attendant offered her a glass of champagne.

"Oh, yes, excuse me … thank you." She accepted the flute and savored the bubbles, knowing they'd send her right off to sleep.

"You know, that's why they make you turn those things off," the older German woman next to her, impeccably dressed and carefully peeling an orange with a fork and knife, had interjected.

"I'm sorry?" Charlotte looked over.

"Maybe a decade ago there was some issue with bandwidths or whatever. But modern aircraft are built with the modern world in mind and are not susceptible in the least to anything put out by your little mobile. No, they just tell you that so you have to turn them off, so you won't be distracted in case something goes wrong."

"I see," Charlotte replied. "Thanks." She turned back to her notification settings and let the Frau keep peeling her orange.

Midflight a jolt of turbulence shook her awake. *The phone can't harm the plane. They're just worried that the phone is so distracting that you'll tweet through an emergency.*

"It just didn't add up, Julia. The whole point of this 'Sasha' business was to make it politically unfeasible for the US to support Latvia. To make the American public think the enemy was some non-existent Latvian nationalist terrorist cell, one that played on their darkest fears and insecurities—whether lefties who sympathized with Russian non-citizens against a fascist conspiracy, or conservatives who felt the country under attack by an ungrateful so-called-ally. To do that, they needed a patsy. But why settle for a real patsy, when in the age of the internet you can have the perfect fake one?"

A call came up over the radio: they'd apprehended a man alone in the apartment. Charlotte continued.

"Once we knew Sasha was a Russian operation, I had to look at all the evidence in a new light and assume that everything we knew about it was fake. So what's the simplest explanation? Bērziņš was a patsy. An extremist, aggressive cop, to be sure—but that just made him the perfect straw man. Someone else carried out those murders, in order to frame Bērziņš, who someone then got rid of. And boom! Here are the protests you need to get things started. Throw in a trail of breadcrumbs for me to find, knowing I'd eventually give it to you or the press — and thereby make real intelligence out of thin air."

"We never even suspected." Agent McCandless had been utterly incredulous at first, but the evidence was clear. Charlotte gestured for them to go down to the street. "Let's go meet this mysterious man." She finished her story walking down the stairs.

"So they used me to paint a picture. Once the idea of Aleksandrs as a Latvian fugitive was in our heads, was all over the media, we were primed not to see the facts in their own light. Natalya planned today as the trigger. And they know the most powerful weapon isn't the booby trap, or whatever is hidden in that building. It's the video they'd take and immediately share, showing FBI agents getting blown up by a Latvian whack job."

They reached the street and could see the team was coming down the stairs with the suspect. Charlotte finished as they walked toward the group of agents.

"And the only part of the whole puzzle that had to be real? Thomas. The man who walked in on us at Ocracoke. What kind of lifelong fixer gives up for a bribe that quickly? The guy who 'just drove' had to be a trusted agent of the highest degree in order to put us on just the right path. Someone who could then be in place to film and post the culminating event, from just the right angle at just the right time. And that's him right there, North Carolina accent or not. Hello, Thomas. Or should I say, Boris."

The man glared at Charlotte, the middle-aged loafer transformed into the image of defiance. The agents led him to a squad car.

A voice crackled over the radio. Agent McCandless looked at Charlotte in admiration. "That was the bomb tech. They found an explosive wired into the main door. Enough to kill the entire SWAT team."

CHAPTER 33
Greenwich Village, New York City, January 13

"Hot plate," the waiter warned as he placed the steaming risotto in front of Charlotte, the scrumptious aroma of truffle oil and mushrooms mixing with the heady Beaujolais to overpower her senses, already primed by the thrill of sitting in a crowded back-alley restaurant and relishing the electricity of feeling safe and at home and surrounded by her family.

Their entrees set, Bill proposed a toast. "To our lovely daughter, once again home safe, once again a mystery, once again making us proud." Charlotte held back tears; her father had never expressed pride in her accomplishments. Meeting Heidi and Chuck's eyes, she felt like she was finally coming home.

And yet she felt guilty, guilty at how little she could actually share with her family. They were smart — they could read the headlines about Brooklyn and Latvia, Bērziņš and Daugavpils, and infer that the FBI's calls looking for Charlotte meant she was at the center of things. But she desperately wanted to talk about connecting with Evan, about the thrill of the chase, about figuring it all out. It felt like the new sense of power and confidence she'd gained would have to remain hers alone — or hers and Evan's.

Evan, who still hadn't reached out after forty-eight hours. Whose report clearly hadn't gotten to the FBI before Charlotte could make it to New York in person. Who could be anywhere — from behind Russian lines to some military interrogation room — for all she knew. She'd written him a few emails, but nothing.

Not that she'd had much time to think about it. She'd been on a rollercoaster from the moment they'd arrested Boris, and this dinner was her first break.

"What next?" Julia had asked as they got into the back seat of her official Suburban, tailing the SWAT team back to the New York Field Office. She'd insisted on first names as long as they weren't in front of the troops.

Charlotte laughed. She'd plummeted off an emotional cliff with Boris's arrest, feeling like that was the last step. She hadn't spared a moment to think through what would happen after.

"Well ... we're under attack. But at this moment, we know almost everything about the enemy's plans, and they don't know how much we know. We have nearly a perfect advantage." She thought aloud as they approached the Brooklyn Bridge.

"But it's not a military attack, not one that your average American would recognize as such. And it's not a terrorist attack—9/11 was enough to invoke NATO's mutual self-defense, but is a shadowy conspiracy? No, it's an attack in the information space, the simplest way for a smart opponent to directly target our will to resist. So, it's in the information space that we have to defend, or better, counterattack."

"But what does that mean?" Julia countered. "We're a nation defined by our freedoms. We don't have the propaganda ministries, or mass monitoring, or control of the media ... and our foreign policy ... at least we *try* to define it by our values. How are we supposed to fight, hamstrung by the very freedoms we're fighting to protect?"

"Those freedoms are our very best weapons. We may forget it, but it's American movies that get second billing after Bollywood hits in Mumbai. And Silicon Valley tech companies providing the encrypted apps protestors use to coordinate on the streets of Hong Kong. And … American journalists who are the most ardent critics of our own government.

"All we have to offer, ultimately, is the idea that we are trying to make it work. We, too, inherit a staggering legacy of violence. We, too, groan under the weight of imperfect institutions. We, too, labor against a grossly unjust distribution of wealth. We, too, are home to a lovely, ugly, complex, astounding, roiling mix of identities and races and ethnicities. And yet we try to make it work. We try, we fail, we improve a bit, we keep trying. And the world *wants* to believe in us, for all our faults. We just have to keep the faith enough to keep the wagon trundling down the road.

"So, we may not be able to strike back tactically, move for move on the ground, but morally? It's ours to lose."

Julia assessed Charlotte, clearly unused to someone junior to her speaking so frankly. "As long as we stay true to those freedoms. So what do you suggest? Total transparency?"

"Exactly. Release as much about what just happened as you can without compromising the investigation, right away. Flood this story with journalists. Flood Latvia with journalists. The 'ground truth' may not matter as much anymore, in an era of deepfakes and Twitter bots, but the more observers, the more accurate the mean observation."

Charlotte was unsure the extent to which her tirade had the

desired effect, for while it was clear Agent McCandless was now firmly in Charlotte's camp, the twenty-four hours after the raid had a been a blur of doctor's visits and interviews, one examination after another. She hardly had a chance to catch her breath, let alone check headlines on what was happening in Europe or ask about the progress of the investigation.

So she was surprised when, the next evening, Julia told her that her parents were outside waiting for her, that she had three hours for dinner, then had to get right back. She ran downstairs and straight into their arms, bawling at the relief of seeing familiar faces, overjoyed to feel loved. They'd piled in a cab and headed straight to her favorite Italian place.

Charlotte was well into her risotto, cherishing the warmth and the company, halfway listening to her mother's excited rambling about potential wedding venues and the chances she'd be able to convince Caitlin to hold a second reception in New York, when her father directed the conversation back toward her.

"So Charlotte. Have you given any thought to what comes next?"

Oh boy. Here we go. "To be honest, dad, I really hadn't yet. Kinda been caught up in things."

"Well," he continued predictably and without any reference to her response, "you know there's always a place for you at the business. Our clients would really respond well to someone with your credentials and experience. You know we've been starting up a whole new 'ethical investing' fund I'm sure you'd love being a part of."

Charlotte struggled not to actually roll her eyes. If it were possible to define a single fund as "ethical," then what did that say about all the other ones, or the industry as a whole? The thought repulsed her, and she struggled out a gracious, non-committal thanks.

"And Caitlin tells us you've reconnected with Evan," her mother chimed in. *That little ...* Charlotte swallowed her indignation with a large mouthful of risotto. "How is he doing? Is he still in the Army?"

Charlotte gave the best, vaguest answer she could, not wanting to dive too deep lest her mother see through her nonchalance. Besides, it was an operational risk to discuss Evan when she didn't even know where he was or what he was up to. And a personal risk when every mention of his name tapped into her urgent need to see him—and the same feelings of abandonment that had clouded the last six years.

"Well," Heidi responded, "we'd sure love to see him again." She winked.

Charlotte really did roll her eyes at that, which then settled on an Asian family getting seated at a table across the room. They were certainly speaking English and carried themselves like Americans. And yet all four were wearing construction-style face masks. She was used to seeing groups of Asian tourists traipsing about New York with masks, but it was somehow startling to see a group so clearly American doing the same thing. She pointed it out to her family.

Chuck perked up, aggressively checking them out. "Must be that Kung Flu, you know?" He cackled at his own joke.

Charlotte looked back down at her risotto. Family they may

be, and lovely to feel loved. But between the greed, the gossip, and the casual racism, she just couldn't stand the privilege. It was time to get back to her life.

CHAPTER 34
Acela, New Jersey, January 16

Charlotte leaned against the window of the train, watching the bare treetops race by on the three-hour Acela from New York to DC. Every so often a messy squirrel's nest or a murder of crows would punctuate her view, but mostly it was just an endless line of boughs striving toward the sun, waiting for spring to reawaken them with new purpose.

Four days she'd spent at the New York Field Office, in interview after interview. At least this time she was treated as a trusted colleague, not a devious suspect. Indeed, she started to notice a certain kind of look in the hallways, and by two or three days in, when the story was all over the news, random people started coming up and thanking her. Of course, nothing took away from the fact that she was locked in a building. And still no word from Evan.

The only distraction besides dinner with the family had been feeling her phone buzz: it had been going wild since she'd gotten her old number back, with everyone from Alycia and Beth to old college roommates hearing through the grapevine that Something Was Afoot and reaching out. She ignored most of it, largely just wishing it were Evan, and not wanting to say anything public until she was more sure of herself.

But there was one that stood out. Charlotte felt the repeated buzz of an actual call as she sat in the cafeteria with Julia, and was surprised to see it was Margaret. Out of instinct, she was about to swipe to receive the call when she caught herself. *I owe this woman nothing*, she realized. *Her staff is broken, her powers undone.* She swiped it to voicemail.

Later, alone in her hotel room, Charlotte listened to the message.

"Charlotte, Margaret here. Given everything that's happened, I just wanted to let you know we're making your old position available. There's a place for you on the team. Please give me a call."

Charlotte smiled to herself. Short, to the point, devoid of any regret or apology or even human touch: classic Margaret. There was no way in *hell* Charlotte would go back to working for that woman, especially not after what she'd pulled. But it was nice to at least know she had an option beyond working for her father.

In all, the four days were an exciting glimpse inside a counter-intelligence task force handling the denouement of a major attempt against America. For the most part, she just tailed Agent McCandless, sitting in on every meeting and watching the entire case get prepped to turn over to prosecutors from the Department of Justice. But the more interesting part was getting to influence the organs of the federal government as they creaked into action to counter the Russian scheme.

By the afternoon of the 12th, the story was plastered across every global news outlet. Russia vehemently denied any involvement but, regardless, had completely lost the initiative. Over the coming days, as journalists and observers piled into Daugavpils, the raw number of eyewitness accounts overpowered Russia's ability to shape events. Which is not to say that the continuous churn of internet crap abated one bit; only that, under scrutiny, Russia lost its ability to throw up smoke and mirrors as it moved its chess pieces about.

The US Department of Defense released satellite photos

showing a massive Russian troop buildup on the Latvian border, the echelons of tanks clearly poised and ready for the flag to go up. Daily tabloids sold like hotcakes with images of German paratroopers digging foxholes around the Daugavpils airport and a French aircraft carrier transiting the Danish Straits. Most encouragingly, the Latvian government, assured of NATO support, came off the defensive, and released an official statement condemning the massacres, regardless of who committed them. The Russian nationalists getting their news from *Kanal Rossyi* may never believe what they saw as conspiracies, but there was no denying the official summit scheduled to discuss the protestors' grievances, the visit to Daugavpils by the Latvian President and her ethnically Russian Minister of Labor, the slow decline in the size of the protests. After just four days, it was clear the crisis was on its way to resolution.

And yet Charlotte wondered—what about Natalya, and Misha, and the rest? Had they just bundled up and gone home? The Latvian police would be able to roll up some of the partisans, but the ringleaders would have no trouble escaping. Would they just chalk this one up to bad luck? Russia had made an enormous wager on the success of a small deception, and if it hadn't been for Charlotte and Evan's bad—or good—luck, Moscow would have been throwing Daugavpils a welcome home party. So what was their next move?

Charlotte's role in the endgame got smaller and smaller, and by the morning of the 16th it was clear she had played her part save for testifying in Boris's eventual trial. Julia pulled her aside after lunch.

"I imagine you're ready to get home."

"You said it. I'm worried about Evan."

"I hear you, but I wouldn't be. He's just in the hands of a bureaucracy with a much more rigid process for handling these things. If something had gone wrong, we'd know. You'll hear from him soon enough."

"I hope. He and I need a real vacation together."

"I'll say. Charlotte, here is an Acela ticket to DC for this afternoon. I'll give you a call in a couple weeks to talk over what comes next—but this case will take months, if not years, to come to court."

"I'm honored to help out any way I can."

"On that, Charlotte. I know you're out of work. Take a break, think things over, go on a proper vacation. But, when you're ready, you have a place on my staff."

"Huh?" Charlotte was stunned.

"You have a real knack for this. There's no way to shortcut becoming an agent, but if you're willing to work as a researcher or assistant in counter-intel, I'd love to have you right away. I think you'd like the work, and you can see if it's right for you and go from there."

"But ... won't I need a clearance?"

"We granted you an interim one to work on this project and can expedite the investigation that's already open. You'll be making beans, but—"

"I'm in. When can I start?"

Julia laughed. "Take a few weeks. We can discuss it when I call."

"Wow, um ... thank you."

"No, Charlotte, thank you. The country owes you. But Charlotte—"

"Yes?"

"I do need you to sign this NDA."

Charlotte laughed on the inside, scribbled her signature, and gratefully accepted a ride in a Bureau Suburban to Penn Station.

Three hours later she was dragging herself and the meager luggage she'd acquired over a hectic four days the last few blocks to her house. It was cold, it was late, the gorgeous brick sidewalks weren't helping, she missed Evan, her ribs ached, she was exhausted, and all she wanted was to get in her bath with a glass of wine and watch something utterly inane until she drifted off. She could relax. It was all over, and she had a future again.

She opened the door, greeted by an enormous pile of mail and a flickering light. *Back to the real world.*

She stepped in and turned to close the door. A gloved hand blocked it open, and Charlotte's stomach dropped.

CHAPTER 35
Northwest, DC, January 16

Natalya emerged through the doorway, immaculately disguised as a DC housewife out for an evening stroll. "Sit down," she rasped. Fear gripped Charlotte with a resounding shudder—gone was the thick Russian accent, replaced by that of a posh English boarding school. Charlotte went into the living room and sat on the couch, petrified at what was coming. Natalya took a seat across from her, back to the wall and facing the door. She glared for a moment, then transformed her face into the most generous smile.

"I hope you are happy, Charlotte. We were this close to accomplishing something very simple, just supporting our people. Nothing you Americans didn't do in Texas, in Hawaii, in Grenada. Or anywhere else you decide it's worth caring about your made-up 'human rights.' But now you've gone and stuck your nose in our business, so the world is on the brink of war." Charlotte squirmed, doing her best to remain emotionless. She tried to focus.

What was Natalya doing here? How had she even gotten into the country? How had she found her home?

"Never mind the havoc you've caused me, personally," Natalya continued. "I always liked you, Charlotte. Felt like you and I read from the same page. When I saw you in Daugavpils, I wanted so badly for it to have been a coincidence. But knowing you—that is to say, knowing myself—I knew you were onto us. I tried to give you every chance to leave, to save yourself. Because you don't deserve what's about to happen. But we are all adults; we endure the consequences of our actions. And I, having failed to provide the necessary distraction through Operation Sasha, now find myself with the unenviable responsibility of tying up the loose ends." Natalya cracked a conflicted, dominant smile. Charlotte braced for what was to come, willing her exhausted body to help her brain function.

"So now you have a choice. Come with me. You'll have to leave everything, right here, right now. I won't tell you where you are going or what we'll have you do—only that you'll become part of our solution to this problem. Of course you'll have to make statements, and you'll forever be remembered as the most treacherous double agent since Mata Hari. But I'll take you under my wing, and you'll have a future. And"—she took a small vial from her pocket and placed it on the coffee table before Charlotte—"you won't be dead. I'm sure you've heard of Novichok? Of course you have. Then you know that it takes only a deep breath …"

Charlotte was stunned beyond the ability to think. She stuttered.

"It is a very simple choice, Charlotte. What will it be?"

Both options were beyond the pale. Both options were repugnant, but Charlotte especially hated to admit to herself that there was even a choice …

There was a soft knock at the door.

"We ignore it," Natalya demanded. "What is your choice?"

There was a second knock. Charlotte glanced back at the door. When she looked back, Natalya was calmly pointing a pistol at Charlotte's head.

Charlotte willed herself to hold Natalya's gaze, to not give an inch. If she was going to die, fine. But it would be at Natalya's hand. And she'd damn well leave as much evidence as she could.

The sound of scuffling outside was followed by the unmistakable "click" of a key turning in the lock. Charlotte saw Natalya's eyes flick to the door, and she dove for the floor.

The pistol went off with an enormous CRACK and a searing pain cut through Charlotte's arm. She hit the ground, hard, and rolled toward Natalya's feet, seeking only to get some skin stuck under her fingernails so the investigators would have an extra clue. She heard a rapid succession of pops, somehow much quieter, and Natalya's scream.

Grabbing at Natalya's legs, Charlotte clawed at her skin, breaking it and covering her hands in blood. "CHARLOTTE!" Someone was yelling for her. Not a British accent. She turned her head and saw several men emerging from the kitchen. *There were men in the kitchen?!?*

Then a strong hand was helping her to her feet, to take a seat on the couch. Her hands were covered in blood, her arm was streaming, she was completely dazed. She looked up and saw Evan across from her. He hugged her close.

She just stayed like that for a minute, regaining her bearings. When she opened her eyes, she saw her home was full of men in tactical gear, a crime scene team … completely flooded. So much for the bath.

She let go of Evan and looked at Natalya, who was still dazed from the intense tasing and rubber bullets. One man was reading her Miranda rights, handcuffing her and getting ready to lead her out. Natalya glared at Charlotte, but as their gaze broke, Charlotte was sure she read in her eyes something beyond anger: an unmistakable glint of victory. Charlotte shuddered and turned to Evan, hugging him again.

"Evan, what happened?"

"Within minutes of me getting to the embassy, everything was in motion. The Ambassador pulled out every stop to mobilize what we could inside Latvia, and I was on the phone with the General in charge of the entire European Command within hours. Honestly, I was amazed at how quickly everything moved."

"But when I got to New York, it was as if they didn't know," Charlotte interjected.

"That's the rub. I couldn't speak directly to the FBI until the official report had gone through and we had permission from the highest levels to coordinate. The legacy of decades of good civil rights litigation is that it is remarkably hard for someone like me to work directly with a domestic agency. So all they really got from me was the address, which apparently they already had. They didn't even know you were on the way."

"So you heard about what happened to me?" she said with a smile, remembering how enjoyable it was to get tackled with three cracked ribs.

"I did. And from the 13th on, I was talking to Agent McCandless every day."

Charlotte was stunned. "You what?!" Had Julia been playing her that whole time, as well?

"That's right. We're both sorry. But it was Agent McCandless who thought through the whole scheme and predicted they'd make a play for you. We weren't sure it would be Natalya, but we were certain they'd try. We had the Suburban that drove you to Penn Station make a few calls on a radio channel we know they monitor, and had security teams on you the whole way. It worked perfectly."

"But … how could you be sure they wouldn't just … and how did Natalya know I was here?"

Evan continued. "They had our passports, remember? And we knew they'd try to take you alive, so they could put you right back onto the chessboard. That's why we couldn't tell you. I'm really sorry about that Char, I really am. I'm not really sure how Natalya got into the country, but I'm sure we'll figure it out soon enough."

Charlotte was stunned. "So what you're saying is you used me as bait?!? One second longer and I—"

"Not bait, darling. Just a profile Natalya couldn't swipe left."

CHAPTER 36
FBI Headquarters, DC, March 6

Charlotte walked into the darkened conference room, carefully holding the oversized cake aloft as the group crowded into the work area and began to sing: "Happy Birthday to you …"

It was Julia's forty-fifth birthday, and Charlotte wasn't about to let this chance to celebrate her new boss just pass on by. She'd stayed up late baking, struggling to resurrect long-neglected techniques as Evan berated her from the living room: "Don't forget to add the anthrax, darling. What this country needs is another good bio-weapons scare."

She'd somehow cobbled it together, unsure if the outcome would be worth the time invested or measure up to the respect she held for Julia after her first four weeks working as her personal assistant. The pay was barely enough to cover her rent, but feeling like she was a part of something that mattered made it worth dipping into her savings. And, for the first time since she was twenty-five, she'd let go of her pride and let her parents help out, even if just a little. And keeping Evan around definitely cut down on dating expenses.

After Natalya's arrest and a visit to the doctor, she'd asked him to stay over, and from then on it was only a question of how much time they spent together. Evan had an unpredictable and brutal work schedule, once leaving for over a week with only a few hours' notice. But then he'd have stretches with nothing much at all, and once she consented to giving him a key, Charlotte discovered the pleasure of coming home after a long day at her new job to the smell of roasting brussels sprouts or a lavender oil bath. They'd worked in a weekend in the Shenandoah, an evening in New York, and three days on a beach in Puerto Rico. It was heaven.

The only real hiccup had been thinking about anything beyond a few months. Any time it came up, Evan got a little cagey. He said everything he could to reassure Charlotte, but there was definitely something coming up: a move, a new assignment, a deployment, something. She knew his lease was ending soon but really nothing else beyond that. But Charlotte wasn't the same twenty-five-year-old, and she was OK with accepting that uncertainty as the cost of spending time with her man. It was clear he was all in, in any case.

Caitlin had, of course, been completely against the whole thing, her suggestion being to make him do something over the top to show his commitment. Typical Caitlin behavior, of course, but Charlotte felt there was a grain of truth in it. If Evan really cared, maybe he should pick up some of the rent, or help her out … she wasn't sure. But that was OK.

One way Evan had already shown up, to be fair, was by linking Charlotte up with a professional to talk to. In the long, easy days of late January, as she felt the stress melt away and began to reflect in earnest, she was most troubled by the memory of standing over the man she'd bloodied and maimed in the hotel, and her complete lack of regret. She hadn't even been defending herself — she'd attacked him from behind — so it was nice to start working through her feelings with someone who knew how to help.

As the group finished the song, Julia took a deep breath and blew out all forty-five candles. Charlotte moved in to cut the cake, and amidst the happy din, someone turned the lights on, illuminating the workspace where they were gathered. Photos and maps adorned the walls, interspersed with wild dry erase spiderwebs and the occasional printout of a meme. It was the home of a task force hard at work.

As Charlotte handed slices around, Julia approached. "Thank you, Charlotte, this is truly lovely."

Charlotte paused and looked at her new mentor, conscious of their setting. "No thanks needed, ma'am. I'm just glad to be here. Anyway, you deserve it."

Julia smiled. "So tell me, honestly. Where do you think we stand? I don't want to ruin the festivities, but I haven't had the chance this week to ask your opinion. Do you think we'll ever turn Natalya?"

Charlotte looked at her, feeling valued and confident. "Four weeks ago, Julia, I would have said that it was just a matter of time before Natalya turned." She paused. "And last week, I would have said 'I'm new here, ma'am, and have no experience with interrogations on which to base an opinion.'" She smiled as Julia appreciated the self-awareness.

"But now I'm standing here with a piece of cake in my hand, so I'll give you my honest opinion. I think Natalya's about to turn. And I think that's been her plan all along."

Julia stood, evaluating. "I appreciate that," she declared. "Let's revisit that on Monday."

Charlotte smiled. "Happy birthday, and have a good weekend."

"You too, Charlotte."

A few conversations later and she was walking home, the

early spring weather making the mile trek almost pleasant. She touched base with Alycia, who was again single but at least thankful it was finally spring so she could really start dating again, and left Beth a message proposing a gym sesh together on Sunday. She hopped up the stairs to her door, seeing it open before her. Evan greeted her with a big kiss.

"Another week completed by our resident badass. Welcome home." She hugged him close and dropped her bag on the floor. He took her by the hand and led her to the kitchen, where her gaze fell across the replacement egg boiler Evan had found, to a gorgeous spread of cheese and a sweating glass of rosé. She looked at Evan, lovingly.

"Char, there is something I'd like to talk about if you have a moment. Or would you rather wait?"

She considered delaying but figured she'd rather have anything requiring thinking done so she could relax. "No, go for it. What's up?"

Evan sat down on the new sofa Ted had purchased to replace the one she'd managed to bleed all over. She plopped down beside him.

"So, you know my lease expires this week. I'm pretty much moved out—it's not like I have all that much stuff, anyway—but here's the thing. I was planning on subletting a buddy's spot in Dupont while he's deployed. But with all this COVID drama, it looks like his timeline is getting pushed back a few weeks, so—"

"So you're asking if you can crash here?" She completed his sentence.

"It would only be until he leaves."

Charlotte considered her response. On the one hand, she'd love to have Evan here. Love to smell him every morning, love to share evenings, love to feel like he was in that inside place in her life. On the other, she was still protecting herself by being OK with his comings and goings. If he were to move in, they'd really have to face the hard question of what their future held.

"Three weeks, Evan. That's all you get. I'm really excited to have you around, but I don't want to talk about moving in together until … you know."

"I do, Char. And thank you. We'll have a great time, and I'm sure I'll find a new place by the end of March."

AFTERWORD

Thank you for reading *The Right Swipe*! It has been a tremendous joy bringing this project to fruition, and I truly hope you enjoyed your time with it.

The Right Swipe is a work of fiction. In no way should this work be taken as a "leak" or insight into real-world happenings; while the events described herein are entirely plausible, this story is meant to entertain and inform, not to reveal. Any resemblance the characters bear to actual persons is coincidental. *The Right Swipe* also does not represent the views of anyone but the author.

Please, please review this book on Amazon! Should you want to learn more, please visit the book's website on Facebook or at TheRightSwipeBook.com.

ACKNOWLEDGEMENTS

This book is the product of nearly four years of dreaming, research, plotting, false starts, and lost confidence. It grew out of a work of love, a fun gift for someone very dear, but quickly became an emotional outlet as I struggled to make sense of the chapter of life I was in. It sat completed for two years before I found the confidence to bring it into the world; two years during which BLM, Belarus, and QAnon vindicated its premise. So I have nothing but the deepest gratitude to all those who've supported me in this journey.

Most importantly, I'd like to recognize my wonderful friends in Latvia and eastern Europe, whose generosity and warm welcome taught me so much about this fascinating corner of the world. For inspiration, I must also recognize Erskine Childers and Timothy Snyder, authors with the firmest grasp of the play of fantasy on our world.

To my editing and art team—copy editor Lisa Dusenbery and illustrator Agnese Priekule—my deepest appreciation for your patience with my fickle needs. To the coworkers and colleagues who tolerated my raving—JT, PM, AG, NT—and only made fun of me a little. To my beta readers— AB, JR, CB, JM, JN, E2, SM, LR, RS—I will never be able to express how much your support meant, especially for those who had to put up with the steamier moments of the early drafts. To JK, whose professional expertise gave me the final burst of confidence. And to my entire family, and not just for letting me use the cabin—you were there for me during the COVID summer, and I can't wait to be there for you too, soon (and thanks to G for the title)!

A, I can't wait to explore the dream of collaboration we shared for a few hours on Vashon. Your talent is an inspiration, so I cherished your approval and enthusiasm. Here's to finding time during your sabbatical …

To a campfire duck à l'orange.

And to the real-world Charlotte, whose remarkable mind and questing spirit inspired this book—thank you. I cherish you.

ABOUT THE AUTHOR

The author, writing under a pseudonym, is a veteran of United States government operations in eastern Europe and elsewhere. Their experience, while not limited to the types of events described in *The Right Swipe*, inspired the arc of the story.

Learn more at TheRightSwipeBook.com

Made in the USA
Monee, IL
09 September 2021